MY BODY IS CALLING

A Novel

Sonya Harris

Also by Sonya Harris

Guilty Pleasures

What readers are saying!

"This book depicts the true essence of a woman in search of peace, love, and happiness, and all the dynamics she encounters on her mission." –Breeze, An avid reader

"I enjoyed it…it was sexy." –Thomas Green, Author of *Courting Miss Thang*

"Sonya Harris has crafted a novel that encourages one to look within…*Guilty Pleasures* is an enjoyable read that truly lives up to its title." –RAWSISTAZ Reviewers

"Reading *Guilty Pleasures* again was like reading it for the first time. It had me feeing like I knew these people or could understand exactly their pain." –Actress LaTamra Smith

"*Guilty Pleasures* invites you into a world of revelation, love, and reality. This is a novel to read."
–Saadia Coleman, Educator

MY BODY IS CALLING

A Novel

Sonya Harris

Sayha Publishing

Library of Congress Control Number.: 2009903135
ISBN: 0975445820
ISBN: 9780975445822
Sayha Publishing

My Body Is Calling is a work of fiction. Names, characters, and incidents
are products of the author's imagination or are used fictitiously. Any
resemblance to actual events, locales, or persons, living or dead, is entirely
coincidental.

At the time of publication, every effort was made to provide accurate website
information, telephone numbers, and statistical data. The author does not
assume any responsibility, or have any control over changes that occurred
after publication. The author also does not have any control over or assumes
responsibility for the websites or their content.

DISCLAIMER

This novel is not intended to give medical advice or suggest treatment for medical conditions. Readers should not: 1) Substitute the contents in this body of work for professional medical guidance or 2) Make any health decisions without first consulting with a doctor or licensed healthcare provider.

The purpose of this novel is to raise and promote health awareness, spark dialogue about social and health issues that plague women, and inspire them to take personal responsibility for their emotional, and physical health.

What you don't know about your body might hurt you.

ACKNOWLEDGMENTS

I am grateful for living another day to see this project come to fruition.

To readers who embraced, enjoyed, shared, and recommended my first novel, *Guilty Pleasures*, thank you for your support and patience and I trust you know that sometimes life doesn't go according to "our" plan. However, stay your course, compete only with yourself and you will never lose!

Book clubs, booksellers, book reviewers, fellow authors, book event planners/promoters, libraries, and the media, thanks for keeping literacy alive in the community and beyond. Books build knowledge. Education empowers.

A special thank you to Shana Capone, LaTonia, Sonia Monique, and Leslie for your input at the start of the project. Author C-Note, thank you, I truly appreciate the referral. Tsha, thanks for contributing authentic details during my research process. My late cousin and my loudest cheerleader Barbra Daniels – you are missed! Cuzzo Randy...a good look is a good look! As always, Ma (Mary Harris), I am proud to make you proud.

In closing, there will be more to come if it is in "His" plan for me.

Visit www.sonyaharris.com for updates and events.

Again, *thank you!*

DEDICATION

To my #1, Jocelyn Kristina: Sweetie Pumpkin Pie, walk through life with both eyes open, and let faith guide your way. Know that you are an individual with a voice. Know when to use it and don't lose it. I want you to know that when you were 5-years-old, you said you wanted to be an artist, and even a scientist. Always BELIEVE that you can be anything you put your mind to, so don't walk in the shadows of others. Let the light inside of you shine! I will always be in your corner. Love, Mumma. :o)

CONTENTS

PROLOGUE
MIND, BODY, SPIRIT

Simone Miller was miserable. Her head was spinning like a Ferris wheel in reverse. Her emotions went haywire when she got her period. It made her bladder as unpredictable as New England weather. She was bloated and achy and didn't know what to expect from one pang to the next. She pressed her thighs together, hoping the pressure would stop the excruciating cramps.

Over-the-counter pain relievers—Tylenol, Advil, and Pamprin—were futile. The pain worsened with each dose, so she flushed the capsules down the toilet and got into bed with a heating pad.

Given that her thirty-fifth birthday was three months away, Simone's first thought was, *I'm getting old.* Her second was, *my body is adjusting to fleeting time.* Then she checked herself out in the mirror.

Contrary to her youthful appearance and charismatic personality, she was far from a spandex flaunting spring chicken sashaying around like she was new money fresh off the press. Reality. Cellulite, a supermodel's nightmare, had already begun to dimple her belly all the way down to her thighs. So much that, she had grown to despise even the mention of cottage cheese.

One thing couldn't be denied: Simone's body was in dire need of medical attention. Mentally, she dealt with the pain for as long as she could before deciding to call her gynecologist.

"I'd better call my doctor," she said, convinced the time had come to take action against the painful cramping. Simone telephoned her gynecologist, Dr. Theery, to make an appointment for a thorough pelvic exam to investigate what might be causing baffling aches in her lower abdomen, and sometimes her womb.

After the call, Simone placed the telephone back on its cradle with a sick feeling in her gut. The way her luck ran bad most times, she didn't expect the preliminary diagnosis to be good. The phone rang as soon as she put it down. She thought about not answering, until she recognized Portia's number flashing in the Caller ID Box, which meant a report of domestic violence was brewing. Simone had to decide whether to brush aside her issue to listen to Portia moan and groan about Lonnie beating on her again. In mid-thought, Simone's Nextel rang. She ignored Portia's call to pick up her cell. Keisha's mobile number blinked on the screen. Simone knew a salacious scandal was on the horizon and chuckled, "Hmm. I wonder what married man Keisha has blackmailed for cash and designer shoes this time." Next, she received text messages from her sister Susan: One asking to borrow money for a private matter, another complaining about her flip-at-the-mouth daughter Monica. Simone texted back: The bank is closed and Monica just needs a classic ass whooping.

Aggravated by social demands, Simone prepared for a warm shower. Standing naked in front of the floor length mirror, she palmed her Georgia brown ass to make sure it was still supple and sexy. To her delight, it was. She slid her slender and elegant fingers over her clean-shaven Lady— a pet name for her womanhood—stopping intermittently to tantalize her clit. In an instant Simone was wetter than Seattle on a stormy day. Her doorbell rang, interrupting her private time. *Who in the heck came here without calling?* She wondered, slipping into a bathrobe.

Simone ran downstairs and looked through the peephole. To her surprise, her ex-lover Andy was outside pleading for make-up sex. Simone gave him ten seconds to leave, threatening him with a restraining order for stalking her. Andy called her bluff. Caressing his hard-on, he spoke with Billy Dee confidence, "You know you want it. Now open the door."

The wetness between her legs became a bubbling inferno. *Heck*, she thought, *a one-night stand with an ex would be a-first.* Feeling her spirit weakening for the flesh, Simone leaned back against the door, slid to the floor and prayed for strength.

"Damn it, Andy! I have company." She yelled, only partly lying. "Now leave me alone before I call the cops!"

Andy left, but promised to return.

Simone dashed to her closet and pulled out her "company", which was stashed in a velvet box tucked out of sight. She then moistened all ten inches with her tongue. Simone was more than ready to tear the sheets off the bed thinking mechanical pleasure could be better than what any doctor could order. But, just as she was about to thrust her secret pleasure deep into the sugary crevice of her Lady, the bearer of bad news rang to inform Simone that death had stolen another soul.

1

HOMEBOUND

Two weeks later.

As she sat on the Boston-bound flight from Atlanta, Simone's mind traveled back to where troubles of her heart began. Andy Williams was bad news—real bad news—from the moment she laid eyes on him six years ago at the house party of a mutual friend. At first glance, it was lust on a two-way street. Andy was just too handsome for words to do him justice. Simone liked her men fine, impeccably dressed, creditworthy, and streetwise enough to know peddling illegal merchandise was the quickest route to a ten-year bid in jail. She didn't get a thug vibe from Andy. In fact, his dangerous charm had Simone convinced he was too strait-laced to even steal Cable. But stealing pleasure while Simone slept was his fatal offense.

Nothing promising developed from their first encounter. Nevertheless, after unexpectedly seeing Andy's fineness on a boat cruise in the historic Boston Harbor, it became obvious that the devil had manifested their destiny.

Partying on the upper deck in front view of Andy and his dog pound of three buddies, equally handsome in their own right, Simone yearned for Andy's touch on her womanly body. She shamelessly gyrated and swayed her hips to the rhythm of R&B, reggae, and hip-hop soul. She twirled around and shook her curvaceous rump like she was perched on a washing machine churning in spin cycle. To say she carried on like a Jezebel with persistent sexual needs would have been an understatement in the Red Light District, where prostitution, drugs, and crime flourished. Her risqué antics were outright desperate. She wanted him, and that night, six years ago, she was not gonna be denied. Andy was the one.

Timing was everything, which made the pursuit of affection a no-brainer considering Simone had recently ended a tumultuous courtship with her skirt-chasing, car-obsessed first love, Clay Marshall. The scars from that volatile union had healed, but Simone was wounded emotionally and harbored a cynical view of man-woman relationships. Still, that negative outlook didn't deter her desire to be held by somebody. Andy was that somebody. Between his charm and her longing for intimacy, Simone just had to have Andy and didn't know if he was worthy of her woman-with-needs act. She didn't care as long as he was willing to be her guilty pleasure for one night. Andy, on the other hand, was smooth and cavalier with his lustful intentions to get between and stay between Simone's thighs and screw her Lady dry.

Slow and steady the little head in his pants led him to Simone. Andy could've had his pick of the female crop on the boat. But she was the "special one" caught in the crosshairs of wall-to-wall, nonstop body slapping sex in every position— upside down, front, back, sideways. They did it morning, noon and night until the dopamine in Simone's brain lost its potency.

Over time, as sex became a must-have-on-demand for Andy; it became a chore for Simone. His sexually sociopathic, red flag behavior became unbearable for Simone after he violated her body while she slept. She woke the next morning to the grim discovery of Andy's crusty sperm smeared over her butt cheeks. After Andy thought it was kosher to use Simone's ass for DNA target practice, their emotional rollercoaster of a relationship came to an abrupt halt. The callous manner in which he ejaculated on Simone's ass enraged her. For the first time, she truly accepted that, to Andy, she was only good for one thing: sex. Humiliated by his brazen selfishness, she plotted to flatten his car tires, scratch hateful words from the hood to the trunk, pour sugar into his gas tank, and glue the door locks so the heathen would know what it felt like to be victimized.

Simone was disappointed in Andy and their quasi-relationship, which never evolved beyond sex. When she finally blessed and released the bond, she thought they shared, from her heart, she knew her feelings for him wouldn't fade overnight. But she had to start somewhere. Even though she'd threatened to serve Andy with a restraining order, the possibility of jail time didn't deter him from calling and texting Simone to the point of harassment.

Fifteen minutes into flying time, the pilot's baritone voice boomed from the PA system and nudged Simone's thoughts out of a past that continued to haunt her present.

"Ladies and gentlemen, this is Captain Briggs. Once again, I'd like to welcome you aboard Flight 509. We've reached our cruising altitude of thirty-two thousand feet. Estimated flying time is two hours, forty minutes, but a strong tail wind could put us at the gate early. The current temperature in Boston is a rainy fifty-seven degrees. Enjoy the trip. Looks like it's going to be a smooth one."

When the seatbelt indicator flashed off, feeling like she could benefit from a stretch, Simone unlatched her safety belt and bent forward to relieve stiffness in her lower back. She then stood up and opened the overhead storage compartment to retrieve a chenille blanket from her carry-on bag. As usual, the plane was colder than an icebox.

Simone was on her way home from another visit to the state of Georgia. She had already made the journey south several times to pursue employment and job offers that didn't pan out. In the relationship realm, just about every other man Simone encountered on the streets of Atlanta, in the malls, in corporate offices, seemed to be gay. Her pessimistic side thought the odds of making a love connection there were slim to never. When she assessed the pros and cons of leasing her house, complete with state-of-the-art kitchen appliances and gorgeous hardwood floors to move there, it didn't make sense. Simone realized relocating to another state with no roots would require serious planning from finding gainful employment to securing affordable housing. Not to mention, it would take more than a bad breakup to run her out of town. Atlanta's rich ethnic culture, progressive black pride, and the splendor of all-you-can-eat buffets quickly lost its allure.

This last visit to Georgia had another purpose; Simone had paid her respects at her friend and former Fairmont University roommate Traci Horton's, mother's funeral.

For the duration of the flight, Simone reminisced in her journal about time spent with Traci. She was happy to see marriage had been kind to her. Nearly ten years after meeting each other freshman year, Simone was still man less. She sadly glimpsed her bare ring finger. A woeful feeling of eternal loneliness swirled in her head, *If marriage and happily ever after were meant to be, they would've happened by now.* She thought as she tried to push out of her mind a peculiar pain that she had been experiencing in her womb, near her uterus during PMS. Every time Simone survived a bout of symptoms, she prayed they would go away for good. But they always resurfaced to break her into fragile little pieces she thought would never find their way back together.

It was only a matter of days before her gynecology appointment. With her luck these days, she wasn't expecting a good diagnosis.

2

HERE TODAY, GONE TOMORROW

During the taxi ride home from Boston's Logan Airport, Simone wondered what sadness the rain would bring with it and why it often rained after deaths and during funerals. *Rain seems to make losing a loved one hurt even worse than their unexpected passing. It's a shame how I never really appreciate life, until death steals away someone close to me or someone I know, like Traci's mother.*

Traci's mother, Doreen, was sixty-six years young when she suffered a cerebral aneurysm and collapsed face-first on the dinner table, narrowly missing a plate of collard greens. Sadly, no one in the family had advised her to seek medical care when she complained about a migraine that wouldn't subside, even after she had taken the prescribed medication. Unresponsive, Doreen was rushed to County Hospital where she underwent grueling hours of surgery, but died on the operating table. The chief surgeon determined a blood vessel in her brain ruptured, resulting in a hemorrhagic stroke. When the doctor quizzed Traci about Doreen regularly taking migraine medication she couldn't answer the question honestly.

She thought faith and prayer would strengthen her mother's will to heal, but God had another plan.

The taxi hit a pothole and shook Simone out of her thoughts. Simone palmed her achy stomach. She worried a little that God might call her Home next. Meanwhile, her conscientious driver concentrated on the rain-slicked road. Surprisingly, he didn't attempt to tell her a funny story, a bad joke, or why he drove a taxi for a living. He didn't even gripe about the Red Sox losing to the Yankees. Instead, he silently merged onto I-93 South.

Simone looked out of the rear passenger window at the raindrops streaking the glass. She marveled at the historical Boston skyline, a breathtaking view stretching from downtown to the exclusive and very wealthy Back Bay. The weather beacon above the Old John Hancock insurance building was the standout landmark in one of the wealthiest sections of Boston. Its beacon was stable neon red, the signal for steady rain in the forecast. As the taxi got closer to Exit 11B, heading toward Simone's working-class neighborhood of modest single-family homes and manicured lawns, the skyline transformed from tall magnificent structures to black tar rooftops, telephone poles, and empty dark space. It started raining harder. Water dripped down the window and blurred her vision. Rooftops and telephone poles became nearly invisible, but darkness remained unchanged. The driver sped up and hit a few bumps on the off ramp. He traveled west along Gallivan Boulevard approaching Gunther Road. Closer to home, Simone's thoughts switched back from wealth, rooftops, and the rain to her cramped, bloated belly.

3

TIME HEALS ALL WOUNDS

The driver parked in front of 51 Gunther Road and killed the engine. Simone stepped out the cab and hummed, "Home sweet home at last."

The driver rushed to retrieve her bag from the trunk. Simone wanted to hurry him along so she could take a hot shower, but she stayed silent and let him earn the tip that he was working so hard for.

When she tipped him, money broke his silence. Long in the tooth, he beamed his appreciation. "Thank you, Miss. The pleasure was all mine."

"You're welcome. Happy driving," she replied.

He quickly got in the car and cruised away.

Curbside, Simone looked around. Gigantic birch trees swayed in the faint rainy breeze. There wasn't a single person roaming Gunther Road. Not even Snow, her adopted stray cat, was out scrounging for food. As much as she couldn't bear the humidity that usually came with precipitation, rain in any form—drops, drizzles, torrential downpours—was a blessing in disguise. No matter if it was light, heavy, or a passing sun shower, the wet climate seemed to have a stifling effect on crime in the city and surrounding communities. Burglaries, shootings, stabbings, and murders declined, compared to when the weather was dry and goodness forbid hazy, hot, and humid and crime spiked out of control. Simone hummed, *Rain, rain, don't go away. The more it rains the more community members will live to their life expectancy.*

In the process of wheeling her luggage and forcing her sluggish body up the walkway, a dark sedan with tinted windows and hardcore beats thumping inside careened down the street and held Simone at the door. She stalled to see if the car would make a sudden stop in front of her property before she inserted the master key. The last thing she needed was some desperado wielding a knife, a gun, or a Louisville Slugger to do her bodily harm for the measly dollar and fifteen cents in the cute wristlet dangling from her arm. The car didn't stop, but intrusive Betty Bonita, head of the Neighborhood Watch Committee, turned on her porch light and poked her nose outside the door. As usual, Ginger Snap, her Beagle loped at her feet.

"Welcome back, Simone. Every time I look out my window you're going and returning from a trip," Miss Bonita laughed.

"There's a whole world to see, but it sure feels good to come home." Simone replied in kind.

"Okay, I won't hold you. I just wanted to let you know that I watched your place while you were gone. Now go on in and get out the rain because if you are anything sweet like me, your sugar is gonna melt," Miss Bonita advised, standing on her porch grinning.

Simone wished her a good night, unlocked the door and wheeled in the luggage. She quickly secured the deadbolt before disarming the security system and switching on the ceiling light. Relieved to be in familiar surroundings, she surveyed her cozy living space and admired portraits of her budding nieces, Monica and Sasha; her rambunctious nephew, Dallas; and many academic accomplishments tacked to the wall in matching wood frames, lightly covered in dust. The drooping Pothos, her very first plant, positioned on the side table was dying a slow death from thirst. Watering it ranked high on her list of things to do before going to bed.

The message counter on the answering machine was flashing. She had four messages. Simone parked the luggage next to her wet shoes on the welcome mat and walked across the timber floor to review the call history. Respectively, her recruiter from Crown Employment Agency, her mother Claire, Women's Hospital, and the word "Private" appeared in the small screen. The unknown private party got the big delete. She then pressed play.

"HELLO, SIMONE, THIS IS RYAN TODD CALLING. QUEST FINANCIAL WOULD LIKE TO EXTEND YOUR TEMPORARY ASSIGNMENT FOR ANOTHER WEEK. CALL ME IF YOUR PLANS HAVE CHANGED, OR SHOW UP ON MONDAY. MS. HEDLEY IS EXPECTING YOU."

She waited for the next message.

"CALL ME THE MINUTE YOU GET OFF THAT PLANE, THAT WAY I'll KNOW IT DIDN'T CRASH."

Simone huffed. *Just like Mother to take it to the extreme.* Annoyed, she shook her head and waited for the next message.

"MISS MILLER, THIS IS DR. THEERY'S OFFICE CONFIRMING YOUR THREE O'CLOCK APPOINTMENT ON MONDAY. IF YOU CANNOT KEEP THIS APPOINTMENT, PLEASE CALL 617-555-CURE TO RESCHEDULE."

Playing back the messages, Simone was pleased to hear the recruiter verify that Quest Financial had extended her transaction settlement assignment. The extension couldn't have come at a better time because her emergency fund was slowly decreasing. Satisfied with the good news of employment, she plunked down on the sofa to rest her tired feet.

Comfortable where she sat, Simone mused at the insane notion of Andy welcoming her home with a dozen yellow roses, a cup of Vanilla Nut tea, and a hair-raising massage to secure him a place between her sheets again. Time ticked closer to the ten o'clock hour. Another moment of weakness lingered. She cast a long glance at the telephone expecting Andy to call pleading for one more chance to be a better man. Time ticked on. She was getting sleepier by the minute. The telephone didn't ring. Her custom two-story Colonial stayed as still as the darkness lurking outside. Fleeting thoughts of Andy was just the lonely nagging inside her head. To resist the urge to call him, she fetched her journal from her travel bag. Simone started keeping the journal during freshmen year of college at Fairmont University. She wanted to record how life had changed for her since that blessed opportunity of witnessing people who looked like her making the most of their lives. She also wanted to document her relationship track record. In the event she bore an unexpected blessing of a daughter, she'd have an unofficial family heirloom of relationship "dos and don'ts" seeing that personal experience is the best teacher of life lessons. Simone covered her lap with a chenille throw and began to read a promise letter she had penned after her last break up with Andy.

> *Dear Me:*
> *Don't ever change to please anybody. Don't take flack from anybody. Don't turn the other cheek. Remember, Dad has already punched Mother in hers and left welts on her face. The first time a man violates your body, strikes your face, foots you in the tail, calls you any name other than the name you were given at birth, shames you with other women—or men— leave, start loving you again, and don't look back.*

Simone then stuffed the journal into her lingerie drawer for safekeeping, undressed and sat on the toilet. In addition to stomach pangs, passing waste through her bowels was now painful and time consuming. Another change she blamed on the perils of aging.

Minutes later, Simone lathered up in her glass encased shower. She scrubbed her sienna complexion to exfoliate the skin. She scrubbed so hard, the wiry ball of mesh almost unraveled. Yet, her soul still felt dirty.

Feeling sad and emotional, Simone couldn't hold back the salty tears that blended with the water streaming down her face and over her protruding stomach. Lonely moments like these Simone wanted to sing her troubles away, but knowing she couldn't hold a note to save her life she cried instead.

Simone emerged from the shower and headed straight to the dressing room to ogle her potbelly in the mirror. She administered a thorough once-over, up one side of her and down the other. She looked sadly at the stretch marks that could chart a marathon on her ass, and the weariness that had replaced the glow in her eyes. More salty tears trickled down her cheeks, seeped between her lips, and left a taste of anguish in her mouth.

Simone couldn't deny the element of truth when she saw it unfolding on her waistline, hips, and thighs. She frowned at her changing body, then thought, *there's nothing to gain from beating myself up until I know for certain whether stomach pangs and the bulge on my waist are detrimental to my health or just an indication that I need to hurry up and get back in the gym!*

A moment later, Simone knelt down at her sleigh-style bed and prayed for strength to handle the emotional, social, and physical changes she was going through. After her talk with God, she crawled under the duvet, still unable to push worry totally out of her head.

4

TOO MUCH OF A GOOD THING

Simone had barely closed her eyes when the telephone rang. It was 11:09 P.M. when she reluctantly brought the receiver to her ear, she heard Keisha Bailey sobbing hysterically on the other end like a mother whose only son was shot dead, execution style. Simone suspected her troubles were the result of a married man refusing to leave his wife for the twentieth time. She was convinced Keisha wouldn't stop chasing a meal ticket until a fed up wife broke an ankle stomping money hungry Keisha beyond recognition.

Simone befriended Keisha while working part-time at a local bookstore. She learned early in their friendship that Keisha had an affinity for successful married men and their fat wallets. Keisha claimed some of her conquests were for entertainment purposes and most for the sole purpose of keeping her rent paid and food in her stomach. She'd sworn up and down that her married lover was in the final stages of divorcing the wife, kids, and his dog if he had one.

Last time they'd e-mailed, Keisha had raved that Simone's visit to see her in New York was a-must so they could take in a Broadway play and dabble in a treat at some cigar bar she started frequenting looking for fatter wallets. For one reason or another, the trip never happened and Simone hadn't heard from Keisha until now, as she sobbed hysterically about possibly having a Sexually Transmitted Disease (STD) and the consequences of unprotected sex.

Simone practically fell out the bed and bumped her head on the floor listening to Keisha's story of how wearing down the springs in a Sealy Posturepedic mattress, with her married lover Gordon at the upscale Millennium Hotel, had gone so terribly wrong. When Simone probed for more details, Keisha said that initial tests revealed that she had a STD but that preliminary tests were inconclusive. Simone didn't bother wasting her breath to ask whether she had practiced safe sex. Common sense had already told her that a hunger for a man in a finely tailored suit enticed Keisha into irresponsible sex. The cynic in Simone suspected, *Don't ask, and don't tell* was the modus operandi at the swank cigar establishment where Keisha hunted for married men with fat wallets on the prowl for female company with no strings attached.

Simone put aside her own physical issues to focus on Keisha.

"Stop crying, Keisha. It could be worse. You probably discovered just a harmless bump that won't go away."

"I can't stop crying. Don't you understand? I'm damaged goods. Why didn't I insist on using a condom? I should have kept the lights on when we were screwing to make sure he was disease-free. At least I would've noticed his infected penis." Keisha sobbed on her soapbox of sorrow.

Playing the devil's advocate, Simone reasoned, "Well, if he was infected, it wouldn't have mattered if he'd worn a condom because a prophylactic doesn't guarantee one hundred percent protection. Only abstinence does. I thought you knew that."

"My doctor said the same thing. I wish I had known then what I know now." Keisha sniffed and blew her nose.

Simone secretly wondered if seeing a tainted penis on the perimeter of her vagina would have discouraged Keisha from the high stakes of casual sex since somewhere on a luxury car lot, there was probably a shiny Mercedes convertible with *Keisha B.* already engraved on the vanity license plate.

Truth is, Simone really didn't quite get Keisha even though she accepted her as she was, wallet chasing and all. Nonetheless, home wrecking didn't bode well with Simone because it wasn't like Keisha didn't have the wits to earn big bucks and star power as a celebrity publicist, her lifelong dream. Keisha's résumé noted interviews with big-screen actors, R&B legends, high profile rappers, top runway models, and music industry moguls. She had the total package and could easily have made it in Hollywood. The camera loved her diamond-shaped face, high cheekbones, and stunning stargazers. She had the looks and a brick house body to stop New York traffic at rush hour.

Considering the circumstances, Keisha didn't deserve to be judged during her personal crisis. She was human and made mistakes as Simone had so many times with men she thought loved her more than they loved cooked food. Only faith could make them both stronger after learning another life lesson the hard way: Indulging in too much of a good thing can't buy happiness. Like love, it starts within. Keisha was entitled to the benefit of the doubt. So, nonjudgmental Simone listened and let Keisha cry on about her unfortunate predicament until near daybreak.

A small part of Simone felt like she had cheated in the game of love and suffered only minor scrapes and bruises compared to karma coming full circle in the form of a possible STD the way it had for Keisha.

When the sun nearly rose on their conversation, Simone had already checked out mentally and decided it was time she got some sleep.

"Keisha, I'm going to bed now. Call back if you need me."

"Okay. Thanks for lending me your ear. I'm going for a second opinion."

"Smart idea. Keep me in the loop so I know what's going on and if I can do anything to help you through this ordeal. Sleep tight."

"I'll try."

Simone returned the phone to its cradle and thought, *whoever coined the phrase, it's cheaper to keep her, should have included the unlucky-with-love mistress is as disposable as a soiled diaper because married men don't cheat for keeps.*

17

5

PICKING, SQUEEZING, AND SCRATCHING

A month before her heart-to-heart talk with Simone, Keisha had noticed a small bump growing on her labia. During the first couple of weeks of living with the growth, she picked at it and scratched at it to see if fluid would seep out. Frustrated, she stopped picking, squeezing, and scratching to inspect the growth more closely using a small mirror and a high beam flashlight. During the inspection, Keisha didn't notice any fluid, except her skin appeared to be slightly irritated from the excessive picking, squeezing, and scratching.

She dismissed it as acne and started using home herbal concoctions to get rid of it. Keisha gently applied black seed oil to the area. A few days later it became a bit scabby at which point she applied a dab of raw Shea butter and continued applying small amounts until the scab went away. Soon after the first bump disappeared, a smaller one appeared, and she repeated the same inspection and treatment process. Instead of the new bump going away, it seemed to rebel and get bigger.

She tried to stifle its growth with more black seed oil and Shea butter, both potions were ineffective; that's when she drove straight to Urgent Care for professional analysis.

The inexperienced resident on duty diagnosed the bump as a "harmless pimple" and recommended that she consult a dermatologist. Keisha wasn't prone to acne. She didn't have a solid reference for an accredited dermatologist in New York, so she researched her insurance provider's website for skin-care specialists based on her zip code. She chose a doctor at a reputable practice, accessible by public transportation.

Reputation and convenience didn't prevent the visit from being horrible, second to a root canal. Not only wouldn't Dr. Erman let Keisha complete her sentences, his impatient beady glare whenever she tried to ask a question pissed her off. His snappish responses, quick analysis, and zeal to perform a future surgical procedure without answering questions to her satisfaction had Keisha rushing to leave. Before she could reach the elevator, the silver-haired receptionist posted at the front desk nearly tipped over furniture stumbling to bombard Keisha with copies of an in-depth article authored by Dr. Erman.

Keisha slowed her strut to the elevator and took the article and read the title. *What Women Need to Know About HPV (human papillomavirus)*. She scrunched up her nose like something smelled rotten and furrowed her tapered brows in confusion.

"HPV," Keisha said, turning to the receptionist. "Ma'am, what's HPV, and what does it have to do with a growth on my vagina?"

"I'm not authorized to discuss medical matters. Direct your questions to Dr. Erman. He's the best in his field."

"Never mind." Keisha figured questioning him would be wasted time.

"It's your choice. But, hopefully you can find some answers right there in your hand."

"Perhaps," She sighed.

Keisha left the doctor's office, hopped on the subway, and decided to pass the time reading the entire article. After perusing the details, she was completely freaked out. She learned that genital human papillomavirus is the most common sexually transmitted infection in the United States. There are more than 40 HPV types that can infect the male and female genital areas. HPV can also infect the mouth and throat. Most people who become infected with HPV do not know they have it. The virus can be passed on to a partner during sex. According to the Centers for Disease Control and Prevention, most people with HPV never develop symptoms or health problems. The article also featured information about a HPV vaccine to be introduced, in the near future, as a preventative measure for young women.

Keisha was in disbelief one minute, seconds later her face was wet from tears. All she knew going into her dermatology appointment was that she had a tiny bump on her labia. She'd only wanted to hear Dr. Erman say, "Ms. Bailey, we've taken care of the growth. There's nothing to worry about. You can leave now." But, no such words were spoken.

Keisha could not accept the truth. The HPV revelation was too stressful for her to handle living alone in a big city where she had resigned to build a career on the fast track to earning money, power, and VIP status as a celebrity publicist.

Forty-five minutes after leaving the doctor's office, Keisha entered her rented apartment and closed the door to shut out the world. She dismissed the unpleasant encounter with Dr. Erman who left her with no meaningful answers. She picked up the phone, and made an appointment with her primary care physician, Dr. Akeheart, hopeful that a subsequent exam would somehow refute a HPV assumption.

6

TOMORROW IS NOT PROMISED

It was Saturday morning, the day after Simone's candid talk with Keisha. She woke to the phone ringing.

"Good morning," she answered, frowning at dusty furniture and wood floors in need of a polish.

"Welcome home. Shower and put some clothes on. I'll pick you up in an hour." It was her friend, Portia.

"Portia?" Simone said, still half asleep as she rolled out of bed. "What time is it?" she asked, opening the drapes and peering out of the window. Outside the ground was still wet from the evening rain. A kiss of dew rejuvenated her parched lawn and gently coated birch leaves with a glistening sheen.

"Time to get up and catch a sale. Get dressed so we can hit the mall, splurge a bit, and have a light lunch."

"Sounds like retail therapy. I have to pass. I'm on a shoestring budget and don't know where my next nickel is coming from."

"Tightwad, how much is lunch going to cost you, a million bucks?"

"Portia, that's not the point. I don't need to buy another item I'm not going to wear or use. I'm running out of closet space as is, and my emergency fund is dwindling."

"Quit with the poor mouth excuses. You're hardly broke. Be ready when I get there."

Making her way down the staircase to prepare a fresh cup of Vanilla Nut tea in her state-of-the-art kitchen, Simone's call waiting beeped.

"Portia, hold that thought for a sec." Without checking the Caller ID, Simone clicked over and zinged, "Speak!"

"Now, I know I raised you better than that."

Simone plunked down on the sofa, bracing for the third degree.

"Good morning, Mother."

"Mornin'. How was the funeral?"

"Sad, moving, and heartbreaking. Saying the final good-bye at graveside was the hardest part. When the pastor recited, 'Ashes to ashes, dust to dust, we condemn this body back to earth,' Traci was inconsolable. It unnerved me to watch her husband Brent struggle to keep her from jumping into the burial plot with Doreen's casket."

"Have mercy." Mother Miller groaned. "That must have been a sad sight to see."

"It was. How have you been? Hope you're taking your blood pressure medicine."

"Never mind all that," her mother scolded, and launched phase two of her third degree. "When were you gonna call and let somebody know you got back safely?"

"Mother, I was going to tell you. I just hadn't gotten around to it yet."

"Well, you should've called. Had me up all night watching the news thinking your plane crashed."

"You're right. I should've called as soon as the plane hit the tarmac. You didn't call to hassle me about it all morning. You must want something. What is it?"

"Run me to Wal-Mart so I can pick up a few odds and ends."

"What time?"

"When you get here, and don't wait too late. It's already nine-thirty. The day's just about over."

"Give me a chance to wash a load of laundry. See you soon."

Fed up with everybody demanding her time, Simone clicked back over.

"Portia, I need a rain check. My mother wants me to take her to Wally World. I'll call you from the car."

After satisfying her hunger with a bowl of bran cereal and a tall glass of calcium-enriched orange juice, Simone grabbed her luggage to wash the dirty clothes she had accumulated during the trip. In the interest of time, and to keep her mother off her back, she washed the whites only and put them in the dryer on high heat. While the machine roiled through its cycle, she showered, dressed, flattened her growing bangs, and brushed the rest of her hair into a tidy ponytail. Putting the spic-and-span shine back into the wood floor had to be put on hold, especially if she expected to make it to Tresses Hair Salon before someone else beat her to the last walk-in appointment.

Simone called Portia on the way to pick up her mother. Portia didn't answer her house phone or the mobile phone so Simone left a voice message at both numbers.

Twenty minutes later, after Simone had dropped her mother off in the cleaning section of Wal-Mart, Portia returned her call.

"Hey, Simone, you got a moment? I really need to talk to you about some personal turmoil."

"Portia, are you crying? I can't hear you. Speak louder!" Simone shouted into the phone as their wireless connection faded in and out. They weren't able to talk at great length because the poor reception inside Wal-Mart cut their conversation short. When the call disconnected, violent images of Portia's abusive boyfriend Lonnie played out in Simone's mind. She envisioned brutal kicks, punches, and profanity spewing from his insulting lips. Staring at the LCD screen on her cell phone, Simone hoped that for Portia's sake and her sanity, she was calling to complain about breaking a strap on one of her pricey designer handbags because Lonnie wasn't worth the salt in her tears.

Simone meandered into the CD section to browse the latest Top Ten releases as Mary J. Blige blared over the speakers singing with passionate conviction about playing the fool, going through changes, being free from stress, and no more drama in her life. Simone surrendered to the undying impulse to sing along with the music until Mary's soulful voice blended with a frantic, young mother screaming at her unruly child for sliding across the floor on his knees and crashing into a display. The red-faced woman, snatched him up by his shirt, pulled his pants down, and beat his bare ass. The electronics department cashier picked up the phone, and announced a number code over the loud speaker. Within a matter of seconds, store security confronted the woman. The chaos reminded Simone why she was childless, and ran her out of the music section to meet her mother.

Watching Claire take her sweet time pushing the shopping cart up and down aisles and listening to her bemoan about her bunions burning her feet because she wore the wrong shoes was driving Simone absolutely bananas.

Ten minutes later in the slow-moving checkout line, Claire asked Simone, "Can you drive me to the package store for mama's usual 'cause these wild bad kids running all over the place, keeping up noise, and breaking stuff, got my blood pressure up?"

Package store was a code name for liquor store. Claire called her usual brand of alcohol nothin', which was synonymous for none of Simone's business.

The request put Simone in the awkward position of having to say no to Mother Miller, the matriarch, the cotton and steel of the Miller family.

"Mother, you know what the doctor said about chasing your blood pressure medicine with liquor."

Claire clutched her purse tightly against her sagging breasts, "Simone, um grown. How many times I gotta keep telling you that? Stop being so hard on the ears."

"But, Mother we won't pass any liquor stores on the way back anyway."

"That's an ugly lie. A package store is on practically every tenth block, right alongside them chicken joints and junk food shops taking over the neighborhood. Now are you gonna take me to the store or not?" Claire bowed her head and wrung her hands, in a ploy for sympathy. "I sure get thirsty for a taste of somethin' when I'm home alone."

Simone knew better than to honor her mother's request for something unhealthy. If she gave in then she would have been guilty of possibly shortening her life expectancy, which was about 70.2 years, according to government statistics.

"Well?" her mother fussed, sensing her play for pity had failed.

Simone shook her head.

Waving a finger to and fro, Claire gave Simone a tongue-lashing that was heard three lanes over from their cash register.

"I don't appreciate being treated like um the child. I pay the cost to be the boss of my body, and if I wanna drink, then um gonna drink! Now, take me home and drive like you got some sense because He ain't ready for me yet."

In the parking lot a few minutes later, facing the woman who had pushed her out into the cruel world against her will, Simone thought carefully about what she wanted to say because speaking her mind more than she should might cost her a few teeth from a good ole fashion whooping which she was all too familiar with from childhood.

"Mother, what will it take for you to trust my driving? I got you here safe and intend to get you home in one piece."

Getting into the passenger seat, Claire tightened her seat belt, and said tersely, "Then stop yapping and drive, or let Jesus take the wheel."

Pedal to the floor, Simone was sorry she asked the question and did everything in her power but defy the laws of gravity to arrive at her mother's house in record time. She rushed to put the bags on the kitchen table and sealed a tender peck on her cheek.

"Take your blood pressure medicine. I'll call you later. Bye."

Mother Miller yelled at Simone as she was rushing to her Camry. "Don't bother ringing my phone" and then she slammed the door.

Five minutes to spare, Simone sped off to Tresses for a wash and set with a splash of juicy gossip on the side.

7

A SPLASH OF GOSSIP

Tresses was a modest salon located in the heart of the community on busy Blue Hill Avenue. It offered typical services one would expect in an urban shop from relaxers, roller sets, faux lashes, and permanent coloring to stylish weaves, cuts and trims, and, of course, gossip—juicy and scandalous gossip. The gossip factor didn't put Simone off. In fact, she appreciated it because, although TraNeese, the owner and lead stylist, was accommodating and talented, her tendency to yap time away was Simone's constant reminder to be mindful of what she said, whom she said it to, and how much she said knowing that words often had a way of being twisted in translation.

With that thought in mind, Simone walked in admiring the pastel sand textured walls beautifully decorated with seashell inspired art and posters of women with beautifully styled hair. An aluminum wind chime hanging above the entrance resounded a smooth, melodic tune announcing her arrival. TraNeese took a break from curling a client's hair to welcome Simone with a look of exasperation.

"Hi, Simone. You're lucky I had a cancellation. Otherwise, I would've been closing up after Mrs. Glenn."

Simone assumed Mrs. Glenn to be the silver-haired woman planted in the styling chair getting a hot press and curl.

Simone signed the appointment book and thanked TraNeese for taking her as the last customer. She capped the pen and made herself comfortable in the reception area fanning through a hair care magazine.

"You getting the usual?" TraNeese asked.

"Auburn streaks and shorter bangs would be nice," Simone answered without looking up from the magazine.

TraNeese elevated her voice at Simone. "Do you see what time it is? I ain't tryna be in here all night applying color. How about I trim all them split ends, and give you a protein conditioner, and a roller set? That cool with you?"

Simone stopped browsing the pages. "Maybe next time then," she mumbled.

"All right. Go to the shampoo station. I'll be with you in a minute," she ordered.

Soon after TraNeese cashed out Mrs. Glenn and booked her follow-up appointment, her aggressive fingers went to work shampooing and conditioning Simone's hair and scalp. After she rinsed the conditioner, there wasn't one tangle left behind. Simone's shoulder-length mane was relatively snarl-free, which was another reason she patronized Tresses. TraNeese stocked the salon with top-of-the-line products that didn't knot up Simone's stubborn hair to the point TraNeese had to get heavy-handed tussling with it like she was fighting in the streets.

TraNeese's cell phone rang. She answered the call pointing to the grooming stool for Simone to sit so she could trim her bangs and then set her hair. Simone sat and towel wiped excess water trailing down her forehead. TraNeese stood over Simone talking loudly into her phone while she styled her hair.

"Robert why are you calling my job with this nonsense?"

"TraNeese, I'm returning *your* call. You left a message asking for help with sports, uniforms and all kinds of extra shit that should be covered by the money that I give you."

"Hold up! What you give me only covers basic needs. Must I spell those out for you?"

"TraNeese, shut up and listen."

"No. Robert, you dialed *my* number so you need to hear what I've got to say. The child support you *agreed* to give barely helps cover food, clothing, toiletries, school supplies, and other day-to-day stuff. Nathan is growing up and wants to participate in activities outside of school. I'm not denying him fun because you're too cheap to part with your money."

"I'm just getting by myself and I've got a business to run."

"Robert, please, I don't want to hear your story. In case you've forgotten I've got a mouth to feed, a body to clothe and a mind to entertain. His name is Nathan."

"TraNeese you're being vindictive because I've moved on."

"Motherfucker, you're talking like I've been stalking you. I'm glad you moved on. So stop making excuses for being a deadbeat dad and help take care of our son. Just write the check and mail it to me. End of discussion."

"Fuck you. I'll write the check when I write the check."

"You're three weeks behind. Hurry up and write it before family court has to intervene to help you get your priorities straight. And don't call me at work anymore complaining about your financial obligations."

Simone listened as TraNeese threatened to take her son's father to court for delinquent child support payments, before ending the call and slamming the phone on the counter so hard, the battery cover flew across the room.

TraNeese groaned, "I swear arguing with that sorry motherfucker always gives me dry mouth. She then popped a stick of sugarless gum into her mouth. When she offered Simone a piece she declined.

"No thanks. I couldn't help but overhear what you and Robert were arguing about."

"Sorry about that, but his stingy ass never wants to pay child support and he's always got an excuse about why he's late."

"May I say something about the situation?"

"Go ahead."

"In my opinion, if the roles were reversed, and Robert had primary custody of Nathan, he would understand the logic of why you expect him to pay child support on time. I mean after all, as children grow up they need more and want more, so naturally the financial needs would increase too. I don't know, maybe it's just me, but I don't understand his resistance to supporting a child that he helped make. My father was a stand-up man. He didn't need a court order to do right by his children."

"Mine either. But, hey, it's my responsibility to make sure Nathan's needs are met. Hold your head still."

Handling a pair of cutting shears, TraNeese began to shape a bang slightly above Simone's brow. She clipped split ends from the sides and back. She then spun the stool around so Simone could see herself in the mirror.

"That cool?" she asked her in a tone that said it better be.

"I like it."

"All right, Missy. Here you go."

Pleased with her approval, TraNeese handed Simone the roller and pin caddy. Simone placed the plastic bin on her lap, and passed the rollers and pins to TraNeese to speed up the process as they chatted.

"Simone, you didn't hear this from me," TraNeese said, indicating she was about to broadcast somebody's secrets. "Do you know my client Sherrie?"

"Can't say I know her personally outside the salon. What about her?"

"Well, the way it was told to me by someone in her *circle*, Sherrie got caught out there sneaking around with another woman's husband."

"Caught out there how?"

TraNeese stopped parting Simone's hair and waved the rattail comb to stress what she was fixing her lips to say. Gossip dripped from her sinning lips and waxed Simone's thirsty ears. TraNeese shamelessly blabbed on and on with so much more to say about the drama, more than Simone cared to hear. It wasn't like Simone hadn't heard an earful about Keisha's whirlwind trysts with married men and so-called estranged husbands. But TraNeese was in full-gossip mode and showed no signs of slowing down.

"Simone, I swear Sherrie must've been under the spell of some good ding-a-ling to max out her credit cards buying that man Hugo Boss suits, gold cufflinks, premium tickets to the Super Bowl *and* the NBA All-Star game. Can you believe she even thought about financing a candy apple red Cadillac for his jive, married ass?"

"A Caddy?" Simone repeated in disbelief and pursed her lips. "Mmm. Mmm. Mmm. The ding-a-ling must be certified platinum *plus*. Let me stop running my mouth before you get me caught up in their BS."

"The ding-a-ling ain't the clincher. I haven't even gotten to the good part yet."

"There's more to this saga than a ding-a-ling?" Simone asked, getting comfortable in the chair. "Do tell. Spill the tea."

TraNeese snaked her neck then brought it to a slow halt. "*More?* That's not the worse part of her sticky situation. Sherrie is waist deep in debt. Her spirit tank is so low you might think that man steamrolled her twice with a Hummer."

"Now that's the kind of ugly God doesn't like."

"Simone, if you think that's ugly, it gets even uglier. Sherrie bought that married man a pair of two-tone alligator shoes for his birthday! What's uglier than buying shoes for a man, especially one you ain't married to?"

"No! Not the womanizer of all womanizing shoes! I should know because my daddy owned three pairs! I don't give a rabbit's tail if the ding-a-ling is knockwurst thick, a mistress ain't supposed to buy someone else's husband shoes. She practically gave him his walking papers back to his wife or to his next mistress's Valentino handbag to empty."

TraNeese spun Simone around to face her, and shrilled, "Hello!" TraNeese then spoke, her voice going up an octave or two. "I tried telling Sherrie not to empty her bank account trying to keep that leach of a man! She didn't listen to me and bought the shoes anyway. Then the parasite had the audacity to get indignant when she begged him for money to pay the bills he helped create."

"And how did the gold-digging punk respond?"

"That good for nothing so-and-so told Sherrie that he didn't need another dependent because he already had a nagging headache at home."

Simone shook her head disgustedly. "That's a damn shame. And worse, the sponge was never Sherrie's to have, hold, and keep. Married men should be off limits, and they need to stop acting like they're seventeen and sowing their wild oats again. I know one thing, that womanizer is lucky Sherrie didn't go upside his head with a pot and pray about it later. As for the shoes, she would've been better off sending him crawling back to his wife after she'd rammed her foot up his trifling ass."

"Simone, instead of Sherrie bashing the con artist with a pot, she pretends to be pregnant and is acting conflicted about whether or not to keep the imaginary fetus."

"My goodness, if faking a pregnancy isn't the lowest act of desperation to keep a worthless man, I don't know what is. How is the glutton for punishment holding up?" Simone asked.

"Depressed, stressing about those credit card bills, and scheduling hair appointments she can't keep because she's broke and can't pay me. You know me, Simone. I don't do credit. I got bills of my own to pay."

"I hear you. Oh well, hopefully Sherrie will learn money can't buy love and happiness, at least not the kind she was shopping for when she sacrificed her self-esteem for temporary affection that left her pockets empty and her mind close to a nervous breakdown."

"You can say that again. So, have you heard from Portia? I usually see the hardest working woman in the cosmetics business at least once a week for a wash and blow. Come to think of it, I haven't seen either of you in church. Y'all better get right and quit backsliding."

It was Simone's turn to suck her teeth at TraNeese's hypocrisy.

"Gossip queen, I was born right. You got more nerve than a thief cashing my tax refund check, to tell me to 'get right' as much as you gossip."

TraNeese curled her lips. "Mmm hmm. Whatever, Ms. Morality, you don't have a problem listening to my gossip."

Simone shook her head in disbelief. "How can you judge my Christianity when you keep telling yourself that gossip is information? I always knew you were a delusional Christian."

"Anyway, so did Portia tell you that Lonnie ain't working again and can't collect unemployment?"

"Portia hasn't said anything to me about what Lonnie is or isn't doing. Ouch! Not so tight." Simone pulled her head away from TraNeese's grip. "You know that's my sensitive spot. Be gentle."

"Sorry about that." TraNeese said, not really sounding sorry at all.

"How's Nathan doing in school?" Simone changed the subject.

"Horrible! I spanked his tail with a switch for bringing home Cs and Ds last quarter. "

"TraNeese, beating him with a switch might just make things worse for him. Have you talked to Nathan about it? He has a voice and deserves to be heard."

TraNeese sucked her teeth. "Talking ain't doing any good."

"Have you visited the school to make sure he's in a healthy learning environment?"

"How am I supposed to visit his school when I got a salon to run?"

"You should take a deeper interest in his education. Your involvement is invaluable. Research has proven that family involvement enhances the academic and social welfare of a child, especially for students of color. Please try to attend every parent meeting and open house. Missing one meeting can give a false perception that you're just another single overwhelmed parent disinterested in her child's education, and we both know that's not true."

Simone softened her tone so as to not sound too preachy.

"TraNeese, now that the salon is closed on Mondays, maybe you can visit Nathan's school and speak with his teachers and request to see his assessments. If he's entitled to academic support before, during, or after school, you can make sure he's getting it. If necessary, stop his extracurricular activities, including sports, until his grades improve. Be polite, persistent, and firm, and put your concerns in writing if necessary. This is Nathan's future we're talking about. It's your responsibility to make sure he gets the best education possible so he is academically and socially prepared to compete for a good job, a career, or a trade."

"I suppose I could do all of that if I were superwoman." TraNeese sighed.

Don't be so hard on yourself. You're a single mother who owns a thriving hair salon. As far as I'm concerned you've already surpassed superwoman status. You're a success story. You should be proud. Talk to Nathan. Don't give up on his education."

TraNeese shook her head. "I'm through talking. Nathan is gonna live with Robert now that he and Lucette are playing house. With Nathan in the picture they can be a complete family."

"Who's Lucette?" Simone asked, surprised at the revelation.

"This young chick Robert is shackin' up with. The same chick he was running around with behind my back."

"Since when?"

"Since Nathan was born. My baby wasn't but eleven months old when Robert started running around on me."

"How'd you find out?"

"I checked his cell phone bill and noticed the same number popping up whenever he claimed he had to check on his mother or forgot contracts at the office."

Simone rolled her eyes, and smirked, "Typical lies of a sloppy cheater. Did you confront him?"

"Why you think we ain't together anymore? Intuition told me to check his Blackberry after he started taking it to the bathroom with him whenever his sorry ass was home to use the bathroom. Before Robert got a clue about what I was doing, I wrote down the date, time, and length of every call to the same number for months. One night when he got in from *allegedly* retrieving contracts from the office, he practically tore a path in the carpet rushing to shower. That's when I decided it was time to clamp down on his dick. I sealed the call history in an envelope and left it on his side of the bed. When Robert finished washing away the guilt, he picked up the envelope and asked 'What's this?' My answer was 'Who is she?' Then that son-of-a-witch politely reminded me that we weren't even engaged to be married."

Simone couldn't believe her ears. "Wow! Talking about perspective. Did you go upside Robert's head with his Blackberry just for the hell of it?"

"I did better than that. I packed my belongings and took Nathan to my parents' house. My mother was happier than a pig in slop to have us under her roof. Now that my baby is growing up, his shoes and sneakers are more expensive, and Robert got the nerve to keep Lucette glamorous like Jennifer Lopez, while his firstborn plays second fiddle to his piece of tail. Every time I drop Nathan off, the conceited heifer poses at the door in pricey designer clothes like she's paying the rent where she spreads her legs."

"TraNeese, in all honesty, if Lucette is spreading her legs for Robert, she probably deluded herself to think she's paying more than her fair share. How young is young anyway?"

"Twenty. Half his age."

"Maybe Robert is going through a midlife crisis."

"He can call it whatever he wants, but I told him if he takes sick and can't do for himself, Lucette ain't gonna wipe his ass and neither will I. Mark my words, she's gonna leave when he can't keep her fabulous anymore."

"TraNeese, the young ones always leave so don't think for one second Robert doesn't know what side his bread is buttered on."

She grumbled, "I don't care about his bread if it's not buttered on the side of bonding with and supporting Nathan. And I'm not gonna settle for Lucette's crumbs. I ain't no pigeon. Nathan's gonna live with Robert. I need a break from the single parenthood."

Simone shook her head. "Now I know why I don't have children. Who needs the aggravation of begging a poor-excuse-for-a-man to own up to his responsibility?"

"If it takes the legal system to force Robert to provide for Nathan, then that's what I'm prepared to do. And Missy, why you don't have any children? Is it because you don't want to mess up that petite body of yours? "

Simone opened her jacket and revealed her bloated belly. "TraNeese don't pretend like you can't see these saddlebags hugging my waist."

"Child please. What's wrong with a little bit of fat? Men like it."

Simone rolled her eyes, "So they say. Anyway, it's not that I don't want children. I simply choose not to push any babies out until I'm convinced children are what I want along with putting someone else's needs above my own. As self-centered as it may sound, it's the truth. But, every now and again maternal instincts flair up but they fade just as quickly."

"Simone, every woman should have at least *one* child."

"I really don't want the motherhood piece of the American pie right now. I'd rather travel halfway around the world with a companion wedded at my hip."

An hour later Simone paid TraNeese but didn't schedule any appointments her dwindling cash flow wouldn't let her keep. She left Tresses thinking about paying Portia a surprise visit to find out if she was weeping earlier about breaking a strap on one of her designer bags, or if Lonnie was spewing profanity, throwing punches and karate chopping her down again.

8

AMERICA THE BEAUTIFUL...
LAW & DISORDER

Simone left Tresses completely satisfied with chic wispy bangs across her tapered brows. As she started the engine a police cruiser shot up Blue Hill Ave., the central artery to the back roads and mean streets of the inner city. She drove off hoping the officers were racing to see who got the last jelly doughnut and not to a fatality.

Simone drove north to nowhere in particular awestruck by the countless makeshift memorials she encountered along the way. The after-effects of ridiculous turf wars appeared in the form of weathered teddy bears, deflated helium balloons, and spiritual candles burned to their wicks. Heartfelt sentiments were strewn about sidewalks, secured to weathered trees, power boxes, and street lamps. I LOVE YOU, WE LOVE YOU, R.I.P., and YOU WILL NEVER BE FORGOTTEN, were scrawled in paint to tag the location of the death of loved ones in the wake of senseless violence.

Death was all around, and the devil was plotting and planning to steal another young life. The haunting sights made

Simone want to know, *What was really going on in America the Beautiful.*

These public shrines were heartbreaking reminders of all the work to be done. The onus was on the community to advocate for better gun control laws and to oppose the proliferation of liquor stores and fast food joints to affect change for the better.

"There is hope. I believe there is still hope," Simone sighed. Detouring at the intersection of Blue Hill Avenue and Seaver Street, she drove a quarter mile to the Fort Hill section of Boston.

Fort Hill was a secluded community in the heart of historic Roxbury of generational Black American families who had not yet been displaced by the influx of former South End residents who fled their quintessential neighborhood because of condo conversions, and as secret as they'd like to have kept it, they could no longer afford the pricey brownstone rents. Fort Hill was a unique place so steeped in American history from as far back as when Black Americans were called Negroes.

Simone's discontent with the dysfunctional gentrified state of the community rumbled in her head, *If only children of color knew all their history. Not only the strife, injustice, and inhumane treatment of their ancestors, but also their rich contributions to the "free world" known as America. If only it meant something to Blacks that crime is escalating in predominately minority communities, while less than a stone's throw away, a "mixed community" boasting median incomes upwards of six, seven, and quite possibly eight figures is seemingly unscathed.*

Arriving at Portia's condominium complex, Simone had pulled one of Portia's stunts by showing up at her condo without first calling.

Getting out of the car, Simone called Portia. Portia's soft spoken, childlike voice filtered through the line.

"Hey Simone."

"I'm downstairs. Buzz me in."

When the door clicked opened, Simone entered the building and climbed the two flights to Portia's unit.

Wearing a fuchsia jogging suit, and dark sunglasses, Portia greeted Simone at the threshold and hurried her inside like she was a fugitive. Inside, everything was in disarray. Books, invoices and contents of her Blush cosmetic case were littered about. Portia's voice was the first clue that something was wrong, disorder in her living room was the next.

"Is everything good with you?" Simone asked, standing in the middle of the living room admiring Portia's contemporary décor. A mocha colored loveseat, sofa, and chair set were draped with ivory and turquoise chenille throws. Cream curtains covered floor to ceiling windows. Beautiful ethnic art was showcased on the alabaster walls. Vibrantly colored throw pillows nestled on the loveseat and chair brought the room together.

Portia made her way to the sofa, and flopped down.

"This place looks like a mini tornado blew through it. I didn't see your car outside. Is everything good with you?" Simone asked again.

"Nice bangs," Portia said, picking up the remote control to turn on BET. Half-naked women pranced around in stilettos and skimpy bikinis with hair all down their backs while a popular rapper, rhymed over hard-hitting beats about money, exotic cars, and beautiful women. Portia cranked the volume up as if it wasn't already deafening.

"I didn't ask you if you like my bangs. I asked if everything is good with you. I called you from the car en route to Wally World and left a couple messages. You called me back sounding weepy, but we were cut off. Turn that off please, so we can talk."

Portia groaned but turned off the television.

Simone sat next to Portia on the sofa, clutching a pillow against her stomach. "You still haven't answered me," she reminded Portia. "Is everything good with you?"

"Yes. If you're hungry, sautéed shrimp and rice are in the kitchen. Help yourself." She offered, changing the topic. But Simone wasn't fooled.

"I'll take you up on that offer if you remove those glasses and prove everything's okay."

Relentless pounding on the door interrupted their conversation.

"Portia, let me in before I tear this door off the hinges!" a gruff male voice boomed.

"What in the name of Jesus!" Simone yelled as Portia rushed like a racehorse to the door.

Lonnie, Portia's controlling and socially inept lover, barged in. Built like a gladiator—broad and nearly two hundred plus pounds solid—he stumbled forward before catching his balance then started barking at Portia.

"What in the hell took your dumb ass so long to answer the door?" He looked at Simone, then back at Portia. "Don't play your childish games with me just because you got company. When I knock once, your stupid ass better open the door, and not a minute later!"

"Lonnie, how was I supposed to know it was you? I didn't buzz you in?"

"You *must* be deaf. I'm gonna say this one more time, when I knock once, your stupid ass better open the door, and not a minute later!"

If Portia earned a dollar every time the obnoxious bull cursed this, that, and the other, she could have retired from selling cosmetics to the French Riviera.

The whole scene was making Simone uneasy. She didn't know when fists and furniture would start flying in her direction. Lonnie was pissed about waiting and she had no idea what else had rattled his cage, but if he didn't calm down she was going to call the police and have the tyrant thrown in jail.

Simone's gut told her that things were about to get crazy. She slipped out her cell and dialed 9-1-1. In the middle of Lonnie and Portia's quarrel, Simone heard the operator ask, "What's your emergency? Hello. Hello." She wanted to say something, anything that would have made Lonnie quit acting like a bully, but a lump in her throat kept her silent. She ended the call and switched the ringtone to vibrate in case the operator called back. But Simone kept her finger on the redial button, just in case.

While Lonnie cursed at Portia daring her to get flippant so he could slap the spit out of her mouth, Simone turned to Portia and whispered, "If Lonnie makes the wrong move, I will knee him in the groin so we can escape to the nearest police station." The closest precinct was about four minutes away.

Portia snapped at Simone. "Let me handle this."

"I'm not one to mind your business, but I thought you said you broke it off with—"

"Don't say another word." Portia said, cutting Simone off. "I got this under control."

"Really?" Simone fumed while Lonnie maintained his big, bad bull stance. She had seen his kind many times before: Unemployable, unmotivated, fatherless, and spiritually bankrupt. Lonnie's demeanor was the epitome of the so-called gangbangers clad in menacing black hooded sweatshirts wreaking havoc in the streets. As far as Simone was concerned, Lonnie was as vulnerable as a homeless man panhandling to fund his next meal. Simone couldn't act like she didn't know exactly how the chaos was going to shift to pleading and begging for forgiveness. After all, she had been there and back dealing with Andy's emotional abuse for three hellish years.

Lonnie finally acknowledged Simone's presence after seeing the disappointing looks she was shooting his way.

"Simone, let me explain what's going on. I have nothing but love for Portia—.

Simone cut him off. "I'm not the one you need to convince."

Portia shouted, "Lonnie, please leave!"

"Why should I leave? Earlier you said we should discuss where this relationship is taking us. If we're going to build toward the future, then let's talk."

"There's nothing to talk about anymore. Lord knows I'm tired of talking. Now leave. Go." She said, shooing him away to the door. "Get out *now!*"

"You don't mean any of those words." Lonnie said, then turned to Simone. "I'm a good, man, Simone."

Simone looked at Portia. "I should go and let you two work through your differences."

In response, Portia reached into the pocket of her sweats and pulled out her cell phone. "Leave Lonnie—now!"

"Or what?" he barked, his hands forming fists at his side.

Hmm. Where did all that love go? Simone wondered. She knew their history. Lonnie could no longer get unemployment because he wasn't enrolled in college or trade school and was running out of options. But judging from the spanking new Air Jordans on his feet, Simone would have never guessed that Lonnie hadn't worked steadily in almost a year. She was willing to bet the high-end sneakers had to set Portia back a couple of Benjamins. Lonnie probably figured that Portia made enough money for both of them as a successful beauty consultant selling Blush Cosmetics. Meanwhile, Portia had given years to the relationship and still loved Lonnie, despite being used as a punching bag. Portia probably hoped she'd taken her last beating in exchange for the sneakers. .

While Lonnie and Portia argued back and forth, Simone inched over to a heavy looking vase in case Lonnie did something stupid like physically assaulting Portia.

An unexpected banging on the door surprised Portia, Lonnie, and Simone.

"Boston Police. Open up!"

Here we go again! Portia thought as she heaved a heavy sigh of relief and opened the door. Two male officers, one White, the other Black, were outside, Officer White did all the talking.

"We got a call from one of your neighbors about an altercation here." Lonnie choked on humble pie. Their Glocks, mace, and billy clubs kept the bull in check. While Portia explained that she asked Lonnie to leave, but he had refused, Officer Black looked Simone over like she was a seafood menu.

"May we come in?" Officer Black asked gawking at Simone with a pair of hypnotic eyes that could have put her to sleep standing. The sight of a manly man in uniform made her hungry for more than the shrimp and rice in the kitchen.

Portia stepped aside, invited the officers in and closed the door. Once inside, their eyes scanned the room. Officer Black smiled a Crest White smile at Simone that revealed cavernous dimples in his cheeks. She grinned, longing to know if his lips were buttery soft or slippery when wet. Meanwhile, his partner extracted a pocketsize notepad and pen from inside his jacket.

"Did he hit you?" he questioned Portia.

Portia responded, "No."

"Are you sure?"

"Yes."

"Officer, he didn't get physical with her. I've been here the entire time trying to keep the peace," Simone added.

"What's behind the sunglasses?" officer Black inquired.

Portia removed the stylish shades to prove she had nothing to hide except "pink eye" in its healing stages.

"Conjunctivitis. It's contagious. I may have caught it from one of my clients." Her statement sucked the air out the room, as everyone took a step away from her.

Officer Black turned to Lonnie. "Sir, is this true? Did she ask you to leave the premises?"

Lonnie smirked. "Actually officer, she *begged* me to stay."

"You lying, no-good asshole. Go on about your business!" Portia blurted out.

"Portia let them do their job," Simone soothed.

"Sir, I asked you a question. Did she ask you to leave?" Officer Black repeated, authority anchoring his words.

"Man, I ain't come here looking for no trouble. We had an argument about me using up the gas in her car. I drove to the service station to fill it up and returned it with a full tank. Next thing I know, you show up. I ain't even do nothin'. I ain't tryna get in a jam with the law."

Portia snapped, "Lonnie, that's a lie! You took my car without permission and told me you were going to bring it back when you got good and damn ready."

That explains her mood change earlier today from shop-'til-I-drop to Weepy Willow, Simone thought.

Lonnie turned to Portia, his nearly two-hundred-plus-pound body rigid with anger, as he clenched and unclenched his fists. Noticing the change in Lonnie's posture, Officer White intervened.

"Buddy, let's step outside and talk for a minute."

Lonnie stepped into the hallway. Officer White followed him. Officer Black shut the door behind them then recorded Portia's personal information: full name, date of birth, and telephone number onto his notepad. Simone stayed nearby for moral support and to bat her lashes at Officer Black.

Ten minutes later, the door opened and Officer White walked in and handed Portia her car keys.

"Ms. Davis, I don't think you have anything to worry about. Your *friend* was advised to leave the premises and warned that if the police are called again, he'll be arrested for trespassing."

Portia gave him a big smile. "Thank you, officer. I feel better knowing he's been warned. But, knowing him, he won't take it seriously."

Officer White nodded, "Don't hesitate to call 9-1-1 if he comes back. Have a good night."

Officer Black smiled at Simone as he left the condo. Portia closed and locked the door then turned to Simone.

"What sleazy kind of charade was that? You need to sit your hot ass in a bucket of ice because you were making me moist. But, I must admit he was fine. Did you see the buns on him? They were tight with a capital T."

"Portia, when our eyes met I was too mesmerized by his Crest White smile to even notice his other assets. I bet his velvet voice would melt me away between the sheets. I wonder if he's single and if tall, buff, and luscious prefers his catfish broiled or deep-fried."

"I don't know but it seemed like you two had already slept with each other. Chemistry was oozing out of your pores. Spill the hot tea. When? Where? How many times did y'all get it on?"

"Portia please. It was a shameless case of lust at first sight for me. What the attraction was for Officer Black I will probably never find out."

"Never say never in a city as small as Boston. Are you going to eat?"

Simone looked at her watch. "I'll pass. I'm not hungry. Thanks. And you shouldn't be alone tonight. Stay with me. I'd feel better knowing you're okay."

"I doubt Lonnie will come back. If it's one thing he fears, it's losing his freedom like his father did for killing his mother when he caught her cheating in their bed."

"Yeah, I remember you telling me that horrible story. Living that nightmare as a child could be the source of Lonnie's anger. I hope he gets the help he needs."

"I do, too, Simone. I pray on it every day. So, are we still on for your doctor's appointment?" Portia asked changing the subject.

"Monday afternoon. Three o'clock sharp."

"Count on me being there."

They hugged and air kissed their good-byes.

9

CLOSURE

After a warm oatmeal bath, Simone had a cup of Vanilla Nut tea and settled on the couch in front of a sappy Lifetime movie about affairs, heartbreak, and champagne. Much to her discontent, there was no joy watching relationships deteriorate on screen, and there was absolutely no joy witnessing make-believe heartache either. The disappointment Simone suffered with Andy was Emmy-worthy drama compared to the spice of Hollywood fiction.

An hour into the movie Simone's cell rang startling her awake. She had dozed off like an old drunk on the couch with the television watching her. Paranoid, she hastily sat up and scanned the room. Living single in the city would do that to an independent woman like Simone, who had started sleeping with a box cutter for protection.

The clock above the television read midnight. Instead of ignoring the phone and taking her tired self to bed, she picked up. When she heard Andy's voice she almost hung up again.

"Andy, what part of restraining order do you *not* understand?"

"Sweetheart, calm down. I'm calling to say I miss you and want to see you."

"Andy, I'm not about to fall for your I-miss-you crap. You're scheming for makeup sex." Simone then proceeded to impart some knowledge on him. "I hope you don't think I've forgotten about that disrespectful ejaculation stunt you pulled. So please leave me alone if you don't want a court order barring you from dialing my number again."

"Simone, quit acting like you don't miss me as much as I miss you."

"For the last time, Andy, what do you want?"

"I couldn't sleep. Whenever my head hits the pillow, all I think about is your pretty smile. I miss everything about you. Please, I need to see you."

Suddenly, warm moisture engulfed Simone's Lady. *Darn, what is it about this man's charm that makes me so horny?* Of all the men Simone had dated, Andy was the most charming of them all. Fearing what she was feeling between her legs was too wrong to be right, she quickly blurted out, "Good night, Andy."

"Simone, when are you going to stop running from your heart?" he asked, trying to keep her on the phone.

"When the devil stops pursuing it," she joked.

"Cute. What are you wearing?"

"Nothing. I was getting ready to take a bath before you called, she lied then she undressed to make part of what she said true.

"Why so late?"

"I had company," she fibbed again, stepping out of her thong.

"Company like who?" Andy asked, like he had a right to pry into her personal affairs.

"None of your business, that's who," she sassed to let him know he had crossed the line.

"You're right. I didn't mean to pry."

It felt so good to hear Andy speak the truth for once. So good, she sauntered to the bathroom stark naked, switched on the light, and rushed to the mirror above the sink. Simone stared at her reflection thankful that she still loved what she saw, except for the hideous bulge she had been battling on her waistline.

"Sweetheart, are you really wearing nothing?" Andy asked.

"What do you think?" she teased.

"It's not what I think. It's what I want to know."

Simone surprised herself and threw out her Lady bait. "Come over and see for yourself."

Andy chuckled. Why, so you can have me locked up? I'm not stupid. Nice try."

When he didn't bite right away like she thought he would, she upped the ante and sprinkled the bait with colorful memories of their sexcapades.

"Partner, don't you want to love me down until the sun comes up? Remember when the nookie was so delicious to you? Remember how I had you howling at the moon? Remember when you cried for more? Remember?"

Andy chuckled. "Sweetheart, are you all right? You're going from one extreme to the next. Restraining orders. Wearing nothing. Talking dirty. Have you been drinking?"

"A girl gets lonely sometimes." Simone pouted, circling her finger around the areolas of her breasts, preparing to delve into the crater of her sexual prowess with every intention of reeling Andy in to avenge his unforgiveable transgression.

"I thought you had company earlier?"

"And I thought you would remember how I can make you moan and bust all kinds of nuts. Remember when we used to watch us tearing the sheets off the bed? I'm setting up the mirror as we speak. Remember when I used to suck you until you came in buckets and howled at the moon? Remember when I used to talk *sooo* filthy, grimy, and nasty, pleading for you to tell me how deep you wanted it to go or if I should make it magically disappear down my throat?"

"Do I ever," Andy whispered.

"Remember when I'd get down on my knees and delight you with my mouth?"

"Sweetheart, you mean when you got down on your knees and made me say, pretty, pretty please? Boy, oh boy, do I remember," Andy moaned.

Simone smiled, envisioning him massaging his shaft until it swelled and hardened.

"Tell me more," he moaned into the receiver.

"Remember when you were so deep in the sugary tunnel of my Lady? Remember her?"

"Damn right, I remember. A gentleman never forgets a sophisticated lady. Sweetheart, I'm on my way."

Simone sneered at the phone. *Just like I knew he would be. Let the games begin.*

"Andy, give me twenty minutes to freshen up."

"I'll give you ten!" he shouted excitedly.

"Fifteen," she replied running upstairs to the bedroom.

"Deal. See you in fifteen."

After brokering a deal with the devil, Simone hung up and smiled to herself. "I've been waiting patiently to even up the odds. Vengeance will be mine."

She returned to the bathroom and freshened up. She gargled and rinsed with peppermint Listerine. What used to be a roller set flopped into a complete beautiful mess, but looked presentable when she tied a silk headband from the hairline to the nape of her neck. Strands of hair brushed her feminine shoulders. "I am one vivacious, sexy woman," Simone said, strutting to her lingerie drawer in search of the most tantalizing, peek-a-boo thong in her private collection.

She slipped into a sheer black bodysuit thong and put on a brand-new face, applying cleanser followed by moisturizer that she worked in upward circular motions, exactly how Portia had trained her. In addition to being a good friend, Portia was Simone's prayer partner and beauty consultant. Lastly, she wet her lips with ginger gloss, and wrapped her body in a knee-length silk robe. She spent the remaining five minutes before Andy arrived mentally preparing for a night of deception and much-needed closure.

The doorbell rang. Staying true to never letting her guard down, she peeked through the peephole and saw Andy and everything about him she loved to hate, and everything about him that she wanted to change.

On the count of three, she slowly opened the door to meet a look only a man in heat could give. Something about Andy was different besides a slightly more muscular build. His alluring appeal that attracted Simone on the boat cruise was back. His dangerous charm was even more addictive. A part of Simone wanted to hate him, but she didn't have it in her heart to hate someone she once loved and perhaps still loved.

Standing at the door grinning like a sex hound, Andy adjusted the collar on his leather jacket a little too pompously for her taste and provoked Simone to slap his face. The loud slap echoed in the room.

"How could you treat my body that way?" she yelled.

Andy held her wrist before she could slap him again, twice as hard. Simone wanted to slap him for every year she had tolerated his abuse, three long years of head games and endless bickering.

"Once is enough!" Andy shouted, sounding hurt. "I was wrong. I did something disrespectful. Do I have to apologize a thousand times before you forgive me? Simone, I never meant to hurt you."

"You're hurting me now," she snarled, scowling at his hand tight around her wrist.

Andy released her arm, invited himself inside, and then closed the door behind him. In the foyer, he stuffed his hands into the pockets of his jacket and pulled them back out. Simone wondered if that was a self-control mechanism to keep from knocking her five-foot-five body into the wall.

"Simone, was this a set-up, a sick ploy to antagonize me into striking you so you could call the cops and play victim?"

"You had it coming!"

"Now that you gave it to me, are you satisfied? Can you finally let go of the past?"

"Andy, I won't be satisfied until you tell me why you ejaculated on my body."

"Sweetheart, can we sit and talk about it in a civilized manner?"

Simone ignored his question and left him standing impeccably dressed in perfectly creased slacks, sporting a gold plated watch. Feeling a touch of victory, she sat down on the couch. Suddenly, the room fell empty with silence. Andy eased over to where she sat and hovered over her like an ominous cloud.

"Are you gonna sit down or stand all night?"

Andy didn't say anything. He just stared at the tip of his shiny Johnston & Murphy shoes before sitting down on the opposite end of the sofa. A moment of calm passed before he spoke.

"Sweetheart, I don't know what to say anymore. I had a good woman in my life and didn't treat her right. I guess I was scared."

"Scared of what? I don't bite."

"Like hell you don't. When you get mad your tongue can slice through a slab of concrete. You chewed me up and spit me out every time you couldn't get your way, and you haven't changed much either. You're still a spoiled brat, and that's what I love about you the most."

"Andy, you didn't appreciate me this much when I was your doormat. I refuse to be a prisoner in the game of love again, especially after what you did to me. It was awful and degrading."

"Do you hear us? It's one o'clock in the morning, and we're fighting like an old married couple."

"Except we aren't married." In fact, no man had ever asked Simone to meet him at the altar.

"Would you have married me?" Andy asked sweetly, tugging on her heartstrings.

"You know you weren't ready to settle down, at least not with me. You didn't want to invest in the whole cow. You only wanted the milk I was willing to give so freely, and when I rebuffed your sexual advances, you took what you wanted from me anyway." Seeing that Andy hadn't changed at all, Simone stood up headed to the door.

"Partner, time for you to go, I've got things to do in the morning," she said, her hand on the doorknob.

Andy didn't budge. Instead, he spread his arms across the top of the sectional like he had chosen the style, color, and financed it.

"Before I leave, you have to answer my question. Would you have married me?"

"I'll give you the answer on your way out," she quipped.

"Sweetheart, come sit down." Andy patted the spot next to him.

"No. You should leave."

"It's also Saturday night. When are you going to stop stressing over tomorrow?"

"When I die."

Andy chuckled behind a charming smile. "Somehow I knew you'd say that." He stood up, walked over to Simone and opened his arms to her. "Can I hold you for old time's sake?"

"What if I accidentally turn you on?" she asked, trying not to give in too soon.

"Oh, I get it now," he said angrily, like he had her all figured out. "You lured me here, greeted me practically naked, slapped me, and expected me to hit you back so you could do me dirty."

"Andy, no amount of dirt can cover up your track record. I have two words for you: restraining order."

"Woman, stop the intimidation tactics. I don't need a domestic charge looming over my head. Now can I get that hug?" His persistence reeled Simone in.

"Okay, but don't say I didn't try to warn you when you're standing before the judge."

Simone yielded to his embrace. They cuddled for a minute, maybe two.

Her eyes were closed.

Her juices flowed.

His chin rested on top of her head.

The sugar between her legs threatened to cascade down her thighs.

Andy spoke softly as he brushed his fingers gently through her hair. "Beautiful, it feels like you're naked under this silk robe."

Simone felt him harden against her. Pressing against the crotch of Andy's slacks was an enticing forbidden temptation. She shaped her lips into a triumphant grin. "Someone seems to think so."

"Yeah, he's got a mind of his own," Andy said proudly.

Simone knew if she didn't move away she would be in a world of trouble. "It's time for you to be on your way." Simone reached for the doorknob. Before she could touch it, Andy whisked her off the floor and to the sofa where he laid her down. He kissed her ever so lightly from the ankles to her thighs. He stopped to find her looking at him with longing eyes.

"Sweetheart, we don't have to take this any further if you don't want to."

"If you've got a condom, please don't stop."

Two hours later, they were on round three in the shower as Simone kneeled low to engulf all of Andy.

Andy then lifted her up and wedged her back against the shower wall as she locked her legs around his waist. He then cupped his manly hands on her ass and shoved his hardness deep inside her. It hurt so good like it had never hurt so good before. Immersed in the pain of pleasure, Simone gyrated hog wild knowing their session wouldn't last forever. Head thrown back, she tried to breath against the cascading water as Andy pounded in and out of her. When he released, thunder seemed to rumble and sizzle through the sky. Panting, near breathless, Andy eased Simone down and then ripped open another condom eyeing Simone. "Sweetheart, are you up for round four?"

Exhausted, Simone turned off the water, and slipped out of the shower and into her robe. "I'd much rather settle for a round of sleep."

Andy stepped behind her and wrapped his arms around her pudgy waist and begged, "Pretty please, thickness."

"Pretty please *nothing*!" Simone tore away from his hold, and went downstairs heading straight for the door. Andy followed, still wet, tucking his shirt into his slacks.

"Sweetheart, slow down. Did I say something wrong? I wasn't making fun of your body. I know how sensitive you are about it. Talk to me. I don't wanna leave knowing you're upset about something, especially after the magic we just shared."

At the foot of the stairs, Simone faced him with tears in her eyes. "It wasn't magic. It was a poor excuse for a roll back down memory lane."

"It was our fresh start. It was special."

"No, Andy, I'm afraid that's where you're wrong. It was closure. Now you should get going. Daylight will be here soon."

After ushering Andy out the door, Simone went to shower. Standing under the running water, she vowed to bless and release him from her heart. Life was too short for second chances and she wouldn't give Andy one even if he begged from his deathbed.

Although the shower was rejuvenating, Simone was still pooped, so pooped she shut off the ringer on every phone in her house.

With time passing so fast, she knew another manic Monday would arrive before she could put a dent in the mattress. For that reason, she decided to forgo church the next morning and sleep Sunday away.

10

FORGIVE ME, BABY

"Give me my car keys, Lonnie. I need to go to the hospital and see about my eye," Portia pleaded. It was 3 o'clock in the morning.

"Bitch, screw your raggedy eye. You weren't thinking about your damn eye when you were showing your ass in front of the police, now were you?"

She laughed and plastered a sly look on her face and boldly said, "Whatever."

Lonnie hit Portia again, causing her skin to redden under the sheer foundation. She winced but forced a grin on her face.

"You used to hit harder than that. Is that all you've got tough guy?"

"Bitch, you better shut your mouth before I take these keys and bust you in it!"

Calling Lonnie's bluff, Portia pursed her lips into a Botox pout. "Like I said, whatever. Just give me my keys!"

Lonnie got in Portia's face and spoke through clenched teeth. "I'm not gonna tell you again. If you think I'm playing with your flip ass, say something else. I'm tired of you talking down to me like I'm some punk." Lonnie balled the keys into his fist and pounded his broad chest like he was king of the jungle trying to intimidate his prey. "I don't care how much money you make, what kind of car you drive, or what God you pray to. The same way you get your knees dirty praying to an invisible man, I expect you to get them dirty for me!"

Lonnie then pushed Portia so hard she fell back limp on the bed. He then threw the keys at the bureau, grabbed Portia's hair and yanked it until tears fell from the corner of her eyes.

"Bitch, get up and show my dick some respect," Lonnie commanded, unzipping his jeans.

Portia fell to her knees and worked up a pulsating pleasure in his loins until he exploded in her mouth. She spat his semen into her hands and wiped it on a towel. Standing over her trembling five-foot-eight frame, Lonnie ordered her to strip and sprawl on the bed on her stomach. He then picked up his belt and used the thick strip of leather to beat her. Portia bawled in response to the punishment she had become accustomed to in their dysfunctional relationship. Lonnie then ordered Portia onto her back, and demanded she spread her legs until they hurt at the joints. She did as she was told. Lonnie proceeded to satisfy his salacious appetite with his tongue. When he was finished, Portia lay shaking on the bed. Sitting up, he reached for his cigarettes, fired one up, took a long satisfied drag, and then blew smoke circles above his head.

Portia watched him, hoping he would hold her in his masculine arms. Instead, he turned to her and whispered tenderly, "Baby, I'm sorry. I didn't mean to hurt you. I don't know what came over me. I wasn't myself. Can you forgive me, baby?" Lonnie didn't even wait for an answer before taking another drag on his cigarette.

Without questioning him about his physical abuse, Portia just smiled, "Of course I forgive you Lonnie. But if we're going to have a future together, I really want you to consider the anger management counseling that we talked about to help you get past your strained relationship with your father.

Lonnie responded by violently mashing the cigarette in an ashtray before gripping Portia's arm. The pressure made her grimace. "If you keep talking that crazy anger management shit, it's gonna hurt a lot worse. There ain't nothing wrong with me. Don't keep bringing up my father. To me he's dead! I have no love for that evil man after he killed my mother. And one more thing, try leaving me, I will hunt you down and break your legs to make sure you never walk straight again. Now get on your knees and worship my dick."

Suddenly, leaving Lonnie Albright was not an option. Once again, Portia assumed the prayer position and acquiesced to his demand.

11

GIRL TALK

Six o'clock on Monday morning, the clock radio on Simone's cherry wood armoire blared Gloria Gaynor's women's lib anthem, "I Will Survive." Simone woke up dog-tired. Jetlag and romping with Andy had her feeling like she'd gone five rounds with Laila Ali. She was tempted to roll over, put a pillow over her head, and stay in bed.

"It sucks that weekends end!" Simone grumbled, peeling back the cover and sliding out of bed to mute the alarm. After taking care of her biological needs and showering, Simone headed to her walk-in closet. Perusing several outfits, she settled on black flats, gray pants and a lilac blouse that didn't fit too snug in the hips, waist, or rump.

On her way out, Simone munched on a cinnamon raisin bagel and sipped Vanilla Nut tea from a travel mug. The streets were slick with dew as she drove to Quest Financial, the leading mutual fund company in the nation. The fickle New England temperature hovered above the fifty-degree mark. Motorists moved along at the pace of a funeral procession. Streaks of vapor exiting tailpipes were the only things going somewhere fast that morning. The gas gauge teetered close to the E zone. Simone could already tell the journey to her temp assignment was going to be a mind numbing commute. Short on patience, she banged on the horn.

"Move the car, you idiots," she shouted. "Come on! Move it! I'm running late for work!" The driver one car ahead waved a hand in his rearview mirror telling her to relax. "Yeah, yeah, freak you, too," she yelled.

Pressed for time, Simone swerved into the breakdown lane to make two speedy calls on her cell. The first call was to Crown Employment Agency.

"Good morning, Ryan. There's been a family emergency. I have to take the day off. I'm sorry for such short notice."

"Don't apologize. I understand. Please let me know if you need more time."

"Thanks for understanding. I'll be sure to call if I can't make it tomorrow."

The second call to her sister Susan ended as Simone climbed a short flight of stairs to Susan's house. She rang the bell and hid behind her back a gift she had been meaning to give her nephew Dallas for winning the show-and-tell contest at school.

"Dallas. Get the door. And remember what you learned about strangers!" Simone heard Susan holler.

Dallas poked his head through the curtains and saw Simone standing outside. "Mummy, Auntie Simone isn't a stranger, is she?"

"Don't be silly. Open the door." Susan ordered.

"Good *morning*," Simone sang, strolling in. "Come give Auntie a hug with your fathead self." When Dallas moved closer she hugged him with one arm and used the other to hide the gift behind a plant.

"Why aren't you in school?"

"Because."

"Because what, young man?"

"Because I'm sick. I woke up this morning with a hurt tummy and did Number Two a lot..."

"Okay. Okay. I get it. You don't look sick to me. I think you're faking it." Simone laughed playfully and pinched his chunky cheek.

Dallas squirmed away from her fingers and grinned, showing off his missing front tooth, "Nuh-uhhh, I'm not faking."

"Nuh-uhhh?" she repeated. "Snaggletooth, what kind of alien word is nuh-uhhh?" she asked, strolling to the kitchen with Dallas at her side.

He shrugged his small shoulders. "I don't know."

"What do you mean you don't know? I thought English was your favorite subject and that you get all A's on your spelling tests?"

"English is my favorite subject and I do get all A's. Wanna see some of my papers?"

"Yes. Dallas, I'd be happy to see your work. All A's? This, I've got to see."

He took off skipping down the narrow hallway that lead to his bedroom and vanished from her sight.

"Hey, sis, I thought Dallas was gonna talk you to death," Susan greeted Simone, without turning away from the sink full of dishes.

"Hey to you, too, and what are they teaching him in school, Slanguage?" Simone asked, placing her keys and cell on the kitchen table and then sitting down.

Susan snickered, washed a plate, dried it off, and plucked another dish from the water.

"Nothing's funny," Simone ranted. "Education is no laughing matter."

Still amused, Susan shook her head and washed a casserole bowl.

Simone nudged an index finger against her right temple, "I'm serious. It's what's up here that's going to take Dallas, Sasha, and Monica further than these mean streets. It won't be a laughing matter if they're reduced to hustling on a street corner peddling drugs or begging for spare change, now will it?"

Unconcerned, Susan replied, "As usual, you're taking yourself too seriously, getting riled up over nothing. Dallas and Sasha are passing with honors. I think a C-plus is the lowest grade Monica got last term. She's passing, too."

"Susan, you call a C-plus passing?"

"Yeah. What do you call it?"

"Failure!"

"Sis, for someone with no kids, you're pretty critical— "

"Auntie Simone, I can't find my papers!" Dallas yelled from his bedroom, preventing an argument in the kitchen.

"It's okay, Dallas," Simone yelled back.

Susan changed the subject. "No work today for you either?"

"I've got a doctor's appointment this afternoon. I would've been clocking out early anyway. I guess little Mr. Hurt Tummy gave you the perfect reason to stay home from work. How's the rat race at the nursing home going?"

"Cleaning up behind old folks is getting on my last nerve. I come home and do the same thing all over again. It's like I never leave work. I'm thinking about resigning, and enrolling in culinary arts school."

"Change is always good."

"Yeah, I know. I'll think of something. Since you mentioned your appointment, I've been meaning to ask you about that bulge you've got going on. I noticed it the last time you were over here."

Simone cut her eyes at Susan's wide hips. "You're not exactly Suzie Slim Fast yourself. Turn around and let me see your washboard abs since you wanna point out my flaw."

Susan chuckled, washing the last dish. "That might be true, but at least I have three beautiful cherubs to justify my weight gain. I'm still waiting for your excuse." She finished washing the dishes and turned around.

"Susan! What the fu—" Simone nearly gagged at the sight of Susan's eyes.

Susan's eyes were puffy, and tomato-red. Vivid images rushed back to Simone of a flimsy dress drooping off Susan's skeletal body as she worked Blue Hill Ave. for her next drug fix, smiling a scary toothless smile to close a deal with a random John. Simone couldn't shake the dreadful images of her sister prostituting on the strip, rapping on car windows, hoods, and trunks, hustling motorists for money to feed her addiction. Simone jumped out of her seat, ran over to Susan and grabbed her by the shoulders.

"Whatever you do, *please* don't tell me you've relapsed. Susan, tell me you didn't flush nine years of clean and sober living down the drain. What about Sasha, Dallas, and Monica? They need you drug-free and healthy. Heck, I need you to stay clean and sober because I'm not picking up your maternal slack again. Mentally, I can't do it. I can't and I won't."

"Shh!" Susan shushed Simone with a single finger pressed against her lips. "Don't give Dallas one more thing to be curious about. He's already asking too many questions."

"How else is he gonna learn if he doesn't ask questions? Is that why you're home today? What's going on? Don't tell me nothing either. Eyes don't lie. When did you start using again? Take it from the top. I have until at least two o'clock."

Susan laughed. "Girl, pick up your lip and calm down. I'm not doing drugs again, if that's what you're thinking."

"Well, if it's not what I'm thinking, then what is it?"

"I'm late."

"Late?" Simone echoed, confused by Susan's announcement. "What kind of late got you all puffy-eyed like you've been sucking on a glass pipe from dusk to dawn?"

"Sis, if you didn't want to be pregnant, you'd cry yourself to sleep, too. I'm almost forty-two years old. How would I look pushing out another baby at my age? I'm not starting over with another one. Dallas will be six on his next birthday. It's time for me to live my life. There are things I want to do before I retire, like take cooking classes for starters."

"Cooking sounds fun and creative, but what if you're pregnant? Are you keeping it? I mean, theoretically at your age the baby is at high-risk for Down syndrome, learning disabilities, and who knows what else. Plus, you already got three mouths to feed around here, and the way that husband of yours jumps in and out of jobs, you might have to work nights and weekends to pick up the slack. You already know Mother isn't about to babysit another hollering newborn."

"Simone, slow down. It's not confirmed, yet. Let me worry about it." Susan walked Simone back to the table and sat down across from her. "Now about your bulge."

Apprehensive at first, Simone decided to share what had been going on with her physically. She told Susan about the terrible premenstrual cramping, worse than she could remember since her period started at the ripe age of thirteen. She also mentioned the embarrassing bouts of erratic urination. "And not a word of this to Mother. I don't want to trouble her?"

"My lips are sealed." Susan pretended to zip her lips.

A few hours later, keys jingled at the door and Sasha, Susan's second oldest child, ran into the kitchen.

"Auntie Simone!" she screamed as Simone rose from the table with open arms. Sasha clung tightly to Simone as if she hadn't been held since birth.

"Hi, pretty girl." Simone smiled down at her parted scalp of cornrows. She then stepped out of Sasha's tight embrace. "So, what did you learn in school today? Something meaningful, I hope."

"Oooh, the usual stuff: reading, writing, multiplying, and dividing yucky fractions." Sasha frowned her disdain for fractions and winced, "Double yuck!"

"Well, just remember you are reading to learn, and math is very important because you use it every day. Understand?"

She moped. "Yes, Auntie. I understand."

"Sasha, tell Aunt Simone you got the honor roll last term," Susan was happy to suggest, her eyes partially clear again.

"Mummy, why do I have to repeat what you just said?" Sasha asked, one hand on her hip and the other snapping her finger. "Duh!"

"Sasha, you better take that hand off your hip and quit sassing me! Don't you have homework to do?" Susan snapped.

"Yes, Mummy," Sasha moaned.

"Then go do it."

Before Sasha left to start her homework, Simone took hold of her hands and held them in hers.

"My girl got the honor roll? I am so proud of you. Keep up the good work!" she said as Sasha beamed a big smile.

"Are you proud of me too?" Dallas asked, entering the kitchen on the tail end of Simone's praise. Simone let go of Sasha's hand then pinched his cheek.

"Fathead, what do you think?"

Staring at his feet, he shrugged to imply he didn't know what he thought.

"Of course, I'm proud of you."

"Stay out of grown folks' business," Sasha told Dallas, sticking her tongue out at him.

"You're not grown. How many times Mummy gotta tell you that? Huh? Huh?" he taunted then stuck his tongue right back at her.

"Get lost, Dallas." Sasha waved him off.

"No, he's right," Simone reminded Sasha. "You're not grown. Keep your feet on the ground, head out the clouds, and away from boys until you're old enough to date. Where is Miss Monica? That's who thinks she's grown now that she has bled her way into womanhood."

"Eewww! Gross," Sasha squealed.

"What are you eewwwing about? Your time is coming," Susan snapped again.

"Yep. I can hardly wait," Sasha mumbled, leaving the kitchen to start her homework.

"Now what are you all talking about?" Dallas wanted to know.

Susan snapped at him, too. "Girl talk, that's what! Don't you have a *Little Bill* book somewhere with your name on it?"

"Mummy, you tore it throwing it at Daddy's head this morning. Remember?"

Susan tensed up.

Simone took notice. "Susan, why did you throw..." she started to ask, then reconsidered prying into a family matter. "Never mind. It's not my business. I'll leave well enough alone."

"I appreciate that. Want some peach ice tea?" Susan offered late into the visit more as a diversion than anything else.

"No thanks. Dallas, guess what?" Simone asked.

"Chicken butt," he snickered.

"No, that's not it. I brought you something. Go look in the shopping bag behind the plant by the front door."

"You brought me a gift?" he asked excitedly.

"Well, don't act like it's the first time. It's a reward for winning the show-and-tell contest. Now run along and go get it."

"Yes! Yes!" He double pumped his arm in excitement, and then took off running.

Simone collected her cell and keys and got ready to leave. "Well, I'm off. Of course you know I can't leave without saying good-bye to my little angel."

"You know where to find her. Will another season change before we see you again?"

"Maybe," Simone said hugging her sister before heading to Sasha's room and knocking on the door.

"Go away, Dallas!"

"It's Auntie coming to say good-bye."

Sasha let her in. Walking back to her desk, she asked sadly, "Do you have to leave, Auntie?"

"Yes, sweetie. I have an appointment," Simone answered, closing the door for privacy and walking to Sasha's desk where she was working on her homework.

"Are you stuck?"

"Yes. Fractions are not my favorite. Can you help me?"

"Of course. Let's start at the beginning. Copy down these facts and you'll get better with practice. Ready?"

Sasha opened her composition notebook to a clean page and wrote FRACTION FACTS. "I'm ready."

Simone recited, "A fraction represents part of a whole. Now sketch an egg carton with twelve compartments to help you better understand fractions. We can start by pretending there are twelve eggs in the carton. Then you remove six. "

Sasha used her pencil to shade twelve slots and then she erased six of the slots.

"Wow!" It makes sense now." Sasha beamed with confidence. "So, basically the amount that I start with is the whole and when I take away a piece of it, I am taking away a part or a fraction. And, the whole can be any starting amount."

"Exactly. You're so smart!" Simone gushed with pride.

"Auntie, you should be a teacher at my school."

"Aww Sasha, that's so sweet."

"Are you sure you have to go Auntie?"

I'm afraid so, I have an important appointment."

"Okay, but come back soon."

"I promise, pretty girl," Simone said lightly stroking her cheek. "You know I love you with all my heart, right?"

Sasha nodded.

"Auntie doesn't want to pressure you to talk about family secrets, but your mother seems to be sad. Do you know why she looks like she's been up crying?"

"No. But her and dad argue about bills all the time."

"Do you remember if your dad was home when you left for school this morning?"

Sasha clammed up like an oyster protecting its precious pearl. "This morning? I think so," she finally answered, before going back to working on her lesson.

"Okay. No more questions. I don't want to upset you."

Sasha placed her pencil on the paper and looked at Simone. "I'm not upset."

"Good. Auntie feels better already." Simone scanned Sasha's bookshelf. *Are You There God? It's Me Margaret* jumped out at her. It was a popular book when she was in middle school. She removed it from the shelf. "This was my favorite book in junior high." She said, flipping through the novel and getting lost in nostalgia.

"Mummy said it was the book to read if you got your period and started bleeding from your pocketbook. Eeeew!" Sasha shuddered at the thought. Pocketbook was a nickname Susan used for vagina because nobody is supposed to go in your pocketbook without your permission.

"Absolutely. Did you like it? And a period is not so bad, but I can live without the cramps."

"Nope. Haven't read it yet. Got too much homework and stupid chores."

"Maybe you and Monica should start a reading club."

Sasha perked up at the idea of doing something special with her big sister. The amber in her eyes sparkled bright again. Simone planted a kiss on her cheek. "I've gotta get going. Be good."

She left the room and poked her head into the den. "Bye, Dallas. Keep up the good work in school."

"*Okay*, Auntie. Thanks for my puzzle."

"You're welcome, Fathead."

Simone returned to the kitchen where Susan was prepping a late afternoon snack for Sasha and Dallas.

"I'm taking off now. Stay out of trouble, and don't do anything I wouldn't do." Susan gave her a look.

"Sis, take care of you, and let me take care of me. Drive safely."

"Okay Susan, whatever you say. Just remember those famous last words the next time you need money."

12

KERNEL OF CORN AND WATERMELON

The day of reckoning for both Keisha and Simone had finally arrived. Their doctor's appointments were approximately one hour apart.

Keisha's primary care physician, Dr. Akeheart, practiced medicine at one of the best medical facilities in New York City. When Keisha made the appointment, she insisted that—in addition to the routine Pap smear—she be screened for everything in the STD directory of diseases. Dr. Akeheart gladly obliged Keisha's screening request. By doing so, she was absolved from the responsibility of having to make the suggestion herself.

After examining the tiny bump on Keisha's labia, they discussed the battery of tests that would be conducted at a later date. In the interim, Dr. Akeheart booked another session for Keisha to undergo biopsy laser treatment.

Simone topped off her gas tank and canvassed the medical district several times until she found a parking spot north of the hospital grounds to avoid the outrageous parking fee. She squeezed her midsize Camry between an SUV and Honda Accord. The bumpers nearly kissed. Content with her parking situation, she fed the meter four quarters—confident that sixty minutes would suffice.

A ray of sunlight guided her stroll to the main entrance. At the east wing, she entered the building through a revolving door. Movement was everywhere. Patients, loved ones, and hospital staff were coming and going from all directions. White-coated doctors rushed through the corridors. Wherever she looked someone or something was moving.

Simone boarded the elevator after a swarm of people scurried out. She got out on the ninth floor gynecology unit. The waiting lounge was teeming with a melting pot of women of many nationalities: Asian, Latino, African American, Caucasian, and Middle Eastern. Some were alone; a few had someone there to support them. For the moment, Simone was alone. Portia had sworn that by " hook or crook," she'd cancel her afternoon beauty consultations to be there for moral support. She was usually meticulous about keeping her word and arriving on time. Simone believed she would soon show up.

Simone approached the patient registration desk anxious to learn what was causing spasms that even a double dose of Extra Strength Tylenol couldn't defeat. The pale-faced receptionist greeted her warmly.

"May I help you?" she asked, picking up a sheet of paper containing a list of patients' names.

"Simone Miller. I have a three o'clock appointment with Dr. Theery," she said, studying an anatomy diagram tacked above the copier machine. The purpose and function of every organ governing the reproductive system caught her eye, considering her reason for being in the gynecology unit in the first place.

"Yes. Here you are," the receptionist said, adding a checkmark beside her name on the list. "Have a seat anywhere over there." She gestured to several tweed covered chairs and a matching sofa. "Complete this questionnaire." She handed Simone a clipboard with a pen hanging from a tattered piece of string. "Someone will be with you momentarily," she said and resumed organizing a stack of papers on the desk.

Simone peered over her shoulder and counted at least eight people who expected to hear their name called out, as well. She saw wistful and tired faces, speculating who among the bunch was plagued by the same symptoms as she. It was rude to stare so she asked the receptionist if Dr. Theery was on schedule.

"Sure is," she answered, raking blond strands of hair away from her oval face, while shifting her attention to a middle-aged woman decked out in a corporate power suit. Crow's feet extended webs of wrinkles from corners of her intense eyes. Fine lines boarded her rigid mouth. Simone noticed her nose hadn't left the air since she entered the lounge. The woman stepped up as Simone walked away to answer medical history questions, ranging from previous surgeries, fractured bones, to any known family history of depression, high blood pressure, cancer, diabetes, thyroid disorders, heart disease, and glaucoma.

She checked yes to diabetes, high cholesterol, and thyroid disorders, scribbled possibly to depression, circled PMS, and double-checked lactose intolerance although the aches leading up to the dreaded day were far worse than the onset of gas and diarrhea after enjoying two scoops of ice cream.

A few minutes later, Portia arrived short of breath, practically tearing a hole in the pea-green carpet to greet Simone. Portia was a true friend who always had Simone's best interest at heart. Simone never thought Portia would gossip about their private conversations about love, life, and loneliness.

Simone and Portia cultivated their friendship at New Baptist where they both received the right hand of fellowship. Portia had truly been Simone's guardian angel long before she started keeping company with the likes of Satan, aka her abusive lover Lonnie the Bull.

"Hi there. How are you feeling?" asked Simone's staunchest supporter, who, as usual, was chicly dressed with flawless makeup. Trendy sunglasses accentuated Portia's navy skirt suit to a tee.

"I'm not feeling anything at the moment. Glad you made it. I could use a friend right about now."

Simone scooted over to make room for Portia on the sofa but she didn't sit right away.

"Can I get you anything to eat or drink?" Portia offered.

"No, thanks. I'm still holding on to the bagel I ate for breakfast. Peace of mind will do. Can you manage that?"

"I'll give it my best shot," Portia said, and relaxed next to Simone on the sofa. "Are you afraid of what the doctor might discover?"

"Wouldn't you be if your body was under siege by who knows what?"

"I don't know, but I wouldn't worry. I'd pray. Have you prayed? You had better say yes!"

"No, I haven't prayed yet."

"Why not?"

"No particular reason."

"Need a hug?"

"Nope."

"Forget you then."

"Forgotten."

"You're a trip."

"I've been to Europe."

"Funny. At least you still have a sense of humor." Portia smiled at Simone.

She smiled back. "How's your conjunctivitis?"

"It's healing."

"What's up with you and Lonnie?"

"Not much. I don't take his calls."

"Portia?"

"Yes, Simone."

"What if I can never have children?"

"Where did that come from?"

"Nerves, I guess."

"Simone, don't over think the situation. It could be something as common as a cyst irritating your ovaries. Don't work up your nerves. It could be anything. Don't think about it until you talk to your doctor."

"What about you, Portia? Do you ever think about settling down, having kids, cooking, cleaning, and changing diapers?"

"That's too much work. Maybe I'll revisit the thought when my biological clock starts ticking a little louder. For now, I'm concentrating on building my beauty consulting business."

Simone glanced at her wrist and realized that she had rushed out the house without a watch. She had left her cell in the car. Simone stopped bringing her phone into the hospital a year ago because signs posted everywhere warned of restricted use. She couldn't see the clock behind the desk from where she was sitting. She looked at Portia's arm and noticed she was wearing a bejeweled timepiece that complemented her outfit. "What time is it anyway?"

"Time to pray."

"Quit toying with me. What time is it?"

"I'm not toying. I'm serious. Simone, why don't you want to pray?"

"Look! Maybe I don't feel like talking to myself, that's why."

Portia cracked up laughing. "I know you didn't just say you don't feel like talking to yourself. You are a mess. It's twenty after three," she answered, still laughing.

"Ms. Miller," announced a petite medical assistant standing near the receptionist desk.

Their laughter subsided.

"Well, here it goes," Simone sighed to Portia. Portia gave her a quick hug.

"Be positive. I'll be here when you get back. Portia assured Simone.

"I'm glad you're here." Simone said, grateful that she was.

Simone walked away with her head up and shoulders back. The medical assistant led Simone into a windowless examination room then she checked Simone's vitals and jotted down a few notes on Simone's chart. She then left Simone waiting for the doctor. A few minutes later, Dr. Theery entered the windowless room.

"Good afternoon. "

"Hello," is all Simone said. She was too nervous for small talk. Dr. Theery reviewed the questionnaire then looked up at Simone.

"So tell me about your symptoms."

"I've been having shooting pains in my vagina right before my period. And my stomach has been bloated for months now." Simone took a breath before continuing because it was almost too embarrassing to mention. "I've also been constipated and at times it's so bad that I've spent an hour trying to push it out and I've even had to pull it out."

"I'm sorry to hear you're in so much pain. Coming in was the right thing to do. I'm going to give you an examination and we'll figure out what's going on." Dr. Theery then retrieved a paper gown from a side drawer in the examination table. "Put this on, with the opening in the front. I'll be back in a few minutes," she said, and then left the room.

Simone undressed shivering in the air conditioned room, and quickly slipped into the scratchy gown. Dr. Theery returned after five minutes and positioned Simone on the examination table and slipped her feet into the metal stirrups. Dr. Theery then slipped on latex gloves; applied lubricant to her fingers then quickly slipped them inside Simone. She probed and prodded her inner walls with one hand and with the other hand she applied pressure to her lower abdomen above the pelvic bone. Dr. Theery paused several times below the navel to administer a soft push here, a gentle push there. Little by little, an uncomfortable ache grew inside Simone's womb and she squirmed and grimaced. The pain worsened the deeper she probed. Simone tried to stay strong, but slowly weakened every time Dr. Theery pressed harder and prodded deeper. Her sapphire-blue eyes studied Simone's face.

"Does this hurt?"

"It hurts like hell." Simone gasped. The pain was almost unbearable.

"Take deep breaths and try not to tense up. It's almost over."

Simone drew frosty sterile air deeply into her lungs, and then exhaled it out through her nose, hoping the exam would end before she passed out. She covered her face with both hands to block out the surgical light shining down on her. The heat from the lamp warmed her face. It felt good. Suddenly, the room wasn't so cold anymore.

"There. All set." Dr. Theery withdrew her fingers, threw the soiled latex gloves into the biohazard receptacle, and then washed her hands with antibacterial soap. "You can dress now. I'll be back shortly." She left the room again.

"Goodness gracious. I almost passed out on this stupid bed," Simone muttered, sitting up and then easing off the table. Her vision was blurred because she'd had her eyes squeezed shut. She waddled across the floor until she reached the paper towel dispenser. Once there, she pulled a couple sheets and gently dried the moisture in her crotch. A tantalizing tingle stimulated her clitoris. Simone looked down and mumbled, "Lady, you can't be serious." She ignored the tingle and quickly dressed, then took a seat near the doctor's desk.

Dr. Theery returned carrying a manila folder. She sat in the desk chair and turned to Simone. Simone's heart pounded frantically. She was anxious to learn her fate, which hadn't always been kind to her. She anticipated good news, but there was a fifty-fifty chance she would hear bad news.

"How are you?" Dr. Theery asked.

"All things considered, I'm okay."

Impassive, Dr. Theery showed no emotions. As a trained professional, she was detached from the information she was about to lay on the table.

"How bad is it?" Simone asked. She really didn't want to know how bad it was. Somewhere in her fragile heart, she held onto a glimmer of hope that God would grace her with a clean bill of health.

My preliminary exam shows that there could be a mass of cysts, or possibly fibroid tumors in your uterus, which could explain some of your symptoms. There is a possibility that a small one might be pressing on your bladder causing the excessive urination. However, a routine pelvic exam is not the most reliable diagnosis of fibroids. We'll learn more after a transabdominal and transvaginal ultrasound is performed."

Just the word tumor sucked the wind out of Simone. Speechless, she drew in a heavy breath.

"It's normal to be confused and upset," Dr. Theery assured her.

Simone wanted to protest from the rafters of the building how life was so unfair.

"What exactly are fibroids?" she asked, when she could finally speak.

"Fibroids are usually benign, meaning non-cancerous tumors. They tend to grow in the muscular wall of the uterus, your womb. They can range anywhere in size from as small as a kernel of corn to the size of watermelon. Fibroids are as common as a cold. Women over thirty in their childbearing years are diagnosed more frequently, as well as women who are overweight. African-American women are two times more likely to develop fibroids than women of other ethnic backgrounds."

"That's a fifty percent differential, between us and them. Great, another strike for being Black! Why does race play a factor?" Simone asked.

"Researchers are not one hundred percent certain why African-Americans are more prone to fibroids. Actually, they're not certain why any race is at risk of developing fibroids. If it's any consolation, research is ongoing to detect the origin of fibroids—in particular, what makes them grow, why they shrink and become less problematic during menopause, and why they are more prevalent in women of color. However, there is a consensus in the medical community that a link exists between diet, genetics, environment, stress, and other factors such as hormone and estrogen levels. But again, their origin is unknown."

"Do fibroids compromise fertility?"

"Well, that all depends on their location. The presence of fibroids in the uterus could make conceiving a child difficult, impossible in rare cases, and increase the likelihood of miscarriages. However, other biological factors can cause infertility and trigger miscarriages in fibroid patients."

"Oh my goodness. Thi...thi...this is serious," Simone stammered thinking about all the women in her life, women with children, and there she was over thirty and childless, and perhaps unable to ever conceive.

"Are you thinking about starting a family soon?" Dr. Theery asked, turning to the computer monitor and keypad on the desk.

"Only God knows what the future holds for me," Simone answered, inwardly she agonized, *why did I have that abortion?* The thought of never having children brought tears to her eyes.

Busy typing on the keypad and reading the screen Dr. Theery didn't notice the tears before Simone wiped them away.

"We've scheduled you for an ultrasound this Friday. Does that work for you?"

"Of course. My body is calling. Nothing else matters. To hell with everything and everybody else. The only thing I'm concerned about is the kernel of corn and watermelon growing inside of me."

Dr. Theery smiled as she printed several pages. She skimmed them then handed two sheets to Simone.

"This is your patient radiology referral, and this is a prescription for 800 milligrams of Ibuprofen. Take it as needed to relieve the cramping. Bring the referral with you to the appointment. Drink at least thirty-two ounces of water one hour prior to the exam, and expect to be there for half an hour."

"Thirty-two ounces of water? You're kidding, right? My bladder is so unpredictable."

"It's necessary. Water helps inflate the bladder to capture images of your organs. Try not to worry." Dr. Theery stood up signaling their appointment was over.

"Do you have any more questions?"

"What happens next?"

"The results will be forwarded to me. I will schedule a follow-up appointment so we can review the report and discuss your options."

"I see."

"No worries, okay? It's not good for the immune system. Your goal from here on out is to stay as healthy as possible, and that includes mental health."

"I can't help but worry, not knowing what's going on with my body."

"Well, until we do, carry on as usual. Eat healthy, drink plenty of water, exercise, and get lots of rest," the doctor recommended with a friendly pat on Simone's shoulder as she led her out of the room.

Back in the patient lounge, Portia rushed to meet Simone.

"You don't look so well. How'd it go?"

"I'm not exactly sure how it went."

"What did the doctor say?" Portia pressed sounding anxious.

"Something about a kernel of corn and watermelon growing inside of me," Simone sighed.

"In plain English, that means what?"

"Put it this way, I might be a walking vegetable stand!"

"Simone, just tell me what the doctor said."

"I don't want to talk about it right now. Let's get out of here. This place is depressing me."

They exited the hospital at the east wing and walked to Simone's car. Looking at her watch, Portia turned to Simone.

"I wish I had more time to find out what's going on but I have an appointment with a potential customer this evening. But let's make plans to talk soon." Portia said, then she gave Simone a hug and said their good-byes.

Simone may have arrived at the hospital like a lioness, but a lamb departed not totally convinced God would bring peace her way. Down in spirit, she wanted to scream and shout because she sure as heck didn't feel like dancing in the streets.

13

MANDINGO WARRIOR

Pulling out of the hospital parking lot Simone slowly pulled herself together, and decided that a trip to Jamaica Pond to clear her head and digest the preliminary diagnosis would be therapeutic.

The sixty-acre landscape was the product of an ancient glacier from the 1800s that was nestled in the diverse neighborhood of Jamaica Plain. The Pond, as native Bostonians called it, was a place of tranquility where walkers, joggers, cyclists, boaters—just about anybody who wanted to, could find solace in nature. Today, Simone was no exception.

Staring into the unknown abyss of a health crisis, Simone couldn't stop the tears that poured. Sad and desolate, she slipped out of the car and walked down to the shoreline hoping that the sparkling sunset over the calm water would soothe her. With a heavy heart, Simone realized that backyard barbecues, scorching summer heat, and a spike in crime were but a couple months away.

"Excuse me, Miss." A calm voice brought Simone out of her pensive moment. She turned to find tall, buffed, and luscious

Officer Black standing next to her in a pair of biking shorts that clung in all the right places. His crotch was accentuated with a lump the size of a moneybag. A tight white T-shirt strained to contain a sculpted chest and impressive biceps. Running sneakers were laced tight on his big feet. Simone snuck another look at his moneybag. *I didn't know he had a hidden treasure under his uniform. What I wouldn't give to service the Mandingo warrior and make change for his dollar.*

Officer Black was giving Simone a look that said, he'd be happy for her to service him. He stepped closer to her. She didn't step back. His luscious lips revealed the Crest White smile that had given Simone such lustful sensations pulsating in her Lady. His sexy dimples made her want to strip him out of his tight shorts.

"Fancy seeing you again," he greeted her.

"Likewise." What can I do for you?" she asked, turning on her tough-girl act to shield her grief.

"I stopped running laps to check for the time and realized I left my watch at home."

"Are you asking me to give you the time of day?"

He chuckled "Yes, if you wouldn't mind. Oh, and could you throw in your name while you're at it?"

Simone would have labeled the hunk a bad liar, but she believed he left the watch where he said it was because she'd also forgotten hers when she went to the hospital. She checked her cell phone.

"It's five-forty."

"Thanks. My name's Jeff, Jeff McKinley," he said extending his chiseled arm for a handshake.

While shaking his hand, Simone conducted a quick inspection of his nails, which she was pleased to see were dirt-free.

He'd just unknowingly earned a three-pointer for hygiene and the right to know her name.

"Simone Miller."

Jeff repeated her name. "Simone, I like that. Is it Ms. or Mrs. Miller?"

"It's Ms., and the pleasure would be all mine, but I hear police officers are quite the ladies' men." Jeff abruptly released her hand. She was glad to have it back not knowing where his hand had been.

"Are you serious? I'm gonna pretend I didn't hear that stereotypical nonsense." He turned away from Simone and looked out over the water. "Do you come to The Pond often?" Jeff asked then he picked up a rock to skip across the graceful body of water. Simone watched the rock skip three times before sinking.

"I come here whenever I need some calm and serenity. I'm definitely not here for exercise."

Jeff grinned and skipped another rock across the water. She watched that one sink, too, and then asked, "Did I tell a joke or say something funny?"

"No, but the reaction on your face was, ahhh, kind of cute."

Simone rolled her eyes. "Only babies and monkeys are cute."

He grinned again.

"Why do you keep grinning?"

"Because you amuse me. May I ask you something?"

"The First Amendment says you may."

"Promise you won't bite my head off?"

She turned up her tough-girl act, "Then I plead the Fifth."

"You're fiesty."

Simone gave him a frosty look. "What makes you say that?"

"I can tell by your confidence that you're a no nonsense woman, and I think that's refreshingly sexy."

"You call this flab sack sexy?" She giggled, opening her blazer and pointing to her pudgy stomach.

"Oh, don't be so hard on yourself," he said, skipping another rock across the water.

"It is what it is," she said, full of self-pity.

"Hey, I can see you've got a lot on your plate, and I have another lap to go. I'd better hustle and finish up. My shift starts at seven. Sorry to have bothered you."

She was suddenly sorry to see him go. "You're not bothering me. It was good to talk for a little while."

"Say, before I go, how's your friend?"

Simone wondered if he would get around to asking about Portia. He scored another point for caring about someone other than himself.

"As far as I know, she's still breathing."

"I'm glad to hear she's still breathing," Jeff smiled, before trotting away. Turning around unexpectedly he caught Simone checking him out.

"Simone," he said warmly.

"Yes," she answered with bated breath.

"I hope I'm not being too forward, but I'm very attracted to you. Can we keep in touch?"

Simone was glad he had asked her but she had every intention of playing hard to get. It would be out of character not to give him or any man a hard time. But to her surprise, she said, "Honestly, I'm in a bad space and not open to dating. My doctor talking about kernels of corn and watermelon got my mind all messed up."

He laughed loud and hard. "Corn and watermelon? You're making me hungry."

She shifted from tough girl to Ms. Flirt. "Well, they say food is the way to a man's heart, so I guess that puts me closer to yours, right?"

He smiled. "I meant what I said about keeping in touch. And as for being a ladies man, there is no lady in my life. I've been single since my fiancée decided she wanted more of what I couldn't give her."

"Really? What more was that?" Simone asked, she was curious. A part of her—a very small part —wanted to know where Jeff fell short on the relationship front, even though she wasn't looking to make a love connection at The Pond.

"Time. Something I couldn't always give her when I was working a second, and sometimes a third shift. When we got engaged, crime was skyrocketing out of control. The department was short on manpower because of a citywide hiring freeze. I was working almost constantly and it took a toll on our relationship. "

"I appreciate your honesty. It takes a mature man to admit he screwed up."

"Thanks, now, back to you, Ms. Miller. I don't know if you're involved with anyone, but I'm going to risk asking if maybe we could continue our conversation over a casual dinner, a drink, or a walk in the park? Say, do you work out at all?"

"Nothing consistent. Can't you tell?" she asked sarcastically, directing his attention to her stomach again.

"Your muffin top isn't that bad."

Simone giggled. "Muffin top? Now that is the silliest thing I've heard all day."

"It's good to hear you laugh." Jeff said. He pointed across the water to where the sun was sinking into the horizon in a blaze of golden light. They stood there watching it set, neither speaking. After a few moments, Jeff broke the silence.

"So how about it. You seeing anybody?"

"No, not at the moment. I'm going through a tough time." Simone answered; surprised she was being so transparent.

"Sometimes it helps to have someone to talk to when things are tough. Can I give you my number?"

"I don't want your number, Jeff." When she saw his dejected look, she added, "But you can take mine." She was glad to see those sexy dimples return when he smiled. As Simone gave him her landline and cell number she thought, *He can do the chasing. I'll do the choosing. If he's as interested as he seems to be, he'll call. If not, then from here on out it's all about my fibroids and me.*

Driving away from The Pond, Simone was in a much lighter spirit than when she had arrived. But as she headed home she couldn't stop thinking about what the impending ultrasound would reveal.

Back home, Simone stepped across the threshold just as her answering machine was receiving a message.

"Now who could it be?" she mumbled, hitting play.

"SIMONE. IT'S JEFF. WE MET AT THE POND TODAY. I'M LEAVING MY CONTACT INFORMATION AND

I HOPE, A SMILE ON YOUR FACE. DON'T BE A
STRANGER."

Simone melted inside as she undressed. Her bright smile lit
up the living room and guided her to the bathroom for a
soothing shower.

14

MISSIONARY OR NOTHING!

At six-thirty Lonnie, Portia's "potential client" arrived at her condo, angry because he had lost another employment opportunity. Slamming the door behind him, he ran into the living room pulled Portia roughly off the couch, spun her around, threw up her skirt and yanked down her Victoria's Secret panties then attempted to make himself feel better with anal sex. Something he'd developed a fetish for.

Startled and outraged, Portia twisted out of his grasp, pulled up her panties, and spun around to yell at Lonnie.

"How many times do I have to tell you it's either missionary or nothing?!"

"Come on, baby. Take it easy. I'll be gentle. You won't feel a thing."

When Lonnie tried to turn her back around, Portia kneed him in the groin and yelled, "Get out!"

Lonnie doubled over and howled in pain, "Are you out of your mind?" He grabbed Portia's wrist and twisted it until she cried out. When she yanked her hand away, Lonnie knocked over the lamp trying to reach her but he was still in pain and couldn't move very quickly. Portia dashed for her cell phone and frantically dialed for help, and prayed and prayed the call went through before Lonnie could snatch the phone.

"9-1-1, this line is recorded," was sweet music to her ears.

"Hang up that phone! Hang it up now!" Lonnie commanded. Portia had never seen him this angry. She bolted to the bedroom holding the phone pressed to her ear.

"Caller, this line is being recorded. What's your emergency?"

"Um. Yes. I'd like to report an assault."

"Bitch!" Lonnie growled grabbing her by the arm, causing her to drop the phone. The call disconnected on impact. Lonnie destroyed the phone with one crushing stomp, and then dragged Portia on her heels to her office. Once there he backhanded her so hard, the dog home alone in the unit next door yelped. Portia's head swam like the sweetest hangover Diana Ross sang about. Dizziness wobbled her back and forth, as if the entire room was on an axis. Stunned, she leaned against the desk and attempted to grab for the cordless phone but she was so disoriented she missed. The phone crashed to the floor. Using the full might of both feet Lonnie smashed that phone to pieces, too. Scattered debris and silence were the only things separating Lonnie's rage and Portia's fear.

Portia slipped behind her desk and pulled a loaded pistol from the top drawer. She clutched the weapon unsteadily, pointing it at Lonnie.

"Lonnie, I love you. Don't make me do this," Portia cried trying to hold the gun steady in her shaking hands.

"You must be out of your mind pulling a gun on me and claiming that you love me."

Portia blinked to hold back tears. "I–I–I just want the fighting to stop, that's all," She begged.

Lonnie laughed. Then rage replaced his amusement. Portia realized it was much too late to reconcile with a raging bull about to charge full speed in her direction. She stepped back, positioning the desk between them. Fear sent her into a cold sweat. She felt like a heroin addict going through withdrawal.

"If you know what's good for you, you will put one right here!" Lonnie shouted, pointing to his heart and daring Portia to squeeze the trigger. "Pull the trigger. I have nothing left to live for. Put me out of my misery. Do it now. Bitch!" Lonnie shouted and moved closer to Portia

"Stop! Stay where you are. I'm warning you. If you come any closer, I will cover you with your own blood. I mean it."

Anxious to meet his maker, Lonnie demanded, "Take your best shot. Go ahead. Do it. Pull the trigger he taunted, disguising his fear with boldness.

"No, I–I can't. Lonnie, I love you. We can work things out. I know we can. It doesn't have to be this way." Portia lowered her arm at the same time Lonnie raised his to strike her. Portia reflexively fired. Clear liquid splattered on his forehead and trickled across the bridge of his nose. In absolute awe, he wiped his face with the back of his massive hand, then used that same hand to slap Portia hard across the face, sending her crashing into the wall. The water gun she'd been holding fell to the floor. Portia crossed her arms to protect herself as Lonnie kicked her with his size eleven feet. Adding to her humiliation, Lonnie yanked Portia from the floor, grabbed the very realistic looking water gun, and pistol-whipped her with it. Water splashed everywhere, drenching her clothes and her

French twist up-do. She screamed for help, slipping, sliding, and losing her footing as Lonnie grabbed her and slammed her against the bookshelf. Books tumbled from the shelf and landed all around their feet.

Portia lunged out his grasp but slipped on the wet floor. Lonnie gripped one ankle then the other and yanked her back. It felt to Portia like he'd nearly detaching her legs from their joints. With little effort, Lonnie jerked Portia's body back toward him and then rained punches down on her. Enraged Lonnie crouched over Portia's abused body.

"Bitch, I ought to beat the life out of you!"

Portia didn't flinch. Her will to fight back was forever broken. She didn't even try. What was there to gain from battling a raging two-hundred-plus pound bull already declaring victory?

Before fleeing the scene, Lonnie reared back and kicked Portia. Her body jolted from the sharp impact. When she heard the door slam behind him, she slowly uncurled herself from the fetal position she'd used to protect herself. The pain was almost unbearable. She willed herself to sit up, and when she'd finally struggled to get up off the floor, she smoothed her clothes and hair. She gently rolled her head to soothe the ache in her neck. She tenderly wiped a finger across her lips, inspecting them for blood. Teardrops streaked mascara down her face. Portia didn't even think to face herself in the mirror because she didn't want to see the clown who had made a complete fool out of herself, and gotten beaten because of it.

Instead of coming to terms with reality, she evaluated the chaos in the room. Books, papers, furniture, and boxes of makeup were in disarray.

"Man," she said sadly, "I wish I knew where to find my father, maybe he could talk some sense into me and kick Lonnie's ass so that he knows what it feels like to fight a man."

She painfully limped around books, displaced furniture, and debris to reach the telephone on the kitchen counter. Picking up the phone to call Simone, Portia prayed in a muffled whisper.

"Lord, rescue me from this evil. Grant me the courage to change the things I can and the will to walk away from Lonnie and his ugly ways. Please."

A sudden thumping on the door made Portia jump and drop the phone. Fearing Lonnie had returned to finish her off, she hobbled to the sink and grabbed a knife from the dish rack before tiptoeing to the door, knife poised to hack Lonnie's head off.

"Who's there?" she whispered. "Boston Police."

Portia heaved a sigh. "Just a minute," she said, rushing to conceal the knife between the cushions of the couch. Then she opened the door to greet two officers, one female, and the other male. The female officer did much of the talking and informed Portia they were responding to an anonymous tip about a possible domestic dispute coming from her unit. Meanwhile, her partner gave Portia a routine once-over, noticing her swollen lips. Portia wrestled with the idea of squealing on Lonnie, but she had been so brainwashed by his apologies that she stayed mum to keep him out of jail.

"There must be a mistake. My boyfriend and I had an argument. One word led to another, then he left. End of story."

Neither cop looked convinced. "Are you sure, Miss? May we come in and look around?"

Agitated, Portia got snippy, "If you insist, but you're not going to find anything."

The officers conducted a routine walk through, checking the bedroom, closets, bathroom shower, kitchen, and office. Though the office was a little in disarray, there was no evidence that indicated a crime had been committed, especially if Portia didn't intend to press charges. They left without incident. Portia closed the door and cleaned up. A few hours later it was as if their fight never happened. Nursing her wounds before going to bed, she iced where she knew a bruise might appear on her face. Long sleeves would take care of the rest.

15

IF LOOKS COULD KILL

It was Thursday morning, four days deep into the work-week when the rush hour traffic report blasted through the clock radio at 6:00 A.M. Simone hit the snooze button, then tried to go back to sleep. As soon as she dozed off the alarm sounded.

"Freak it!" she grumbled and shoved the duvet to the foot of the bed. "It's not like I can't use the money." Tired and irritable, Simone eased off the bed to shower and then soothed her dry skin that she'd inherited from her father, with cocoa butter.

Rummaging through her walk-in closet for something slack to wear, Simone opted for pinstripe pants, a white top, and silver accessories to accentuate her neck, wrist, and ears. She then played Eeny, Meeny, Miny, Mo to choose between jet-black leather kitten heels, a pair of pumps, or sensible flats. She chose the flats because they were the most broken-in of the three and her delicate feet appreciated them. Simone slipped into the pants and became woozy sucking in her stomach to close the zipper over the bulge in her belly. The dizzy spell passed as swiftly as it came.

Within an hour, Simone had arrived at the spectacular glass-paned structure of Quest Financial, fashionably early. She rode the elevator to the nineteenth floor where she swiped the magnetic access card to gain entry. Inside the posh office, Simone settled into her designated cubicle and booted up the computer. While the hard drive flashed in and out, going through the typical motions of connecting to the main server, she sifted through a pile of interoffice memos that didn't necessarily concern a temporary employee. In the recycle bin they went and to the bathroom she strolled to empty her bladder.

Returning to her cube, Simone noticed there was a meeting going on in the Vault, the main conference room. At the helm of the red oak roundtable was Mr. Graham, the managing director. In his company Kimberly Romano, his executive assistant, fund managers David Francis and Beverly Ward, and Ms. Hedley, Simone's supervisor.

Mr. Graham was talking rapidly with his colorless hands. Simone was curious to know what was going on, especially since Ms. Hedley was practically stone-faced like she had just been informed that job security was not in her favor.

"Morning." A raspy, male voice startled Simone.

She turned to find Pierre the maintenance man, watching her spying on the meeting. She wished him a good day, returned to her desk, and logged into account services to status fund transactions as well as customer requests for cash distributions. Focused on the task, Simone didn't hear Ms. Hedley sneak up on her.

"When you get a moment, I'd like to speak with you," she informed Simone, as always, curt and to the point.

Simone turned to face her sourpuss supervisor. "Good morning," *to you too,* she so wanted to add. She held her tongue as her mother's wise words sounded in her ear, *Sometimes you gotta bite your tongue to stay out of the unemployment line.* Instead of speaking her mind, Simone smiled and tried to pump her for information. "May I ask what the meeting is about?"

"We can talk in my office," Ms. Hedley answered dismissively before she turned and walked off. Suddenly, Simone was in a bad mood. At her cell-sized cubicle, she took her precious time closing out a pending transaction before logging off.

When Simone interviewed for the Transactions Settlement position, she didn't notice any women of color in the department. From that moment on, she assumed Ms. Hedley would see her as incompetent, or maybe even a professional threat. Simone had read in the book *Work Sister Work* that, "Every sister is not a sister," which she construed to mean, just because they have the same shade of skin, don't expect to be pulled up by the bootstrap, mentored, or favored on any job. Careful not to overplay her assertiveness and rest on previous laurels, Simone reported to Ms. Hedley who was already seated behind her desk.

Wearing a strained smile, she welcomed Simone into her quaint office overlooking Back Bay and all of its quarter-million-dollar brownstones, fine shops, and sidewalk cafes. Simone's attention was drawn to a parade of elephant figurines arranged close to the border of the oak desk. Their trunks were turned up, symbolic for good luck. Oak seemed to be a common theme throughout Quest Financial. Even the lunchroom was furnished with inexpensive oak tables and chairs. Simone kept her focus on the elephants feeling like she was going to need a stroke of good fortune to endure the meeting.

"If you have personal conflicts outside of work, I need to know now so I can consider someone else for the team leader position," Ms. Hedley stated without preamble.

Simone widened her eyes. A job offer was what she least expected to hear. "Did you just say you're considering me for the team leader position?"

"Yes. Are you surprised?"

"Well, I am...It's just that I thought you didn't like...I mean permanent employees have paid their dues much longer than I. Did someone quit, I mean resign?" Simone wanted to know how the position came about because she hadn't heard any buzz around the water cooler.

"No one has resigned. It's a new position. As you are aware, customer accounts have increased twenty percent."

"I read about it briefly in a memo. How does that affect me?"

"Based on my observations, you are qualified to lead the transaction unit. And Mr. Graham is willing to give whomever I hire a generous sign-on bonus."

"Generous as in...?"

"As in five thousand dollars."

"Uh, I need time to consider the offer."

"How much time do you need? Mr. Graham wants the position filled within two weeks, which means I am looking for certainty, not a maybe." Ms. Hedley's statement seemed a little forced, making Simone think they really wanted her for the position.

"Well, in that case, I *really* need to think hard about it before I give you a definitive answer."

"That's fair. Take a few days to review the requisition and other pertinent details." Ms. Hedley handed Simone a document detailing the job description. The semi-private cubicle was the first of many incentives followed by a respectable salary, thirty grand shy of six figures. Strangely, that generous five thousand dollar signing bonus Ms. Hedley stated was undocumented. Simone immediately thought of the cliché, *if it sounds too good to be true, it must be.*

Still skeptical, Simone folded the paper in half and dropped a bomb on Ms. Hedley. "Sorry for the short notice, but I will be taking a sick day tomorrow. I hope that doesn't take me out of the running for the job."

Ms. Hedley frowned, obviously taken by surprise. She then picked up her fountain pen and twirled it rapidly. If looks could kill, Simone's mother would have been planning her funeral.

16

ACNE, PIMPLE, BUMP, GROWTH

Busy scheduling upcoming events and meetings for her boss, Keisha's telephone intercom chirped interrupting her.

"Ms. Bailey, I've got a personal call for you on line one. Should I put it through?"

"Yes. Thank you."

The interruption was a welcoming distraction from the paper cuts she kept getting while sorting paper. Keisha muted the intercom and brought the phone receiver to her ear.

"Keisha Bailey."

"Good afternoon. Dr. Akeheart calling."

"Good afternoon. I've been expecting your call."

"Is this a good time to discuss Pap smear and blood test results?"

"Yes. I don't think I can wait much longer."

"Well, the good news is that your STI screening for herpes was negative. However, after examining you, I have determined that the warts are a low-risk form of HPV, also known as human papillomavirus."

"I don't believe this," Keisha said.

"Please try not to be alarmed. You're still safe."

"Safe? What does that mean?" Keisha was skeptical. "How am I safe with a sexually transmitted infection?"

"Let me clarify what I mean by safe. Presently you are not at risk of developing cervical cancer. The HPV wart strain that you've contracted is not cancer causing. However, HPV is highly contagious, over 5 million cases are reported every year. Given there is no cure for HPV, I strongly advise you to inform your partner so that he or she can get examined as soon as possible, because HPV is transmitted by way of genital contact, and anal and oral sex."

Keisha wasn't ready to accept the truth. "It can't be HPV. Are you sure?"

"Ms. Bailey the tests were conclusive, and denial is normal. Would you like to schedule some time to speak with a mental health counselor? I'd be happy to make that appoint for you today."

"No, that won't be necessary. A head shrinker can't fix this problem. But thank you anyway."

Keisha let the tears fall for a moment then she quickly wiped them away. Returning her attention to the phone she said, "It's a *he*, and I will make that call today."

"Are you sure you don't want counseling? This news can be very traumatic to handle on your own."

"Dr. Akeheart, that won't be necessary. What happens now?"

Keisha listened carefully as Dr. Akeheart explained the treatment process. Afterward, she hung up and sulked in her cushioned chair staring at the wall. Her emotions brought her to her feet and carried her to a picture window where she stared down on the congested Manhattan street littered with pedestrians, vehicles in motion, and some order to the madness of people moving briskly about. Keisha scrambled in her mind to figure out whom, other than herself she could blame for her predicament.

"No one," she concluded. The facts were the facts: her condition was the consequence of enjoying too much of a good thing instead of practicing safe sex. She was now paying the ultimate price. What she'd thought was harmless as acne, bump, pimple, or growth was actually highly infectious.

Keisha sought solitude in the restroom where she wept softly in a stall. After a few minutes of cathartic crying, she regrouped, returned to her desk, and composed an e-mail to her boss, explaining that she had to go home due to a sudden illness. Keisha then powered down her computer, organized her workspace, donned a pair of tinted specs to conceal her misery and rushed out the building before her boss tried to probe her for more details.

Keisha entered her modest apartment, leaving everything she carried at the door. She made a beeline to the telephone. She frantically dialed her married ex-lover's cell phone. When he answered, she started screaming.

"Gordon, you dirty penis rascal! You gave me genital warts!"

"You got that stuff from someone else!" He yelled right back.

Keisha went on a rampage. "Someone else? What do you mean, someone else? Are you saying I didn't get it from you? I haven't been with anyone but you. Get your penis checked and tell wifey before I send her a friendly note about our dirty little secret—"

Gordon cut Keisha off.

"Hello. Hello. Huh! Did this jerk just hang up on me?" Keisha growled, glaring at the phone.

She called him back to continue her rampage.

"Your nasty penis is unclean. I always knew you were bad for my health, bad for my mind, bad for my self-esteem, and unworthy of my heart." Keisha didn't give him a chance to deny her accusation and tell her more lies. As far as she was concerned, he was guilty as charged. No jury in the land was going to overturn her conviction seeing as she hadn't been intimate with anyone in between their trysts. Without any doubt in her mind, he'd given her a STI.

Gordon hung up on her again. Like a mistress scorned, she managed to get him back on the phone and rewound her diatribe. He countered with, "It's over! Good-bye."

Keisha was so upset she started sending all kinds of vulgar text messages; she even threatened to ruin him financially. She was certain she had the ammunition his wife would need to haul her attorney husband into divorce court and sue the boxers off his disease-infested ass.

In one message she wrote in all caps: GET YOUR PENIS CHECKED AT THE NEAREST FREE CLINIC. In the next, she provided the name and address of the nearest location. In her final text message, she typed: PAYBACK IS ABOUT TO BE THE BADDEST MISTRESS WALKING! Keisha then screamed, "time to make a house call to wifey. But first I've gotta call my girl Simone for advice."

17

TELLING LIES AND KEEPING SECRETS

At the end of Simone's workday, she decided to drive downtown to Borders to browse and purchase every book written about uterine fibroids that she could afford. She needed information, lots of it, to help her understand why fibroids developed and why they affected one race of women more than others. She also wanted to prepare herself mentally for any setbacks that would affect her emotionally, psychologically, and physically.

She walked along busy Tremont Street mulling over the job offer. She already knew that any decision she made would be influenced by the results of the ultrasound. God only knew the amount of medical expenses her condition could accumulate. This tempted Simone to accept the semi-private cubicle and hefty bonus, because it would guarantee health insurance and a stable income.

At the crosswalk, she crossed paths with a friend. Denise Hightower, Simone's other prayer partner, looked slim and stylish. She was dressed for success and holding a briefcase. Not one strand of her ready for Hollywood hairstyle fell out of place as she ran to catch up to Simone.

"Oh my goodness. It's *so* good to see you." She greeted Simone, air kissing her on both cheeks.

"Good to see you, too. How have you been? How are the boys?" Simone asked.

"I'm well. Dorion and Dillon are growing. Keeping me busy."

"Love the short and sassy 'do Simone complimented Denise on her modish hairstyle.

"So you like?" Denise asked, fluffing a wedge of hair in the back of her head.

"It works for you. What possessed you to go super short?"

"Yesterday I declared I am not my hair. It was either cut it or go natural. I wasn't ready to keep it *that* real, so I went old school Halle Berry."

"You can never go wrong with the classic Halle short crop. Who did the cut?"

"Jasmine at Studio 64."

"Oh, yeah, I heard about Jasmine. She's one of the top stylists in Boston."

"I see you're letting your wig grow long. You still going to Tresses?"

"Yep, and TraNeese still beats you gossiping."

Embarrassed, Denise giggled off her guilt.

"So what else is new besides your haircut?" Simone asked, changing the subject.

"I'm back at the bank working part-time."

"Why? I thought you wanted to stay home and raise the boys."

"I didn't have much of a choice in the matter. Jackson hasn't sold a single piece of property since February, and he can't stay away from the casino gambling what little bit of commission he does earn from sales. Once the real estate boom tapered off, our debt started piling up. Right now, it's a buyer's market. Homeowners are holding onto their property until the next seller's market comes around if they want to make a profit. What about you, have you found your dream job, yet? By the way, you carry weight well."

Simone cringed at the subtle weight dig.

"Believe it or not, I'm still working temporary assignments, by choice, of course. Teaching crosses my mind but keeps going. Rumor has it academia is overrun with greed and political bureaucracy, too. I don't think I'll ever conform to politically correct standards of teaching that would contribute to the mis-education of children in underserved communities, or anywhere else for that matter. But who knows? Anything can happen. You know me, always hopeful that money and power will stop ruling the world."

"Yeah, well my mother always says positive outlooks are the fruit of life. I'm amazed the temporary staffing pool hasn't dried up at the rate companies have been folding and downsizing since the technology boom went bust. Are you in a hurry?"

Simone checked her watch knowing she didn't have any plans other than going to Borders then home for a warm milk bath and do some very important reading about fibroids.

"Not really. I was on my way to Borders, but it can wait."

"Good. Then come help me find a pair of gold party pumps."

Denise grabbed Simone's hand and practically dragged her to Shoe Warehouse.

"What's the occasion and should you be shopping now that your money is tight?" Simone asked while dodging foot traffic.

"Finances are tight, but we're not at the hand-to-mouth stage yet. Besides, I have a small amount of money stashed away for the boys and me. Jackson doesn't know about it."

"He's not supposed to know your best-kept secrets. Everything ain't for everybody." Simone winked before asking, "How's your mom doing?"

"She's happily planning a soiree to renew her wedding vows."

"That's wonderful. God has truly blessed that marriage. How many years has it been for your parents?"

"Can you believe thirty? I can't see myself staying married to wasteful Jackson for another month. We don't even share the same bed anymore."

"Wow! Sorry to hear that. Trouble must be really brewing on the home front."

Denise mocked, "*Trouble?* Humph, we make *War of the Roses* look like paradise now that Jackson is whoring with blackjack and roulette on a regular basis."

"I can't believe I'm hearing this as much as you, Jackson, and the boys travel and recite The Lord's Prayer as a family. Are you sure you're not over exaggerating?"

"Simone, don't get me lying about my loveless marriage. Love hasn't lived in our house since Jackson carved turkey last

Thanksgiving. And you know what parts of the bird he kept for himself, right?"

"Let me guess: the breasts, the legs, and the thighs!"

"Mmm hmm." Denise nodded. "You guessed right. I left the bedroom after he carved his last turkey, too."

"What happened to the family that prayed together religiously?"

"Jackson pretty much emptied our bank account funding his gambling addiction, that's what happened. We had words about his misplaced priorities, him not spending quality time with the boys, and the fact that I get no love in the bedroom, so I asked him to leave until he got his priorities in order."

Simone's eyes opened wide with awe. "Leave and go where, if you don't mind telling me?"

"I sent the momma's boy back to his momma. That's where he was living when we started dating. I should've known then he didn't want any responsibilities, pushing twenty-eight still living at home. If his mother had her way, she would've bought him a mail order bride if it meant keeping him away from me. I've never cared for that enabling woman. Anyway, it's best he's out of the house and soon to be out of my life because he's still gambling and crying broke when I ask for money to support the boys."

"Denise, this is shocking news. In public, you and Jackson always seemed so happy

"Happy, my big toe. Things are not what they seem. How does that proverb go, believe none of what you hear—"

"And only half of what you see," Simone finished.

"That's the truth. Our marriage was one big facade. I stopped trusting Jackson after I had to question him several times about the same matter and got a different answer each time. Something changed in our marriage. First, I thought it was the seven-year itch, but intuition and snooping uncovered a slew of IOU gambling debts stashed in his shaving kit. Jackson's addiction put a strain on our finances and crap hit the fan and blew back in my face when he chose to roll the dice and stay out all night, *allegedly* at the casino. I have my doubts about that, too, but I'm going to ignore his other bad habit, and file for divorce."

"Is the other bad habit Jackson frequenting the strip clubs?"

Denise hung her head in shame. "Yeah."

"I thought he retired from that cesspool scene after Dillon was born."

"So did I."

"Denise, be grateful for what you have. Stop sulking. Your marriage isn't a total sham. There's always hope if you're willing to work with Jackson to rebuild what the devil tore down. Think of why you said, 'I do,' and cherish those memories for your sons' welfare.

"Honestly Simone, marriage is so overrated. I'm better off single. I have my little tikes, a roof over my head, a halfway decent job, my health, and a super-sized dildo that runs on double D batteries 24/7. So, screw Jackson in his prodigal ass. Pun intended."

Simone laughed. "Ouch, that was harsh. Poor Jackson."

"I meant for it to be," Denise said bitterly.

They both screeched with laughter as they stepped off the escalator straight into a vast space filled with pumps, flats, boots, and athletic footwear.

Strolling casually down the aisle, Simone whispered to Denise, "So, how long do the batteries last in one of those things?"

"It depends on your sex drive. My first handyman broke down before the warranty expired."

"That good?" Simone asked, blushing as though she did not have a secret pleasure at home.

"Daarrnnnnnn good," Denise cooed. "Insert that bad boy, flip the switch, and let him rip!" She shamelessly swirled her hips. Customers spied Denise making a fool of herself, and Simone, too, if she stood beside her any longer.

When Simone shot the onlookers a nasty look they scurried off. Denise saw how fast Simone's ice-queen glare spooked them and she quickly stopped channeling a stripper in need of some training.

"Simone that was cruel."

"They needed to mind their business," Simone huffed.

Denise laughed as they paraded up and down rows and rows of footwear searching for the perfect pair of gold pumps. They slowed down every few steps to admire or scowl at merchandise. Simone resisted the temptation of slipping her feet into an attractive pair of Via Spiga sandals she had been checking out online since the spring collection hit the shelves. After several minutes of browsing, Simone wandered to the athletic section. Thinking about Dr. Theery's exercise advice, she contemplated trying on a pair of Nikes, marked down from the original price. Simone decided not to let the discount tempt her into buying workout gear until she committed to a gym, or even started walking laps around Jamaica Pond.

Denise and Simone crossed paths in the sandal section.

"Guess who's back?"

"Hi, Simone. I saw you over there looking at sneakers. Forget about running shoes and get yourself a pair of party pumps, so we can hang out like we used to. I miss girls' night out with you and Portia."

"Denise, I'm still trying to figure out when and why we lost our spark, our get-up-and-go spirit."

"That's a darn good question. I wish I had the answer. Do you like these gems?" Denise held up a pair of Franco Sartos for feedback.

Simone smirked. "Not crazy about wedge heels."

"What about these sleek and sexy three-inch pumps?" Simone asked, holding a pair of rhinestone-embellished sandals.

"That heel will break my sleek and sexy ankles, too. I can't do anything higher than two inches. Speaking of Portia, have you talked to her lately?" Denise changed the conversation from shoe talk to girl talk, all in one breath.

"Not since Monday."

"Then you don't know?"

"Know what, Denise?"

"I probably shouldn't say anything."

"Then don't. I'm sure Portia will get around to telling me herself."

"Or showing you."

"Showing me what Denise? Stop teasing, or drop the subject. Like I said, if Portia wants me to know something about her, I'm sure she'll tell me."

"You're right. So are you dating again?"

Short and curt, Simone poured salt into a still open wound in their friendship, "Yes and no. Let's not go there because you and I both know you can't hold water."

Denise got quiet. She knew exactly what ignited Simone's sarcastic remark. Simone dared Denise to act like she fell, bumped her head, and got amnesia. She was overdue a few choice words for gossiping with tell-everything Gossip Queen TraNeese about the details of Simone's split from Andy. Once upon a time Portia, Denise, and Simone would take turns hosting prayer parties, and yap about anything under the sun, no holds barred, until Denise lost Simone's trust by repeating what the trio shared in private about the incredible highs and disappointing valleys of life, love, and loneliness.

The truth didn't taste so good to Denise. "Simone, can we leave that touchy chapter in our friendship closed? I was only making small talk."

"No worries. We can talk about anything but my love life, or lack thereof. Now make up your mind about the shoes before we close down the store."

Ten minutes passed before Denise selected an elegant pair of gold sling-back pumps.

The pair left Shoe Warehouse and spent more time together enjoying a quick cup of double roasted coffee. They brought each other up to date about why neither of them had been attending church regularly. Denise refused to worship at New Baptist every Sunday, looking like a single parent, while Jackson lay hung over in bed. Simone confessed to being a self-proclaimed Sunday bedside Christian after she made an unwise decision to get Cable in her bedroom.

When Denise and Simone parted company, their conversation switched to promises of calling, emailing, and planning a girls' night out in the near future.

Making her way to Borders, Simone thought about Portia, and questioned if Denise would intentionally spread vicious gossip or if Portia was telling lies and keeping secrets.

18

SECRET PLEASURE

A couple hours later, Simone was elated to finally be home. While slipping her tired feet out of her shoes she wanted to kiss the shine off the floor. Comfortable on the recliner she tilted back to a desirable position. The footstool elevated her restless feet to a near horizontal position. She closed the windows to her soul and meditated, pining for a man's touch in the worse way. She opened her eyes to unbutton her blouse and slowly massaged her tender breasts. The soft tip of each finger traced rings around her areolas. She paused every so often to rub her hardened nipples.

A pulsating sensation between her legs sent Simone up the stairs to the walk-in closet where she stored a hidden pleasure. She opened the sliding doors, plowed through a stack of shoeboxes, and reached for a velvet container set deep in the rear of the top shelf. She blew off the dust and set it on her ruby red satin duvet. Eager to satisfy a raging libido, Simone quickly closed the curtains for a private session. She then doubled back to the bed, removed the lid, reached inside, and caressed the mechanical dildo, packing double-D power. She slowly snaked her tongue seductively around its tip, and up its splendid shaft, and back down again. Simone gratified herself with Secret Pleasure until she was ready for penetration.

Feeling sensual, Simone lit two cinnamon scented votives in hurricane lamps on the armoire, a magical beam of blue, white, and orange flames sprang up. The blaze beckoned Simone to the bed where she laid on her back. Her head was propped high on two pillows to admire the dildo gliding in and out of Lady. Power stirred and whirled the sugar in her walls as Simone fervently stimulated "the spot." Ecstasy soared her to a climax that was so good, it put her to sleep.

Two hours later, the ringing landline interrupted her nap. Simone reached for the phone. "Yes." She yawned into the receiver, lying back on the bed, with Secret Pleasure still by her side, safe and sound.

"Wake up, sleepyhead. It's Denise."

"What a coincidence." Simone snickered, thinking, *Handyman has nothing on my Secret Pleasure.*

"What's got you so punchy?"

"If I tell you, I'd have to kill you before you tell the know-it-all and tell-everything clique."

Denise sucked her teeth. "Don't start that again. I need to get out. I'm tired of stressing over debt."

Simone offered spiritual encouragement. "God will provide a way. He always does."

"I hope so," Denise sulked. "I'm going to Spades. Want to join me?"

"You know the club scene is not my thing."

"Well, you're letting your hair down tonight. Be ready. I'll drive," Denise insisted.

"Do you mind if I pass? I'm in no mood to dance. I'm exhausted and have some serious reading to do and a long day ahead tomorrow."

"Oh, come on Simone. Don't be a homebody all your life. Live in the moment. Think of it as girls' night out. Drinks are on me, so sexy up and meet me at Spades in an hour."

"Alright, big spender. I can use a distraction. Burning calories on the dance floor might do my body some good. I'll meet you at the door."

Suddenly the kernels of corn and watermelon harvesting in her womb crept into Simone's head as she stood in front of her overstuffed closet. The energy she exhausted searching for something club-ish to wear was ridiculous and mentally exhausting. To expedite the task, Simone opted to wear an animal-print camisole under a black tapered blazer. She forced a pair of hip-hugging jeans over her waistline and pushed herself out the door.

19

BELLY OF THE BEAST

Spades was a popular venue bordering the lower Roxbury and South End neighborhoods. Its historical ties to famous jazz musicians and patrons dated back to the 1930s. The bar catered to a mixed clientele, typically the twenty-five and older crowd. Going to Spades was akin to a high school reunion or a college homecoming. It was popular for live entertainment, stand-up comedy, and rhythm and blues.

Simone parked about a half block away. As she pulled up to the spot another car sped up to steal the parking space. She quickly slid into the spot before the driver could beat her to it. He whipped his bulky Chrysler 300 parallel to her Camry and lowered his front passenger window at the same time she lowered hers to politely remind him of the manners his parents should have taught him.

"Ladies first."

He cranked up a Kanye West track and drove off.

Simone turned off the engine, flipped on the interior light then evenly applied a layer of gloss. She was patting her hair in place when her cell chimed. She suspected Denise was calling to nag about her whereabouts.

Simone retrieved the phone from the passenger seat. Andy's code name Ace appeared on the screen. She frowned and wondered, *Of all people, why couldn't it be Officer Jeff McKinley? I'm not used to wanting a stranger to pester me, but there is something special about him and I can't wait to find out what it is. Perhaps it's his willingness to take me as I am, or maybe that he's serving the community in law enforcement. Of course, his Crest White smile is a winner, but muffin top is the ultimate term of endearment. If he calls, it would be lovely to hear the sweet sound of him saying muffin top a thousand times until love comes down between my thighs.*

The phone rang again and pulled Simone out of her thoughts. The sucker in her answered. The witch in her screamed, "This is not a good time. Bye!" She then shoved the phone in the glove compartment.

Making her way to Spades, cash ruled the entire block as she strutted to the club passing a fleet of Escalades and Range Rovers on the high end; Toyotas, Nissans, and Fords on the low.

At the door, male security inspected Simone's wristlet for illegal contraband. A stocky, wide-shouldered female security guard sporting Queen Latifah style *Set It Off* cornrows, patted Simone down. She seemed to be taking a very long time and enjoying it far too much. The awkward situation escalated to embarrassment as the security woman worked her way slowly back up from caressing Simone's ankles and stopped inches away from her shocked face.

"All set, cutie. Save a dance for me."

Relieved, perturbed, and pleased to have passed the security check, Simone threw the cover charge at the cashier;

snatched up the five dollars she received as change and proceeded to take in the atmosphere. Newly renovated Spades was dimly lit and reeked of assorted liquors, sweat, and hot breath. A four-piece band was dismantling equipment on a small stage. DJ Price played Sade's greatest hits during the changeover from jazz to the Thursday after-work set.

Denise peeled herself from the wall where she was trying hard to be noticed by any man with a pulse. She rushed over to chastise Simone.

"It's about time you showed up! Can't you smell the testosterone in this place? *Darling*," Denise growled, rolling her tongue, "I could use some help attracting attention."

Simone swept the average-size barroom for the likes of Denzel, George Clooney, and Nelly. She didn't remotely see what had gotten Denise so worked up.

"Frankly, my dear, I don't smell testosterone. I see a bunch of Slick Ricks, and Bill Gates wannabes. Now come on, let's snag a table before all the good ones are gone."

Simone strutted off. Denise followed her to the table, trying to keep her boobs in her blouse, and tugging and pulling down her khaki too snug-in-the-hips skirt. Simone gave Denise a disapproving look.

"You should consider Dorion and Dillon and cover up some of that cleavage pouring out of your blouse." While Denise was doing all her tugging and pulling, Simone noticed the gold sandals on her feet. "I see you're wearing the sandals. They look nice."

Denise stopped fidgeting with her clothes to awkwardly lift up one foot, then the other to show them off. "I couldn't wait to wear them," she said excitedly. "Aren't they sharp?"

"Sharp they are. I might splurge on a pair after all."

Denise beamed, "Go for it!"

They sat at a small round table arranged on a narrow path that separated the dance area from the long, fully stocked bar. Denise was getting on Simone's last nerve running her mouth about this man, that man, every man in sight, overcompensating for a broken marriage. Simone tuned her out to spot familiar faces. Patrons ranged from extravagantly dressed, scantily clad, conservative, metro chic, and marvelous. Surprisingly, not one face looked familiar to Simone.

A waiter with a passing tray of drinks reminded Simone why she wanted to sit at the table. Denise bobbed her head and boogied in her seat to the music.

"What are you drinking?" Simone asked Denise, unfolding the five-dollar bill she had gotten back as change. She had only planned to spend ten dollars for the night, and hoped Denise was serious about picking up the tab.

"My usual, Midori Sour." Denise flagged down a striking hazel-eyed waitress who was caught up in the rapture of high rollers dripping in polished gold and platinum-encrusted diamonds. She looked straight at Denise and put up a silent *be right with you* signal and resumed catering to deeper pockets.

Simone grumbled, "It's going to be one of those nights. I feel it in my bones already."

"Simone sweetie, what's wrong?" Denise asked.

"Oh, nothing. Everything is just ducky," Simone lied. "If you say so. Don't forget whenever hazel eyes finds her way to us common folk, round one is on me."

"Round one?" Simone repeated, arching an eyebrow. "Denise, you're celebrating and the ink hasn't even touched divorce papers."

"Relax, will you? In the process of playing the devoted Homemaker, washing, cooking, and cleaning when I should've been pursuing my paralegal studies, I forgot how to dance like tomorrow may never come, and let's not talk about the sun slumping over the eastern horizon before I make it home."

Simone sucked her teeth. "Denise, don't forget Dorion and Dillon need to see their mother in a positive light. Otherwise, they might grow up with a negative perception of women."

Denise ignored Prophet Simone and waved to someone at the bar like she was Queen Elizabeth.

She leaned on the table and whispered as if everybody would have heard what she had to say over the loud music. "I see we're not the only two slipping into the secular world tonight."

Simone wanted to correct her on the "we thing", but saved her breath because she would have been the pot slandering the kettle knowing she didn't go to church as much as she used to.

Instead, she tracked Denise's royal wave to Deacon Brown, a long-standing, unmarried member at New Baptist. Slouching at the bar, he raised his beer to them in greeting. He then discreetly tipped the bottle to Denise. Denise blushed at him with a naughty twinkle in her eyes.

Simone scowled, "Denise, think about the boys."

"Don't give me that look," Denise smirked, scooting her chair back, and pulling down the tight skirt.

"What look is your guilt telling you I'm giving?"

"Be a friend and let me work this marriage thing out guilt-free. I'm going to get the skinny on church announcements because neither of us has worshipped at New Baptist in good while." She winked at Simone. "Maybe there's a relax and release women's conference in the works that we should know about."

"Denise, you're misusing faith to pacify your marital woes."

"And you need to stop turning up your nose every time one of these potential sugar daddies flirts with you. One fling is not going to kill you. See, look at that one over there." Denise pointed in the direction of a man puffing on a cigarette as if his life depended on it.

Simone rolled her eyes, "If I want to date a health hazard with black lungs and smoker's teeth, I'll date Joe Camel."

Denise giggled and looked at Deacon Brown. This time he lifted and held the bottle in midair, his way of saying, "Don't keep a bachelor waiting." She turned back to Simone.

"Order for me. I'll be right back," Denise said and left Simone hanging to get cozy with the deacon.

"I'm going to pray that God doesn't strike you down before you make it over there."

Sade's smoky contralto crooned "Smooth Operator" above the fluctuating tempo of voices filling the club. Her jazzy vocals drowned out a fusion of social chatter.

Simone gazed over the dance floor and noticed every shade of brown, and black on the color spectrum. Men, women, tall, short, stout, and average filled the space.

Simone rested an elbow on the table and leaned her chin on her palm. Being out was better than sitting home alone watching marathon reruns on Lifetime and waiting for her telephone to ring with good news for a change, not like the bad news that was approaching high-stepping and throwing cheap store-bought hair extensions every which way except in the garbage. It was shallow Mya Munroe.

"Simone?" Mya smiled stopping at her table and coiling her messy mane around her finger. "I thought that was you sitting all alone."

"Mya," Simone muttered, tersely greeting the repulsive blast from her high school past.

"How have you been?" Mya asked, slipping into Denise's empty seat.

"I have no complaints," Simone responded.

"You look good," Mya said, flipping a wavy lock over her shoulder.

"Thanks."

Mya was her usual fake self. Every time she flung the synthetic hair as though it was too heavy for her neck, annoyance flared up in Simone. She had neither forgotten nor forgiven Mya for her infamous fax that almost got Simone fired from a job that she had spent over a decade building a respectable reputation as a token employee in the white-collar business sector. Simone had intended to resign on her own accord, not because fair-weather friend Mya almost burned the bridge she built appeasing wealthy clients and working overtime to meet tight deadlines.

Simone silently fumed, *Mya must be out of her conniving mind to think bygones are bygones when she didn't have the decency to muster up a simple apology for her vindictive act.* Simone suppressed her anger and checked her wrist for the time, then she let her eyes sweep the room. She was already tired of entertaining uninvited company. Spades was packed to the hilt and people were still coming through the front door. The jazz session had concluded. The after-work set was in full swing. DJ Price pumped up the volume to blast the latest R&B hits to move the crowd. Every square inch of the dance floor was covered.

Hands swayed high in the air and sweat-drenched bodies did the bump and grind. Hips swerved to the cadence of bass, beats, and drums. Denise and Deacon Brown sat at the bar, throwing back drinks. Even a blind man could see that one more of whatever Denise was throwing back would have cemented her in his lap, humping and grinding up a sizeable erection in his crotch.

Meanwhile Mya detected a bad vibe from Simone's stone cold stance. She gently patted Simone's arm to get her attention.

"Girlfriend…" She grinned with misplaced confidence.

"I prefer Simone," Simone responded. She then looked around for the server somewhere lost in Spades. Annoyed, Simone stopped thinking about a glass of Chardonnay and turned to Mya.

"Why are you still here grinning like we're friends? There's nothing else to talk about. If you don't mind, I'd like to enjoy my night but not in your company."

"*Well,* excuse the hell out of me! I saw misery in need of company, came over to lend a hand, and this is the thanks I get? So much for being a Good Samaritan."

"Did you forget I still owe you an ass kicking for trying to get me fired? If you're here to collect my size eight foot up your behind, I don't have a problem delivering it."

Mya tried another approach.

"I'm sensing some hostility in your voice. It's been about, what? Two decades since our falling-out?"

"It was *exactly* twenty years ago when I came this close," Simone snapped her fingers, "to losing my livelihood, no thanks to your immaturity, *girlfriend.*"

Mya blinked hard at Simone.

Unmoved Simone blinked back harder.

"I thought we could talk woman-to-woman, clear the air and move on. But I guess I was wrong."

"Well, while I'm waiting for the other woman to show up, would you kindly get lost."

"Classy. Real classy." Mya smirked, rising to her feet. "I didn't come over here to listen to you whine about the past. Toodles." She bounced off flinging her extensions.

Denise returned to the table tipsy and giddy.

"I'm glad one of us is having fun." Simone sulked.

Seeing the look on Simone's face Denise asked, "What's wrong?"

"Mya rubbed me the wrong way, as usual."

"I didn't know the phony broad was here. What did I miss?" Denise asked, drooling for gossip.

"A bunch of gibberish. Excuse me, my bladder is calling."

Before Simone left to make a potty run, she told Denise, "Order a glass of Chardonnay for me, if the waitress ever finds her way to our table. You're cut off and I mean it! Here's five dollars for the tip since you're paying." She tossed the wrinkled bill on the table. Denise slid the money close for safekeeping.

Surprisingly there was no line to enter the humid restroom. Normally, Simone would have bypassed the public facility in favor of the pristine throne at home, but her bladder problem denied her the right to choose public or private. At that moment, it was about necessity, not luxury. She walked into the bathroom and nearly smack into Ms. Bad Weave, Maya.

"Long time no see." Mya snickered while drying her hands on paper towel.

Simone ignored Mya and dashed to the nearest stall. The tiny stall was smelly but clean enough for her to stoop and pee. Afterwards, she jammed down the toilet handle with the sole of her shoe, then exited the stall and walked to the sink. Mya watched her coming and stopped fiddling with her hair extensions to make nice.

"You really haven't aged a bit."

Ignoring her, Simone washed her hands and dried them. Mya pressed on to make amends for past indiscretions.

"Simone, can we forgive and forget? I did a stupid thing to express my feelings. What more can I say? We all make mistakes."

"Mya, stupid cannot begin to describe the fall out behind your pettiness. I could've lost my job, my home, my car, everything I worked hard for! Do the words, *'I'm sorry'* mean anything to you?"

"Simone, I said I made a mistake. Isn't that good enough—?"

Simone interrupted Mya. "Listen, do us both a favor, and shut up before you dig yourself deeper in the hole."

Instead of shutting up, Mya raised her voice. "Simone, you said your piece; I listened and deserve the same respect. Now, we've known each other too long to claw at each other like alley cats."

"Putting it that way, retract your claws, I'm through clawing." Simone said and then stormed out of the bathroom with Mya on her heels. Simone turned to confront her, meanwhile Mya narrowed her eyes and stepped forward to face off with Simone. A small group of patrons set the stage for Mya to give Simone a piece of her vindictive mind, a piece Simone wanted her to keep to herself.

"After years of knowing you, I never pegged you to be an unwed mother."

"Mya, what are you talking about?" Simone asked pulling the blazer closed to hide her belly.

"So, how many months are you knocked up?"

"If it's any of your business, I'm not pregnant. I just need to get to the gym and work off some pounds. And you got some nerve showing off your flabby granny arms in that two-sizes-too-small sleeveless blouse."

Mya tossed the synthetic hair behind her shoulders. "I look damn good wearing it, too. Jealous?"

The onlookers watched and waited for a hair-pulling fight to ensue.

"Ladies. Ladies. This is no way to carry on in public." Slurring his words, Deacon Brown intervened to curb the mounting tension. "We're all here to have a good time, are we not? Now, everybody take somebody's hand and let us pray."

Collectively, partygoers disbanded and scattered throughout the club quicker than cats flee water. Meanwhile, the devil was enticing Simone to deck the intoxicated hypocrite smack dab in his nose. At the very thought of asserting violence to settle her differences, she walked away and left the drama behind.

Back at the table, Simone found two empty glasses with traces of the lipstick Denise was wearing. That was her cue to call it a night. She interrupted Denise and Deacon Brown on the dance floor to announce she couldn't find her groove because she never had it and suggested they leave together. Denise showered Simone with alcohol-laced spit as she objected, claiming the night was still young. A few too many of whatever Denise was drinking had eclipsed her ability to reason.

DJ Price had the muscle to keep Denise planted on the dance floor lustfully rubbing her bubble butt against Deacon Brown's crotch. He caressed every curve on her body, as she craved every inch of his rising nature.

Simone said good night and mumbled while walking away, "I know one thing, they're both going to be hung over in the morning if God doesn't get to them first in their sleep."

As she maneuvered through the sweaty crowd, Simone heard what she thought was a balloon popping, followed by glass crashing down on a hard surface. She heard someone shout, "That was a gunshot!"

Seconds later, patrons dove for shelter under tables, and luckily for many, including security, out the door. Women were crying. Men cussed loudly. The club was in chaos. Simone had never been remotely involved in any violence, especially involving gunfire.

In a matter of minutes, Spades became brighter than neon lights in Tokyo's famous Kabukicho entertainment district. Police officers and detectives stormed Spades, clutching weapons. A big, wide burly officer warned, "Nobody move and nobody will get hurt!"

Simone felt at ease and less vulnerable when the police seized control of Spades. From what she was able to see, a nameless bullet cracked the mirrored-glass in the bar area.

On instinct, one responding officer rushed across the floor to investigate if anyone was injured and possibly dead behind the bar. Nine millimeter drawn, he demanded, "If anyone is back there come up nice and slow."

Someone cried out, "D–D–Don't shoot." The bartender appeared staring down the barrel of a service revolver. The weapon-brandishing officer never relaxed his kill-or-be-killed game face. Aiming the weapon spot-on its subject, he cautioned, "Just keep your hands where I can see them."

"Yes, sir." The bartender was sweating profusely as he looked around, amazed to be alive. His saturated shirt clung to his scrawny chest. Fright drained color completely from his face.

Simone searched the room, looking for Denise and Deacon Brown. Mya, she assumed, had slithered to safety the same way she had slithered on the scene. Simone spotted Denise and Deacon Brown cuddling tight in a corner. Terrified, the hazel-eyed waitress cowered on her knees, covering her mouth to quell her cries. Simone was shaking, she had never been so freaking nervous in her life. She thought she had wet her pants.

Leaving Spades Simone cursed, "Damn it! That's what I get trying to fit in where I don't belong when I should've stayed home learning something about fibroids."

20

UNFINISHED BUSINESS

Pep fueled Simone's long strides to her Camry as a small army of goose bumps peppered her arms. As her pace quickened, her anxiety elevated. Unmarked vehicles and paramedic units filled the street. Yellow police tape cordoned off the scene and extended to an adjacent street. Residents converged on stoops and sidewalks in droves. Every major media outlet must've dispatched a crew to Spades in pursuit of their exclusive, breaking news story. In her haste to escape harm's way, Simone scurried through flashing blue lights that tempted her to run to her car. Two feet from the driver's door, she spied a shadow gaining on her.

"Simone, it's me, Jeff. Slow down. What are you doing on this side of town?"

Relieved, she froze in her tracks and turned around. "If it's a crime arrest me," she joked.

Jeff chuckled. "Don't be silly. Let me walk you to your car."

Jeff escorted Simone to her car and waited until she buckled up before closing the door. She started the engine then rolled down the window.

"Thanks for seeing me to my car."

Jeff stooped low on the sidewalk to lean in closer to the car window. "Don't mention it. I wish we could talk until sunrise." He then turned to the commotion outside of Spades. "But as you can see, duty calls."

"Officer McKinley, I understand. Public safety before pleasure."

He smiled at Simone then looked back at a throng of female partygoers passing by talking excitedly about the shooting.

"Hey, handsome," whispered the statuesque, hazel-eyed cocktail waitress from the club.

"Daphne." Jeff nodded. She was clearly delighted to see him and not at all fazed by Simone's presence, nor the chaos that took over Spades.

At that moment, Simone didn't exist. Whoever Daphne was to Jeff, aside from being strikingly beautiful and a lousy waitress, she expected him to say more than just her name. It was obvious by the way she stared at him, before blowing him a kiss.

Simone wanted to catch the kiss and sock Jeff in the eye with it. She really did, especially after watching Daphne strut away like she was a super model. Jeff turned back to Simone.

"Sorry for the interruption. As you were saying."

"I wasn't saying anything. You were about to tell me who Daphne is and if there's some unfinished business between you two." Although Simone had a smile on her face, she was totally serious. To her surprise, Jeff immediately came clean.

"If you're *that* curious, she's someone I dated. It was a brief rebound. Nothing serious."

The cynical side of Simone didn't believe him.

"You know, Jeff, you remind me why I cherish Maya Angelou's poetic pearls of wisdom: 'When someone shows you who they are, believe them the first time.'"

Speechless, Jeff watched as Simone drove away.

Closer to home, Simone felt bad about leaving Denise in the care of Deacon Brown. To clear her conscience, she thought about the pact she, Denise, and Portia made when they became prayer partners: If we arrive together, we leave together. If we go solo, call when you get home.

Thinking about Portia made Simone even more curious about what Denise had said about Portia showing her something, but not as curious as she was about the Chrysler 300 tailing her blasting a Kanye track. When its driver raced to pull up on her passenger side at a red light, Simone sighed, "Not this idiot again."

It was the ill-mannered driver who vied for the parking spot outside of Spades. He motioned for Simone to lower her window. She did, just as the light was about to turn green. He raised and licked the barrel of a gun. "Sexy, how did it feel to almost shit your pannies in the club?"

"You fired the shot!" Simone screamed.

He laughed as Simone sped off.

Further up Blue Hill Ave. she stopped in front of Area B-3 police station, then thought about the code of silence silently killing the community: Snitches Get Stitches. Instead of putting her own life at risk, Simone made a pact with the devil to seal her lips and erase the incident from her mind as if it were a bad dream.

21

SWEET POTATO PIE

Pulling into the driveway, Simone wanted to foot herself in the ass for not leaving Spades when security tripped her Gaydar. Before she could even get out of the car good, her cell rang. She answered, strolling up to the door, hoping it was Denise calling to say she was still in one piece at home with her sons.

"Hello. It's just me calling to see if you're safe and secure at home."

It was Jeff checking to see if she made it home safely. She took the conversation inside to avoid meddling Miss Bonita. Simone disarmed the alarm and slipped out of her shoes. She left the lights off in the room and slumped down on the sofa, preoccupied with insecure thoughts. She had a burning question to ask Jeff. His response would determine if she would take his calls in the future. She didn't want to scare the man off with her self-doubt, but hey, to know her was to understand that she was who she was, and Simone was going to be who she was going to be: complex and as unpredictable as the New England weather.

Crossing her fingers, she popped the question because something about Daphne's cooing and her kiss in the wind, didn't feel quite right.

"Was Daphne your fiancée?"

Jeff scoffed, "No! She was not my fiancée. I told you she was a rebound. It was never serious. Anything else you want to know before my break ends?"

"No. I'm satisfied," Simone said. Although she wasn't happy with his stop-questioning-me tone, she rolled with it to see if Jeff would trip up and lie. The fire in her question still burned. She suspected that something in his milk wasn't clean. Simone was certain that eventually, the truth would curdle and float to the surface.

"Are you sure?" Jeff pressed. "I can forget about food and come to your place so we can settle this face-to-face."

"You don't know where I live."

"I'm a police officer. I can run your license plate."

"You wouldn't." Simone sat up worried that Jeff was the kind of cop who would snoop in her business.

"Muffin Top, I don't have to violate your privacy. You will tell me everything I want to know about you when you're ready to round second base."

Hearing him say muffin top, roped her in for the chase. "You got a pen handy?"

Jeff recorded her logistics and then said, "In case you're interested, my address is 1243 Kalvin Street, in Hyde Park."

Simone made a mental note of his address until she could write it down. They then wished each other a good night. After hanging up, Simone called Denise. Agitated when it went to voicemail, she left an urgent message.

"It's Simone. Please, please call back when you get this. And by the way, you owe me a glass of chardonnay that I never got to enjoy."

She hung up and placed the phone within arm's reach. Laying in the dark, Simone unbuttoned the blazer to massage her muffin top under the camisole. She laughed, "Me, pregnant?" Then she frowned thinking about the abortion that didn't have to happen. Simone curled into a fetal position and wept for the baby she aborted, a rash decision fueled by her me-myself-and-I attitude, coupled with the fact she had no desire to be Andy's baby mama since he wasn't quite ready to claim her as his wife. Then her conversation with Dr. Theery replayed in her head.

"Do fibroids compromise fertility?"

"Well, that all depends on their location. The presence of fibroids in the uterus could make conceiving a child difficult, impossible in some rare cases, and increase the likelihood of miscarriages."

Simone's ringing cell phone delivered her from self-loathing and brought her back to the present. She picked it up wiping away tears from her face.

"I got your message. Let's talk tomorrow." Denise said hurriedly.

Simone rolled her eyes. "Slow down, speedy. Where are you?"

"The Holiday Inn."

"Tsk, tsk, tsk. The divorce isn't even on the books and you're carrying on like you're single. Don't make a mistake you're going to regret for the rest of your life. Dress and go home. Make things right with Jackson. You might not get another chance to save your marriage."

"Simone, it's too late. Deacon *Troy* Brown and I tore the sheets off the mattress throwing down an hour ago. Handyman is history!"

Simone laughed. "If you say so *Stella*. And who's watching the boys while you're getting your freak on?"

Denise giggled. "Dorion and Dillon are with my mother. She's driving them to school in the morning."

They bid their good-byes. Simone went back to wondering what the ultrasound was going to reveal.

A sleepless hour went by. Simone was restless. She couldn't sleep a wink. She attempted to delve into at least one of the books to wrap her brain around coping with fibroids, but depressing testimonies sucked the pleasure out of reading.

Marriages didn't endure. Husbands, lovers, and boyfriends wanted absolutely no part of the misery as their better half's quality of life deteriorated to bouts of hopelessness.

Still restless, after digesting the horrific testimonies, Simone rolled off the sofa and logged onto the computer, skimmed online newspapers, checked the Dow Jones Industrial Average, tackled a backlog of spam, and perused an onslaught of e-mails. Concerned for Keisha's well being, she sent a short message.

IT'S BEEN A MINUTE SINCE WE LAST SPOKE. ARE YOU DOING OKAY? LET ME KNOW WHAT'S GOING ON WITH YOU. BE LIGHT.
—SM

Next, she composed a quick note to Traci to let her know she was in her thoughts. As soon as Simone hit send, an instant message alert from her ever-faithful Internet Romeo appeared on the screen. She could always count on Internet Romeo to help her forget where she was, who she was, and most of her troubles. Sometimes they cyber-chatted for hours.

Anxious to view what he had to say, she clicked on the Read Now icon and relaxed back in the chair.

InternetRomeo: HEY, STRANGER. WUT U BEEN UP 2?
Simmy: I'D BE LYING IF I SAID THINKING ABOUT U.
InternetRomeo: SATAN IS A LIAR.
Simmy: THAT HE IS.
InternetRomeo: I MISS U.
Simmy: AGAIN?
InternetRomeo: CAN'T HELP IT. I'M ADDICTED. COMPUTER LUV.
Simmy: QUIT DREAMING.
InternetRomeo: BE NICE.
Simmy: LAST TIME IT WAS BE NAUGHTY.
InternetRomeo: IS UR MECHANICAL LOVER STILL SATISFYING U?
Simmy: HE SERVES HIS PURPOSE.
InternetRomeo: I CAN DO BETTER.
Simmy: YOU'RE SUCH A TEASE.
InternetRomeo: I AIM TO PLEASE. WHEN CAN I SHOW U?

Before she could type, NEVER IN THIS LIFETIME her buddy alert icon pinged: GrownNsexC HAS JUST SIGNED ON.

Simone forgot all about InternetRomeo. She was wondering why her niece was surfing the web at almost two o'clock in the morning.

Simone had been secretly spying on Monica's cyberspace activity ever since she'd forgot to log off Simone's computer one weekend when she stayed overnight. Simone created a fictitious screen name to lurk in the Noire Planet chat room where she monitored her darling niece's cyber-surfing habits. Ever since she'd overheard Monica bragging about getting "mad chat room play" on the phone to one of her fast-tail friends.

InternetRomeo: STILL THERE?
Simmy: CAN WE TALK ANOTHER TIME? FAMILY CRISIS.
InternetRomeo: SURE. DON'T STAY AWAY 2 LONG.

Simone signed off, then logged back on to Noire Planet under the handle, SweetPotatoPie. Just as she suspected, Monica's frisky fingers were pecking away, hot and heavy, in the Single and Sexy Looking for Fun chat room. Simone could picture the plume of smoke that was no doubt bellowing from Monica's keyboard. She crossed her arms and blew off a stream of disappointment and concern for Monica's safety.

Being late should be the least of Susan's problems, seeing that her maturing, naïve daughter is crying out for attention over the web. The Internet is a dangerous playground, tainted with sadistic predators who entice unsuspecting children to meet offline at discreet locations to satisfy sexual fantasies. Monica probably thinks everyone she encounters online is a friend, or even her age. This Curious69 character has been working long and strong to convince Monica he could give her the rite of passage to womanhood. Sadly, an unsuspecting victim doesn't know what to expect until the encounter actually takes place. By then it's usually too late. Simone turned off her thoughts to join the chat.

Curious69: GNC, WUT TOOK U SO LONG?
GrownNsexC: I HAD 2 WAIT 4 MY ANNOYIN' MOTHER 2 GO 2 SLEEP.
Curious69: U R 17, RIGHT?

SweetPotatoPie: GNC YOU'RE 17?

GrownNsexC: YUP.

Curious69: GNC, R U WEARING PANTIES?

GrownNsexC: A FIRE RED THONG! WUT R U WEARIN'?

SweetPotatoPie: SMH @ GNC & CURIOUS69.

Curious69: A WIFE BEATER.

GrownNsexC: WUT'S THAT?

Curious69: WHO DOESN'T KNOW WUT A WIFE BEATER IS?

SweetPotatoPie: SOMEONE YOUNG, NAÏVE, AND FULL OF POOP.

GrownNsexC: SWEET, THIS IS A 2-WAY CONVO. C UR WAY OUT! C69 AS U WERE SAYIN' B4 THE NOSY WITCH BUTTED IN.

SweetPotatoPie: HE SAID HE'S A LOSER. ROFLMAO!!!

Curious69: SWEET U R FEISTY. I LIKE FEISTY. LET'S HAVE A 3SOME. WHO WANTS 2 BE THE HEAD NURSE? SUCKY. SUCKY. GET IT? LOL.

GrownNsexC: I DON'T SHARE MY GOODIES LIKE THAT.

SweetPotatoPie: SMH @ GNC! ROLLING EYES @ C69.

Disgusted and now afraid for Monica's safety, Simone logged off.

"This cyber chatting is going too far. Time to cool Monica's hot pants before she burns down the house," Simone mumbled, reaching for her cell to call Susan.

"Susan, wake up!"

"Simone, do you know what time it is?"

"Yeah, I know what time it is. That's why I'm calling. It's going on 3 o'clock in the morning and your fifteen-year-old daughter is online talking nasty to an unscrupulous pedophile."

"Monica better not be in that chat room! I told her if I catch her one more time I'm going to take away her computer!"

"Sounds to me like it's time to stop talking and start laying down the law. Straighten Monica out before she starts running all over you, Dallas and Sasha."

On Susan's end, Simone heard sheets ruffling, a bump, and a bang. Susan grunted, "Got damn it!"

"What was all that noise? I hope you're not over there doing something you're not supposed to be doing."

"I bumped my friggin' knee on the nightstand getting out of bed. Let me get off this phone and go handle Monica's grown behind."

"Alright then. Be gentle. Good night."

Thinking about what the ultrasound might reveal, Simone tossed and turned between the sheets until she fell asleep.

22

PRESERVE MY SEXY

The next morning, Simone called out sick then decided what to wear to her ultrasound appointment. It took her less than the usual time to shower and throw on a t-shirt, denim jacket, casual pants, and sneakers. She drank the recommended amount of water for the exam in between taking a shower, getting dressed, and driving to the appointment. The three-mile drive to MRI Solutions in Braintree was a real snooze fest. A construction project had closed down the right lane on I-93 south, stretching from Exit 11 to Exit 18, slowing cars to a crawl. Her pushy bladder felt like a raging body of water pounding and pounding a concrete levee. Simone locked her knees and constricted her vaginal muscles to keep from peeing her pants. Traffic picked up again. She sped up to recoup lost time and traveled southeast until she reached her destination.

Simone was the first patient on the schedule. The facility was virtually empty, contrary to the hustle and bustle at the hospital. She checked in and reported to the lounge. The small open space was peaceful, apart from the buzzing television attached to the wall. Her stomach began to knot up as the water pushed harder for release. She sat down, waiting to be seen and did her best to keep her mind off peeing. Simone concentrated more on getting the ultrasound over and done with.

Her body didn't quite form an impression in the chair before the sonographer, covered in typical blue hospital scrubs, retrieved her from the lounge. Studious frames straddled the bridge of her European nose. Her monologue was limited to, "Good morning. Please, come with me." Her thick accent was probably Eastern European, but Simone couldn't place its origin.

Once inside the radiology unit, they entered dimly lit Room 223 where the sonographer confirmed the purpose of Simone's visit.

"I have you down for transabdominal and transvaginal ultrasounds. Is that correct?"

"Yes," Simone answered.

She then left Simone to undress from the waist down. Simone slipped into the paper gown on the examination table, and then waited with her hands folded on her lap. The sonographer returned wearing a lab coat over her scrubs. She explained how Simone should lay on the table, the procedure that would take place, and which she would perform first. She then methodically pushed, turned, and flipped buttons and knobs on the high-tech sonogram equipment. Simone looked on in amazement and asked questions about the equipment mostly. The sonographer explained in heavily accented English how the expensive machinery could capture the image of foreign growths with the aid of high-frequency sound waves. Intrigued, Simone listened in puzzlement, hanging onto every detail. To her credit, the sonographer was thorough and focused as she multitasked, fiddling with the fascinating equipment.

Katarina was the name Simone was able to read on the identification tag attached to her lab coat. After smearing jelly over Simone's stomach, she utilized a transducer wand to explore her abdomen. The exam was painless, but Simone's full bladder was almost unbearably uncomfortable. After the transabdominal procedure, Katarina allowed Simone to empty her bladder before starting the vaginal ultrasound. Simone was surprised when she was given the honor of inserting the transducer probe into her vaginal canal. Pretending it was Secret Pleasure, she gripped the probe securely, and then slid it deep into her Lady. Katarina took over from there.

Again, the procedure was painless. Afterward, Simone cleaned up, dressed and waited in the sparsely lit room for Katarina to return after checking the film. Ten minutes later, she entered the room, confirmed the presence of fibroids, and stated that Simone would hear from Dr. Theery's office to schedule a follow-up appointment.

For the remainder of the day Simone organized her closet in preparation for the arrival of summer in a few months. Wool dress pants, skirts, and sweaters were neatly folded and packed away in sturdy bins, and later on stored in the basement. She debated whether or not to call Jeff. *What's left to lose besides my mind?* She wondered.

Deciding to take their cat-and-mouse chase to the next level, Simone retrieved Jeff's number from her cell phone call log and called him. Nervous for no reason, she waited breathlessly for the line to connect, her heart thumped furiously in her chest. She didn't know what to say if he answered, especially after all but accusing him of lying about Daphne.

"Well, hello, Ms. Miller. I thought you'd never call. Hold on a sec." Hearing his voice squashed her doubts and dismissed her fears.

"Jeff, if you're busy, we can talk another time." Simone blurted out, more afraid of her feelings than feeling guilty about pulling him away from duty.

"Not a chance. I'm not letting you off this phone. Give me a second."

Simone relaxed when she overheard Jeff whisper to his partner that he needed a few minutes. She felt important.

"I'm back. How are you?" Jeff asked when he came back on the line.

"Well. And you?"

"I don't like to complain, but the soaring murder rate in the city is taking a toll on the entire unit. I could use some downtime."

"Sounds like you could use a hug, too."

"Are you offering?"

"Am *I* offering?" Simone answered, unsure if she were.

"Yes. You. Tonight."

"What time?" Simone asked, surprising herself.

"I came on early, which means my shift ends at eleven-thirty. Your place or mine?"

"Ah. Ah," she stuttered wanting to chicken out. Practicing what she had preached to Keisha was Simone's rule to live by. Her humble abode was off limits to Jeff until she received an invitation to his place *and* an introduction to his family, or friends outside the police department.

Jeff made a new proposition before she could reject his first one.

"I'll tell you what, why don't I treat you to dinner on Sunday? How about the Cheesecake Factory on Route 9?"

"Sure. What time?" Simone asked, relieved.

"Six-ish, seven-ish; you can ride shotgun."

"Let's meet there, at say, six-thirty?"

"If that's what you prefer. Don't keep me waiting."

"Be safe out there."

"I'll try."

Simone hung up feeling a tinge of something for Jeff. A man capable of engaging in conversation beyond sports, his favorite mixed drink, and fast cars had second-base potential. He seemed to be genuinely interested in getting to know her, and not just to get her into bed. "Now," Simone said smiling, "if I can just preserve what little bit of sexy I have left before the fibroids take over completely, I can get Jeff wrapped around my pinky. And maybe, just maybe, I can finally stop obsessing over relationships gone bad as if I ever had a chance in hell of building a happily ever after life with any of them."

Could Jeff be "the one"? Simone wondered.

23

KEISHA B.

Gordon hadn't returned any of Keisha's calls for over a week. She didn't go out of her way to communicate with him either. Ironically, the passing of time made her feel abandoned and lonely. Determined to pry the unadulterated truth out of him, she left a message on his voicemail inviting him to her apartment so they could talk things over like rational adults.

Eight o'clock on the dot, there was a familiar double knock at her door.

"Just a minute," Keisha sang, running around the house in glamorous black lingerie, concealed under her knee-length silk ebony sheath. After finding her pumps, Keisha took a last look in the mirror and primped her hair into a tousled, yet seductive confection. She adjusted her breasts to expose and maximize the appearance of cleavage and reapplied another coat of lipstick. Impatient, her married lover knocked again. She rushed to answer the door hoping to make him thirsty for her love tunnel.

Standing in the doorway Keisha posed seductively to accentuate her curvy hips. She repositioned her leg to flaunt some thigh through the slit of the robe. She then purred seductively, "You've never been one to keep me waiting." Keisha took his hand to pull him inside. "Come in, Gordon. Stay a while. I'll make it unforgettable. Promise," she said, trying to strip him out of his custom sport coat.

Gordon retrieved his hand from Keisha's grasp and readjusted his jacket on his shoulders. Stepping inside he demanded, "Start talking, before my wife calls my cell phone like she's losing her mind."

Keisha glared at him. "You're not staying?"

"No. I can't. She's been on my back, asking too many questions since your juvenile crank call."

"What kind of questions?"

"Typical stuff a wife asks when she suspects her husband is cheating. Preparing clients for trial is a flimsy excuse that can only get me over for so long. I think she suspects something and I can't lose my son behind an affair. He means everything to me."

Keisha exposed more thigh to gain his undivided attention. Hypnotized for a nanosecond, he broke his gaze to look around for somewhere to sit. He then settled down on her couch to end their affair.

"Look, like I told you from the outset, once my wife starts asking questions that means I've gotten sloppy and have to call it quits. I refuse to lose everything I worked hard for while she's reaping the benefits of my blood, sweat, and platinum credit cards squandering money on shopping sprees, and getting her nails and hair done every week. I'm on track to make partner at the law firm. As a Black man in a position to accomplish a career milestone I never thought I'd see in my lifetime, it would be a mockery if my dream were deferred over a piece of ass. I will not jeopardize my chances at the distinguished Bingham, Fields & Poole. I don't care how irresistibly sweet and tasty your loving is. No sex is worth sacrificing my career!"

Keisha got cocky with clear contempt for his I-really-don't-care-about-you attitude. She wanted restitution for time invested playing mistress.

"I see you didn't bring any parting gifts. A simple hello, a goodbye, and just like *that* we're history because wifey is asking questions? Hell, Barefoot Moscato only costs $6.99 a pop," she fumed.

Gordon had arrived empty-handed, no Hallmark Mahogany card, no flowers, nothing to express his apologies and regrets. Keisha was unworthy of even a bottle of cheap wine. One thing was obvious her attire enticed him to take a quick shower so he could burn a thousand calories in a farewell quickie. Folding back the three-hundred-thread count sheets Keisha sprawled seductively on the bed and plotted to inspect his penis for incriminating signs of HPV.

Gordon entered the bedroom towel drying his toned body, the body that Keisha fell head over heels in lust with—after sizing up his wallet, of course. Seeing his glistening pecks and sculpted biceps dripping with water, Keisha hopped up to lead him to the bed, eager to play private investigator on the Posturepedic mattress that had racked up more miles than a Chevy Impala. When Gordon dropped the towel. The sight of his body drove Keisha wild. She pushed him down on the bed and squatted over his washboard abs, bowed down, sucking gingerly on his neck. Her tongue journeyed down his abs, over his navel, and stopped at his penis. Holding his head up for a better view, Gordon drew in a big breath, licked his lips and moaned.

At this moment he wanted oral pleasure more than he wanted to make partner at the law firm. "You're the reason Viagra was invented," he groaned, as he got comfortable and waited for a heart-stopping blowjob.

Keisha purred a sexy purr that would have rivaled Eartha Kitt's signature cat drawl. She sucked her fingertip and wiped saliva on the tip of his penis, then air blew it dry. He trembled and whimpered a symphony of bliss as she gently stroked him, feeling for warts; just one of any size would have fulfilled her mission. He begged for oral pleasure, something he claimed Keisha mastered better than his wife. Deep-throating was Keisha's shameless money earning craft. She was a pro, and never left anything to be desired. On the flipside of her dangerous mission, his magnetic, desirable penis reminded her just how long it had been since they'd actually had sex. Struggling with temptation, she bit on her bottom lip to keep from taking all of him in her mouth. She fondled, explored, and came within a centimeter of tongue-teasing his penis. Keisha moaned deeply, feeling a powerful ocean swelling between her legs. She'd almost given in to it when she felt a wart, a tiny one that would have gone unde-tected had she succumbed immediately to his selfish cries for a blowjob.

Keisha abruptly stopped fondling and exploring, and went in closer for a better look.

"Well, well, well. What do we have here?" she said, inspect-ing his genitals. A wart was in one of the locations described in her HPV pamphlet. Thirty seconds into the inspection,

Keisha then launched into a tirade, followed by a rampage short of ripping out his chest hairs.

"You low-down, filthy, nasty, scum bucket creep!" She yelled, jumping up and throwing things at Gordon. She pitched the table lamp at him, a hand-painted glass vase, and then hurled her slippers. He ducked bolting for the door, grabbing his clothes on the way, and cursing Keisha in his defense.

"What the hell is wrong with you, you psycho broad!"

Keisha yelled back, "You picked the wrong mistress to mess over and calling me a *bitch* was a major no-no. Get out! Go home and tell your wife that you are a walking disease factory. Go!" Keisha kicked him out vowing, "You will soon feel the wrath of my scorn." Gordon had no idea what she was capable of: smashing windows, keying cars, prank phone calls to wives and girlfriends, blackmail sex-tapes, nude selfies, and indecent text messages, was the short list of entries on Keisha's home-wrecking résumé.

Trying to calm herself, Keisha drew in a deep breath, then another one. "Our affair is not over until I say it's over." She swore, and then she grabbed her cell phone to make a long-distance call.

"Caller, I'm unavailable. You have one minute to record your message. Keep it short and sweet. Here comes the beep."

"HEY, SIMONE. LONG TIME NO TALK TO. IT'S YOUR GIRL KEISHA B. I GOT YOUR EMAIL. YOU WOULD NEVER BELIEVE WHAT I'VE BEEN GOING THROUGH. I HAD A BIOPSY ON MY CERVIX. IT HURT SO BAD, I THOUGHT IT WAS

GONNA REBEL AND BURST OUT OF MY VAGINA. ANYWAY ENOUGH ABOUT THAT TORTURE, I NEED SOME ADVICE. CALL ME AS SOON AS YOU GET THIS MESSAGE. CIAO!"

After Simone showered and ate a banana, she returned Keisha's call.

"Hello!" Keisha yelled irritably into the receiver.

"Dang, take the edge off. What's with the funky attitude?"

"Oh, hey, Simone, I thought you were that disrespectful creep Gordon calling to talk trash."

"Keisha, you better stop chasing wallets, there's more to a man than the bulge in his back pocket. Besides, if he's cheating on his wife, surely he's not gonna respect you. What kind of advice are you seeking?"

"Can you believe when I questioned the creep about giving me a venereal disease, he denied it, which means he's probably not going to tell his wife?"

"Keisha, he's probably the arrogant type to think what his wife doesn't know won't hurt her. Oh, and sorry to hear you caught a bug."

"Simone, I caught more than a bug which is why his wife *needs* to know, and I need to tell her without him knowing the information came from me."

"Don't do him any favors. Force the cheating scoundrel to tell his wife. Do you have any pictures of this creep?"

"I think so. Maybe one or two. I'll check. Wait. Why?"

"I'll get to why later. I'm just going to assume you know where he lives."

"I've done a couple drive-bys? What are you getting at?"

Simone didn't pretend to be surprised about the drive-bys. She also didn't put anything above, or beneath Keisha. Simone was convinced that Keisha's sexual abuse as a child was the root of her seeking affection in wrong places. Many years ago, early on in their friendship, Keisha confided in Simone that her father started playing in her pussy when she was barely five years old and kept her quiet with threats and toys. Keisha also confessed that she wished death upon her father every night the child molester tucked her into bed along with a couple dollars of "hush money" to keep his disgraceful secret from her mother. Eight years later, her father crashed head-on into a tree after suffering a heart attack while driving. His death was a relief and a curse for Keisha.

Instead of asking God for guidance Keisha leaned on Simone, someone she could depend on when in a pickle. The HPV revelation brought two old friends together once again.

"My little stalker friend," voiced Simone. "You need to get even. Shake down his pockets and leave him out to dry in divorce court. For that to happen, you must do exactly as I say."

"I'm listening."

"Pictures don't lie, husbands do, and Photoshop works miracles on the web. Get me one picture of his face. We can conduct an exhaustive online search until we locate an image of someone with the same complexion and body type. We don't even need a full body shot to accomplish what I have in store to redirect his future in the legal field straight to Judge Get Right. How soon can you send me his picture?"

"Whoa! Whoa! Wait. Hold on. No freakin' way, Simone. He's a well-connected attorney. He will ruin me if he finds out I had something to do with his downfall. I'm not doing anything illegal that's gonna get me locked up."

"Keisha, did the creep think twice before he dumped you, especially when he may have given you a STD?"

"On second thought, no. He deserves what's coming to him. I'm ready to serve him a lethal dose of scorned payback. Let's do this!"

"And do this we will. A picture might be worth a thousand words, but seeing what I have in store for the Mr. and the Mrs. will leave them speechless. Heck, she might even go blind from shock and awe."

"Simone, you are one wicked witch."

"Saint Keisha, don't get me started on you and your scandalous 'other woman' shenanigans. MISS DO YOU KNOW WHERE YOUR HUSBAND IS? HELLO. MRS. HOME ALONE, YOU DON'T KNOW ME, BUT I KNOW WHO YOUR HUSBAND ATE FOR DINNER LAST NIGHT. HOW'D MY PUSSY TASTE? AND BY THE WAY, I'M THE MISTRESS IN YOUR HUSBAND'S WET DREAMS. Oh, and my personal favorite when a wife brought the beef to your turf: BOOM! BOOM! BOOM! SLUT, I KNOW YOU'VE BEEN SNEAKING AROUND WITH MY HUSBAND. OPEN THIS DOOR SO I CAN KICK YOUR ASS ALL THE WAY BACK TO BOSTON. Should I keep going?"

"Very funny, Simone. You need to be on Comedy Central."

"And you better bring home an Oscar, or I'm gonna disown you."

"Believe me, I already have a place designated on my mantel for the golden statue."

"Keisha, jokes aside. Let's get serious. You don't have to settle for mistress. After you fulfill sexual voids and stroke egos, husbands go home to the wife. As a family, they travel together without having to look over their shoulders. The wife gets the glory of bearing the family name, the right to birth children in wedlock, dibs on bank accounts, retirement pensions, and invited to holiday soirees to hobnob with colleagues while the husbands probably expect you to mingle with bottom-feeder associates."

"Simone, I hear what you're saying, but fried foods are bad for our arteries among other things, but does that stop us from patronizing KFC, and Roy's Fried Chicken?"

Space between the phone lines fell silent before Simone huffed, "Lemons to limes, Keisha."

"Simone, contrary to what you think, *married wallets wanted* is not my motto. I don't need them to prosper. I'm gainfully employed in the entertainment industry. Award-winning actors, rappers, R&B crooners, record label presidents, and industry executives have propositioned yours truly for intimate liaisons. They gravitate to me breathing dragon fire down my neck for excitement that's lacking at home. They don't pay me for sex. I get paid for my time. As the proverb goes: Time is money, money is time. Time doesn't come back. So, if 'getting paid' keeps the lights on, and my feet stacked in Jimmy Choos, what's a mistress to do? Now brains and beauty, tell me the master plan that will leave wifey speechless."

24

BLACK AND BLUE

Stiff as a board from having slept in an uncomfortable position, Simone stood at her bedroom window and peered through the curtains, noticing wetness outside. She found it odd that she hadn't heard raindrops pelting against her skylight before going out for the count. The warm milk bath did her body more than good. Rarely did she sleep through the least amount of noise.

As she was about to step away from the window, Portia parked her silver Volvo close to Simone's Camry. By the time Simone made it downstairs to open the door, Portia was already standing under the porch awning.

"Smooches," Portia grumbled without making eye contact.

"Good Saturday morning and smooches to you, too. Hugs?" When Simone tried to embrace Portia, she backed away as if Simone had the avian flu. "Fine. I don't want to hug your mangy tail either. Come in out of the rain. You know the drill. Leave those wet shoes on the mat."

Portia kicked off a serious pair of come-do-me pumps that had to set her bank account back at least one hundred bucks.

"What brings you out this early?" Simone asked sweeping her hand over the wood furniture inspecting for dust.

"I'm on my way to customer appreciation day at the Plaza. Designer bags are twenty percent off."

"How many more bags do you need? You can only carry one at a time."

"The Signature Tote is my favorite and a must-have. I might splurge on a silk scarf, too."

"Knock yourself out. My money is staying in my pocket. Let me take your coat."

"I won't be staying long."

"Portia, it's wet, and besides, I don't want water dripping on the floor."

"I'll stay where I'm at then."

"You must be hiding something. 'Fess up. You took Lonnie back and he's beating you again, isn't he? Don't lie because you're wearing your usual 'cover-ups': heavy foundation and dark lipstick.

"Not today. Simone. Not today."

"If not today, then when?"

"Never. It's something I have to get a better handle on, but not today."

"What is it about Lonnie you can't get enough of? Is he paying the mortgage on your condo? Help me understand why you keep taking him back. He's mean and hateful. He's unemployed, but of course, you love him, right? The question is why?"

Portia was silent.

"Portia what he's doing to you is wrong and he's not going to stop abusing you until you show him that you won't stand for it anymore. Save yourself and leave."

Portia averted her eyes to the miniature Sweet Lilly portrait gracing the foyer wall, and then shifted her eyes to Simone. "I didn't come here for therapy. I came to say hello and try to get you out of the house. You're not getting any younger cooped up like a recluse. Keep at it, you're gonna end up an old maid perched in your kitchen window knitting quilts and booties for other people's grandchildren."

"What does how I choose to live my life have to do with your self-esteem hitting rock bottom? Let's get back to what triggered this latest tiff between you and Lonnie. Did you say 'hell no' when he asked you to get him a cell phone in your name? Or did he go ballistic when you said you wouldn't foolishly co-sign for another car loan after you financed the Ninja Motorcycle that he totaled?"

"Get a life, Simone."

"I got one, smart ass. Try getting a clue and stop denying your inner peace. Men like Lonnie never change. Once an abuser, always an abuser, it's in his blood, or have you forgotten that his father is doing hard time for killing his mother? Don't empower Lonnie to do the same to you."

Portia's lips started to tremble. Teardrops streaked mascara down her face. The way she strutted her stuff coming up the walkway sure had Simone fooled. She seemed to have it all together, but Simone only saw the illusion that Portia wanted her to see.

"Here." Simone handed Portia a Kleenex. "Get it together. Dry those pitiful tears, and tell me what set Ike Turner off this time."

"Lonnie came into some money. Don't ask me how, because he wouldn't tell me the source of his good fortune. He gave me a few dollars to spend how I saw fit. I added some of my own money to his and splurged on a nine hundred dollar purse. When I showed him what I'd bought, he threw a fit about how I spent the money. I didn't see the big deal because it was supposed to be a gift."

"Portia, I understand your point of view. If it was a gift, he relinquished control when the cash exchanged hands, but I don't understand why he hurt you."

"I'm getting to that. Yesterday my credit card statement was in a pile of mail that I left on the kitchen counter when I took a shower. When I came out the bathroom, the envelope flap appeared to have been resealed, which I found strange because I never got around to opening the mail. Right after I placed it on the counter, I hopped in the shower."

"Naturally, you would question that. Who wouldn't?"

"Lonnie denied opening the mail. But I *know* that he did. Snooping into my personal business crossed the line. I told him I would return the cash gift and that I needed space to focus on growing my cosmetic business. That's when our tempers boiled over into an intense argument. He lost his mind and got physical like always."

"Well, he was wrong on all accounts. He had no right tampering with your mail. That's a federal offense and punishable by law. I wouldn't trust his sneaky ass any further than I can see the nose on my face."

"Tell me about it. From now on, I'm going to hide my mail when he's alone in my house."

"What? Hide your mail?" Simone asked to keep from saying *Fool, who hides their mail and let's a man she doesn't trust in her house?* "Portia, don't be ridiculous. That's no way to live in your own home. Severing ties with the abusive sneak makes the most sense. Don't you think?"

"Simone—" Portia's lips quivered when she cried out— "Lonnie manipulates me all the time. He's such a bully. He has a way of making me feel guilty about everything that goes wrong between us. Nothing is ever his fault. It's always YOU DID IT. IT'S YOUR FAULT. SEE WHAT YOU MADE ME DO. Then he can be sweet as pecan pie when he wants something. I am so bothered by what he did. I will never look at him the same. And then for him to lie to my face knowing he opened and tried to reseal the envelope makes me wonder what else he's been doing behind my back."

"Portia, that's Lonnie's way of affirming his passive-aggressive ways. He has traits of a classic abuser: controlling, verbally and physically abusive, blame shifting, Dr. Jekyll and Mr. Hyde personality, and violent tendencies. I wouldn't be surprised if he hates women. I wonder what his relationship was like with his mother, or if they even had one before she died. Better yet, do yourself a favor, find out if he has restraining orders from previous relationships and be prepared to haul ass."

Portia sniffled and slipped out of her jacket, revealing black and blue bruises on her arms.

Simone took one, long hard look and said, "What an animal. I hope you called the police and filed a report."

"I tried but Lonnie smacked the phone out my hand and broke it." Portia sat dejectedly on the sofa and picked up the Bible on the side table. She glimpsed at a verse or two and prayed silently, her spirit broken, too embarrassed to talk more about Lonnie's abuse.

I'll be right back." Frustrated, Simone left Portia alone with the Bible, wondering who or what bad news besides her own was next to crash down on her like the time bomb waiting to explode in her womb.

In the kitchen, Simone removed a T-bone steak from the freezer, secured it in a sturdy plastic bag, and returned to the living room with a glass of spring water for Portia. Portia accepted the water, but pushed the meat away like it was a smelly diaper.

"Simone, what good is freezer-burned steak for my bruises at this point?"

"It will serve more purpose than staying with Lonnie. Here. Take it," Simone insisted. But Portia shoved it away again. Simone shook her head and sat down next to Portia.

"You got some nerve giving me attitude. First, you interrupt my Saturday bringing your social drama here without calling. Second, you're refusing medical aid like your arms are not black and blue all over. News Alert: Real love doesn't feel like a sack of rocks going upside your head. Now don't get me all worked up behind this domestic violence mess again. I've got my own stress to grapple with and don't need more stress piled on because you choose to worship a loser who can't walk on water and he sure can't part the Red Sea because he's too busy using his hands to beat the color off your behind. Now, do you want this meat pack or what? It's the best I can do on short notice."

Portia yawned looking at Simone as if she was ranting about golf or something else boring and of no interest.

"Suit yourself then," Simone grumbled, returning the meat to the fridge.

"Girls-for-life growing old together, not too far apart. Right, Simone?" Portia asked unexpectedly.

"Of course," Simone answered, returning from the kitchen to sit next to Portia.

"I would be lost without your craziness. You know that, right?" Portia whispered, her eyes again filling with tears.

"I feel the same way about you. Now, come get some love. Never mind. You might collapse and fall apart. I'll come to you." Simone gave Portia a long hug. She could tell that she really needed it. Then they sat quietly holding and comforting each other in the name of sisterhood.

"I needed that," Portia whispered.

"As much as I hate to say it, so did I," Simone confessed, smiling.

"Well, let me get going before all of Boston wakes up. Get dressed and join me," Portia suggested sliding her feet back into her pumps and easing her bruised arms into her jacket.

"I'll pass. I've got things to do. Dust is going to town in here."

"And where is the dust going after it leaves town?"

"Nowhere." Simone couldn't help but laugh.

"Then it'll be here when you get back, so get dressed."

"Portia."

"Yeah, Simone."

"I might have fibroids."

Simone's announcement gave Portia a moment of pause.

"Did you say fibroids?"

"I did."

"What are fibroids?"

Reluctant about discussing her medical condition, Simone changed her mind about what she wanted to say.

"I'll talk to you about it later."

"Simone, you look troubled. Are you sure it can wait?" Portia asked. "The mall can wait. Going once. Going twice."

"Sold. Sit down! This might take more than a few minutes."

Portia and Simone shared personal stories for nearly an hour. Simone opened up about the fibroids, the pain, the bulge that came with them, and the prospect of a permanent job. Portia advised Simone to consider her health and emotional needs beyond the semi-private cubicle, salary, and bonus. After hearing the details, Portia grew concerned about her own health and even considered getting screened being that she was in the high-risk category. Simone mentioned the near-death experience she encountered clubbing at Spades with Denise and confided she was kind of, sort of getting to know Jeff better.

"Do what makes you happy." Portia encouraged.

That advice was Simone's cue to come clean about relapsing in the sack with Andy for closure.

"Don't judge me, but Andy and I had sex for the last time and I *mean* it."

"You horny heifer and you're just now telling me?"

"Everything ain't for everybody. Consider it a privilege."

Confessing was the right thing to do. The foundation of their friendship was trust, and they had come too far to jeopardize it. As Simone was turning over cards Portia owned up to letting Lonnie back into her heart because she feared being alone for the rest of her life. But Simone wasn't prepared for the confession that followed.

"Simone, I wasn't exactly honest about why Lonnie beat me up. It wasn't about money because he's not working. He didn't open my mail either."

"Then what set him off?"

"He got turned down for another job, and tried to take the rejection out on my ass. In other words, he tried to fuck me in the butt, and I'm not with that shit."

"I know that's real. But Portia, if saying no is all it takes for Lonnie to wail on you, then you need to re-evaluate your relationship values to figure out if love is worth physical and emotional pain because you're insecure about being without a man."

"Lonnie has a lot of stress in his life, and as you know he didn't have the best childhood."

"His stress, sick sexual fetishes, and unfortunate childhood should not justify the way he mistreats you. How can you make excuses for him?"

"I'm not making excuses. Lonnie is a good person whether you choose to believe it or not."

"Portia, don't allow Lonnie to make you suffer for his life frustrations. You can do better and you deserve better." Simone sighed.

"Right now I'm doing the man that I love and want to help."

Simone shook her head and secretly hoped in her heart, *Portia, please hurry up and tire of being Lonnie's punching bag before you end up tagged on a cold slab in the city morgue.*

25

RETAIL THERAPY

There were already hundreds of shoppers in the Plaza. Simone couldn't believe she let Portia drag her around spending money like it was falling out the sky. "This place is a zoo. I need to rest somewhere before I collapse from too much exercise running in and out of these stores going broke."

Portia giggled, "I know you didn't just say exercise. Simone you are too funny. I'm hungry. What about you?"

"I'm craving a steamy cup of decaf coffee and a cookie."

"That's bird food. I'm going for Chinese."

"Go for it. I'm watching my cholesterol and sodium intake."

"Good for you."

Sitting in the food atrium, Simone was content with coffee and a moist oatmeal raisin cookie. Portia enjoyed a shrimp and mixed vegetable rice plate from Wong's Eatery. Portia stopped chewing her food to clear her throat. She then mumbled, "We've got company."

Simone wiggled in her seat excitedly. "He'd better be a great communicator and a world traveler. Is he fine? Tall?

Hurry up! Size him up so I can get my mind right before he gets too close."

"Turn around and judge for yourself."

"Portia."

"Andy." She smiled nervously, anticipating Simone's reaction when she heard his name.

"Cheapskate Andy! Shopping? This I've got to see with my own eyes." Simone turned around. Indeed, it was Andy, looking handsome as ever, holding a tray of food.

"I see you've gone from pervert to stalker. What brings you to the mall?"

"Stalker?" Andy repeated incredulously. "Simone, you don't own this place. I happen to be shopping for my mother's birthday gift."

"That's right. Her birthday is in April." Simone, said, feeling a little embarrassed.

"She'd be pleased to know you remember. She asks about you. You should call her and say hello."

"I should do no such thing. Send my regards."

"How come you won't take my calls?"

"There's nothing more to talk about."

"You had a lot to say when you lured me over for...let me see if I can remember your excuse." Andy pretended to think. "Closure, yeah that's what you called our roll back down memory lane."

"Uh, ah, um," Portia stuttered. "I've got an appointment with Vicky. I'll leave you two alone to hash things out." She struggled to stand using her sore arms to push off the table for balance.

Andy offered assistance. "Let me give you a hand."

Portia declined his help. "No. No. No. I can manage. Thank you."

"You sure?"

"Yes, I'm okay."

Simone sucked her teeth. "She doesn't need any help if she's going to Victoria's Secret."

Portia hissed, "Sour pickle."

"Black and blue," Simone snarled back.

"Girls-for-life," Portia conceded, prancing off in her signature got-it-going-on strut.

"Don't worry, your shame is safe with me," Simone said, fixing an evil eye on Andy to counter his pompous grin. Her inner demons battled in her head. *He has some nerve catering to Portia's needs seeing that he wasn't the least concerned about my welfare when I terminated the unplanned pregnancy. He didn't even bother escorting me to the abortion clinic. Bastard!*

In addition to the co-payment, Andy gave Simone round-trip cab fare and wished her all the luck in the world. Her pregnancy was the consequence of being too sexy for her own good. Big hair, perky tits, a barely there skirt, and satin thong invited Andy to have his way with her after dining at a restaurant of his choosing. That memorable date night, Andy worked up a voracious appetite for sex. Nine-and-a-half weeks later, Simone was "with child" and didn't have a friendship ring to show off when her baby was conceived. She wanted to hate Andy so bad for making a fool out of her. She really did.

"Why are you still here? And quit staring. It's rude."

"Can't help if I want who I see. May I join you for lunch?"

"I'd rather you didn't."

Andy sat at the table after Simone distinctively heard herself tell him that she didn't want company. She sucked her teeth, and then sighed; she did everything except move to another table. She didn't move partly because she was content, but mostly because she was tired of running from a failed relationship.

"Come on, Simone," Andy pleaded. "Don't push me away."

"Why shouldn't I? You let me swallow my food alone many nights and didn't care if I choked while you were caught up watching *Sports Center Live.* I'm surprised to see you inside a shopping center. Whoever she is must be extra special because I sure wasn't worth a trip to the mall."

"She happens to be my mother." Andy assured Simone. "And if there were another she, I wouldn't be trying to see if you and I could, you know—"

Simone cut him off and finished what she thought he was thinking. "Work things out, so we can have uncommitted sex for three more years?" She threw back her head and laughed until Andy shut her up with his own profound thoughts.

"Sweetheart, I'm going to be real. You have brains, beauty, and a mean bedroom game, but you're not the only woman with a hole between her legs. Sex is on TV, and on the job. Sex is the woman at the next table fantasizing about her soul mate because that's what you women do, plot and plan your future. But how are you gonna change the way a man eats, dress, and spends his money, then take on a bitchy attitude and cry victim when the plan to live happily ever after— by your rules—falls apart?"

Andy's commentary rattled every nerve ending in Simone's body. Searching her heart for a gentle put-down, she looked at the woman sitting at the adjacent table then fixed her eyes on Andy again.

"Get the heck out of my face, and go give her something to cry about."

"She's not my type. I prefer brown sugar in my coffee."

"White or brown, what's the difference? She's got a hole between her legs, drink up."

"Simone, do you really believe what we had was only about sex?"

"Of course, and by the way, lunch is over. Your inflated ego spoiled my appetite. Simone chewed the last piece of cookie dismissing Andy with her eyes. She collected her trash, preparing to make a hasty exit when Andy sucker punched her in the stomach.

"You still love me, don't you?" He forked another scoop of rice into his mouth, daring her to lie.

Simone was seething mad inside. *Boy, I want to cut him to the bone for testing my allegiance to loving me. I love me, I really do. I just wish I hadn't wasted so much energy trying to get him to love me back.*

"Well, are you going to answer the question?"

"Andy, get over yourself. I've been through loving you. I'm so madly in love with myself I can't stay out of the mirror."

He laughed. "I don't buy that. I know you, Simone. I know what makes you tick. You're strong and resilient on the outside, but I know what breaks you down and makes you cry. You have more issues than the average person, yet a heart so warm it could melt butter. I bet your mind won't let you stop wondering what if we got married. What if we traveled cross-country joined at the hip? What if you hadn't killed our child to spite me?"

"Quit while you're ahead, Andy," Simone warned.

"No. I have some things on my mind that need to be said. I played my part in the abortion, and resent that I let you go through with killing a part of me. You were stubborn. 'Your body, your way.' Isn't that what you told me before purging my baby down a vacuum!" Andy almost yelled, striking a chord close to Simone's guilty conscience.

"Now, wait one minute, you self-centered, *Sports Center Live* fanatic! I don't appreciate you embellishing the truth to cover the role you played in the death of my child, not your child! *My* child!"

"Am I embellishing the truth, Miss Goody Two Shoes? What happened to the truth supposedly setting us free? Look at me." He reached for her chin. She reared back like a cobra, ready to spit venom between his devilish eyes. "Tell me, honestly, that you don't feel anything for me, and I will walk away forever."

"Don't walk. Run as fast as you can. Does that answer your question?"

"No, it doesn't, and please stop being so dramatic."

"Don't tell me what to do! My father died fourteen years ago. You and no other man will ever be the boss of me."

"Simone, let's be honest with each other. I still care about you. If it's over between us, just tell me it's over so I can move on with a clear conscience."

"Andy, you have a conscience? You're no Richard Pryor, but the thought of you caring about someone other than your-self sure is comical."

"Don't antagonize me. Just answer the question!"

Andy thumped his fist on the table, rattling the contents on its surface. Patrons stole a glance, but none loitered for the grand finale. Security—two unarmed guardsmen—patrolled the eatery during the love-hate quarrel and ventured within two feet of their table. Simone stood.

"We're having a friendly disagreement," she stated.

Andy added, "We're cool," for reassurance.

The guards moved on about their duty—no questions asked.

Simone waited until they were out of sight. Once they were a distance away, she spewed venom that never failed to unlock Pandora's Box of unresolved issues with Andy.

"Look, Mr. Williams, I'm going to tell you the same thing I told Clay when I got fed up chasing his elusive affection."

"Your ex-boyfriend has nothing to do with what we had. Leave him out of this conversation."

"Clay has everything to do with it. Truth is, when it no longer pained me to be without him, I gave love another chance with you. I'll be damned to the fire of hell if the two of you are not poster boys for one degree of separation. I had no future with you just like I had no future him. Like you, Clay was too caught up in a 'man's world' to be in a monogamous relationship with me, the so-called 'best woman' that ever happened to both of you. Now, do I think about you? Sometimes. Was sleeping with you for closure the biggest mistake of my life? No, but it's pretty darn close. Am I in love with you? Not one hundred percent. Do I wonder what if? I used to until I remembered that you blamed your family history of failed marriages as the reason you weren't ready to settle down and build a future with me as your wife. Do I want to be happy? Yes, but not with someone who disrespects my body."

"Simone you deserve happiness."

"Then please let me move on in peace. Consider this our last time breaking bread together." Emotionally spent, Simone cried a single tear for her aborted child. After drying her eye she flounced to the restroom, shaking her derriere and didn't bother looking back to see Andy's eyes blazing flames. A few minutes later, Andy noticed her exit the restroom. Simone waved good-bye then made a beeline for the escalator to search for Portia in the crowded mall. Simone caught up with her inside Vickie's dirty little Secret racking up a lofty tab.

"Simone, I thought you and Andy snuck off to book a room at the Sheraton across the street."

"Ha, ha, ha. Not funny."

"Girl, lighten up. We have a choice of bras, pannies, and thongs galore, and you're in Victoria's Secret pouting? Snap out of it and buy something to feel pretty in. Unless you need something extra sexy for Andy, like, say this satin thong." Portia smiled as she twirled the undergarment in Simone's face.

"No. That's not what I need." Simone took the thong and tossed it back in the bin. "What I need is to get back home so I can finish cleaning up."

"Boring. Boring. Boring." Portia sang. "Join me for some retail therapy. It never hurts to buy yourself something special every now and then to take your mind off of bad things."

"It may never hurt but seeing Andy brought back some unresolved issues that continue to haunt me."

"Do you want to talk about them?"

"No. But thank you."

"Then stop sulking and take advantage of the early bird specials before the good stuff is gone."

26

HERE COMES THE PAIN AGAIN

D awn on Sunday morning yielded golden rays of light across the windowpane. Nature was chirping a pleasing lullaby. Elements of dust frolicked in the streaks of brightness reflecting off the walls. Simone eased out from under the heating pad and duvet even though she really wanted to stay in bed all day.

"It's later than I thought. So much for sunrise service, but there's still time to catch the eleven o'clock service." Simone said willing herself up, checking for the time. It was 9:05 A.M.

In the bathroom, hovering over the sink, she swallowed two pain relievers, chased with warm water to help them dissolve. Afterward, she found solace in a soothing bubble bath. Immersed in warm water, she closed her eyes and wished Calgon would take her away—Bermuda, Cancun, Trinidad, Paris, anywhere far away before her excruciating cramps recurred and broke her down physically, emotionally, and psychologically.

Relaxing in the tub, her body luxuriated in the hot sudsy water and a thousand tiny bubbles. Rising steam fogged the pewter mirror hanging over the sink. When the water cooled enough to be uncomfortable Simone released the stopper and drained the tub. Dripping wet, Simone stepped out of the tub as cool beads of liquid trickled down her bronze legs and onto the rug. She wrapped her nakedness in a warm terrycloth robe, tying the belt tightly around her expanding waist.

Standing in front of the mirror Simone turned on the antique hot and cold knobs of her pricey faucet, and then brushed her teeth. Admiring her likeness in the mirror, she examined the adult acne that was usually a dead giveaway that her period wasn't far off.

Simone was at her breaking point. She barely fit into any of her clothes because of her bloated belly. Her frequent urination made driving long distances almost unbearable and she had no idea whether or not she could have children. At that moment a searing cramp doubled her over. She leaned down on the sink but another cramp sent her down to her knees. On the floor, Simone put her hands together and prayed.

Cramps, bloating, and acne, God, here comes the pain again trying to weaken me. I'm holding on with every fiber of my soul, but I can't do it alone anymore. I need your help. Move the fibroids out of my life. Take with them the pang that roars through my womb like a hurricane. Stop it from tearing me apart. Please. Prince of Peace, if you're up there listening to me, I didn't make it this far in life without your grace. Direct my path. Make me wiser, stronger, and determined to defeat the pain. You are my rock. You carry me through this hurricane called life. The power of your presence is the only reason I get up when I fall. I know you didn't bring me this far to let me stay down for dead. I never could have come this far without your grace and for that I am eternally grateful

A few minutes later, Simone used the sink to pull herself up. Holding on for balance, Simone contemplated her next move. She peered out of the small bathroom window, and closed her eyes to create a fairy-tale family in her mind. When she opened them, she saw a depressing sight. Nothing outside resembled the serenity of joy and family. A sandbox for children to frolic and build sand castles didn't exist. Swings weren't swaying in the wind. The only semblance of life were budding tulips, blades of grass, and her stray cat Snow napping under the hedges. Outdoors only told half the story. The other half was trapped inside her custom Colonial. When Simone thought of home, she imagined a safe place. She envisioned love, communication, and compromise, the crushing of scattered Cheerios under her feet, headless baby dolls and Tonka trucks strewn across the floor. There was no place a woman in the spring of her life would have rather been than home, nurturing a family of her own. But after holding down the house for so many years, waking up to solitude in an empty bed and now fibroids, Simone harbored no hidden desire to accept the stillness of the nights and the quiet of mornings. She wanted happiness to be her self-fulfilling prophecy. Happiness had to begin with honesty. At that telling moment, she blessed and released drama, stress, aches, and pains from her heart and decided the time had come to start loving herself again, flaws and all.

Simone felt a smidgen of peace until her cell phone rang. Jeff's mobile number appeared in the screen. She delayed answering not wanting Jeff to assume she was glued to the phone hoping that he would call. She picked up after the third ring.

"Good morning."

"Good morning, Muffin Top. Are we still on for dinner?"

"As of right now, yes."

"Great. I'm working the early shift to make it possible."

"That's nice. I'm actually running late for church."

"I wish I could join you."

"Maybe another time. Speaking of time, it's ten-thirty. I'd better dress and get out of here if I want to get a good seat."

"I'll let you go."

"Be safe out there."

"Pray for me."

"I'll keep you in mind when I bow my head."

27

SITTING IN THE FRONT PEW

A t 10:45 A.M., the first service worshippers were still pouring out when Simone arrived at church at peace with herself. Standing at the front door of New Baptist, she marveled at the traditional clapboard structure that celebrated the legacy of Christ.

"You had better pull your purse strings tight this morning, 'cause it's about money today," a distinguished gentleman forewarned Simone, fastening the buttons on his trench coat.

"Well, you have a blessed day, too." She said warmly before sprinting back to her car where she retrieved another crisp five-dollar bill from her wristlet then tucked the small leather purse under the driver's seat. Walking back, Simone stashed the bills between the pages of her Bible. She then strutted proudly into New Baptist and approached the usher on duty. She handed Simone a service bulletin and politely said, "There's a seat up front on the right. Enjoy the service."

Happy to be in the Lord's house after a long stint of tuning into Gospel TV on Cable, Simone headed down the narrow aisle to the front pew putting a little *umph* in her stride like she was new money fresh off the press. Nobody could tell her otherwise.

Territorial hoity-toities hogged space in the row she wanted to claim for the next ninety minutes, depending on how many saints slowed down the service catching the Holy Ghost.

Poised to annoy them with kindness, Simone beamed a megawatt smile as a motion to sit on the velvet covered bench. All kinds of ugliness coated their uptight expressions. After becoming a full-fledged member of New Baptist, Simone had seen more hypocrisy in her Christian family than politicians who supported gay-marriage rights just to win elections.

They collectively ignored her, waving fans in front of their faces, reading the bulletin, or simply looking away to avoid eye contact. Had it not been for the crucifix suspended over the pulpit, and striking stained-glass windows, one might have thought Simone was not in a church.

A minute lapsed before a member found it in her Christian heart to make room for a child of God. Comfortable on the velvet cushion, Simone smiled at the saint who made room for her, at the same time Sister Pritchard, head of the hospitality committee, called for complete silence as she read announcements and upcoming events from the church bulletin. She closed with a prayer for those who wanted to join them, but couldn't make it that morning. As organ music enveloped the sanctuary the offering tray was passed from one end of a pew to another.

Simone dropped in her contribution. The organ strings slowly ceased strumming. The senior choir director summoned the entire congregation to their feet and led the blessing of the tithes. In spiritual unity, they rose to recite the

Lord's Prayer. An energetic amen followed to close out that segment of the program.

Pastor Cox ceremoniously presented himself at the podium. He checked everybody out and checked himself out, too. He cleared his throat, ready to share his story. Every pastor told a story before introducing the sermon. Pastor Cox was notorious for reciting chapters about his life.

He began with, "Saints, I don't know about you, but I love the Lord."

A unified, "All right now," echoed from the upper balcony.

"Brothers and sisters, this morning I woke up with a terrible headache that had the devil outdone doing me in. Lord knows I wanted to pull the sheets over my head and stay in bed like a big ole fraidy cat."

The congregation erupted in thunderous, contagious laughter. Even the hoity-toity contributed to the joyful noise. The church warmed up from collective body heat. Busy ushers canvassed the aisles in white attire all the way down to their itchy nylons and soft shoes, presenting paper fans to cool worshippers. Simone requested a fan because her pew mates weren't fanning cool air in her direction. Waiting for a fan to reach her, she studied her pretentious seatmates to determine what they thought was so exclusive about them and their holiness. Unimpressed with the likes of Satan, she received a fan and tuned into the sermon, fanning away the heat.

By now, Pastor Cox was deep in his life story. He curled his hands over the edge of the podium, looking all starry eyed at his wife Caroline, the first lady of the church. She was fashionably dressed in a feminine ivory skirt suit. She wore a sophisticated headpiece adorned with an emerald brooch.

"Saints, I don't know where I'd be today without this woman's love, strength, and devotion. Mmm. Mmm. Mmm." Pastor shook his head and grinned lasciviously, as if he could taste the loyalty of his devoted wife. "Brothers and sisters, beside every man has always stood a strong woman who helps him rise when he falls. Above all else, she weathers a storm. My wife's devotion to the Lord is undeniably the wind beneath my wings that carried me here to do God's work this morning. Hallelujah! Thank you, Jesus! Hallelujah!" Pastor Cox hummed in the rapture of Glory while pulpit members encouraged him to take his time praising Caroline.

Meanwhile, Caroline employed her silk hanky to flag off his praise. Simone envied her modesty for no good reason. Pastor Cox moved in short steps away from the podium. As if the script was rehearsed, Deacons on both sides made space for him. Pastor Cox opened his cloth-draped arms, flapped them up and down imitating a hawk in flight. Booming applause engulfed the jam-packed, standing-room-only sanctuary. Even the most pretentious opened their taut lips to join in on praising his free spirit.

"I'm through testifying," he declared, back at the podium as he thumbed through his thick black Bible. "Today, I want to speak to you from the book of Proverbs. Chapter 3: Verse 3, 'Let love and faithfulness never leave you.'" Simone quickly flipped through the pages of her Bible and stopped at the book of Proverbs just as Pastor Cox repeated his words.

"Y'all didn't hear me. I'll say it again. 'Let love and faithfulness never leave you.'"

"Amen!" Sister Pritchard shouted.

Pastor Cox responded gleefully, "Sweet Jesus! That's what I expect to hear after testifying this morning about wanting to give up and stay down when the going got a little rough. Now, some of y'all sitting back putting on airs like you haven't been through changes. Everybody experiences adversity. Some of y'all might even get a li'l thirsty for a sip of something eighty-proof potent every now and again just to cope."

Pastor Cox frowned his condemnation at Deacon Brown. "But I'm not here to judge you!" He then looked around the congregation. "Some of y'all married folk might even gawk too hard at the fruit of temptation and get a li'l enticed to do something you ain't got no business out there doing with somebody that's not your spouse."

A moment of pause muted Pastor Cox after he alluded to the touchy subject of infidelity. "Mmm hmm!" he shouted. "You know who you are because you can't sit still with the truth nibbling at your ears. And some of y'all need to make up your minds where you wanna be: In the club, sippin' on bub, or in church serving the Lord. You can't have it both ways! One foot in." Pastor Cox hopped to put his right foot forward. "One foot out." He hopped and pulled it back. "Doing the hokey pokey ain't gonna fly too long with the *Man*, and I'm not preaching about 'the man' who docks your paycheck 'cause you can't get to work on time for partyin' and shakin' your rumps the night before. You Party All The Time Christians know what I'm talking about. Don't act like you don't know. Been there!" Pastor Cox hammered the podium to drive home his point. "Done all of *that when I was twenty-something.* As a child of God, I ain't too proud to testify. What's done is done. Where's my amen posse at?" Again, Pastor Cox's eyes swept the entire congregation. "Not one of y'all telling me to preach, to straighten those devils out, to say it again this morning. I'm speaking the truth and I can't get support in the Lord's house? Now that's what I call a sin and a shame."

Pastor Cox reached down behind the platform, sipped water from a tall glass, and returned it, seemingly focused on Simone.

"Sister Miller, sure is good seeing you again."

When Simone nodded a subtle hello, Pastor Cox continued preaching.

"Now, I ain't one to gossip," he said, eyeing the congregation once more, "but some of y'all think I'm arrogant and full of myself. Deacon Brown, they call me a walking contradiction and say I think I'm all *that*. Ain't that what they say behind my back?" Deacon Brown nodded his confirmation. "Humph!" Pastor Cox huffed and puffed. "I don't know about y'all, but I never thought I'd see the day when the pot bad-mouths the kettle. And y'all supposed to be so sanctified. Have mercy on me!"

Meanwhile, "Preach!" rang out from the rear of the sanctuary.

"Tell it like it is," boomed from the balcony.

Pleased that a few amen posse members pledged their allegiance, Pastor Cox said, "Now that's what I want to hear. Encourage me to encourage you to get right and stay right. Help me do God's work. Brothers and sisters, I'm going to say a few more words before I take my seat. Trouble doesn't always last. But we wish it wouldn't overstay its welcome either. In times of suffering, be it financial, physical, emotional, or psychological, help," *Bam!* He slammed his palm down on the podium, "is only a prayer away!" He shouted, stepping down from the pulpit. "We all go through trials and tribulations on life's journey." He wandered down the aisles calling out to the congregation. "I see the everyday Christian, cliquey Christian, nine-to-five Christian, politically correct Christian, Gospel-TV-on-Sunday-morning Christian, and the hoity-toity

Christian. Not one of you is exempt from adversity! I'm not exempt. Even our savior Jesus Christ, went through pure—"

"Ooooo, Pastor Cox, hush your holy mouth," spilled down in unison from the choir box.

"Hush my mouth?" he repeated like they had some nerve. "We're all human in here. We aren't perfect in the eyes of God. Who are you trying to impress this Sunday morning? I know it's not me. God is still working on me. Some of y'all are under permanent reconstruction!" He grinned. "The devil ain't the only one who knows what you did last night. God was watching, too." He cackled loudly.

The organ churned out a low musical note to underscore the veracity of his words.

"Brothers and sisters," Pastor Cox drawled, as he strolled back to the pulpit, "We all stumble at one time or another, but it's not about the fall, it's how we respond to being down that makes the difference between whether we stay down for the count or get up and fight. Reach out and touch somebody. Anybody. Turn and join hands with your neighbor. Tell them you love them and say it like you mean it, and don't just say it to hear yourself talk Christian-like on Sunday morning. And please remind our children that they are beautiful and gifted, and talented beyond amazement. Redirect their crooked paths. Encourage them to stay in school. Make them pick up a book and read. Clean up our community just as much as you get cleaned up for the club. If you see a piece of trash dancing in the wind, put your foot down on it, pick it up, and throw it away. Stop the self-destruction and the gang violence in the community. If you see something, report it to the anonymous hotline instead of acting like it ain't your problem because you haven't lost a loved one!"

Gasps traveled from the congregation to the pulpit.

Pastor Cox looked around noticing that he had touched some nerves keeping it real. "Now don't hurt the messenger. I–I–I–" He pushed back with his hands. "I ain't trying to scare anybody, but how many of y'all here today been affected by the random shootings and stabbings making headlines every day? Stand up. Let me see who's suffering in silence. Don't be afraid to share your pain. We are not here to judge. We are here to lift you up in prayer." Practically every member stood up.

"Good gawd almighty!" Pastor Cox looked around in disbelief. "Y'all represent over half the congregation. We must take back our community and fight for our children and our salvation. Amen?"

"Amen."

"Saints, that's all I'm gonna say this morning. The rest is up to you. The time is now. Don't wait until it's too late. Tomorrow is not promised. I'll say it again, and I want you to say it with me. Tomorrow is not promised."

The congregation stood united for peace and repeated Pastor Cox's words.

The collection plate ran its second and last round, Simone added her five-dollar bill and looked around for Portia. She didn't notice her confidante, her sister-friend in the fray of gaudy hats, tired and rigid faces. Simone assumed, *Portia probably came late and sat in the vestibule. Maybe I'll catch her on the way out before she thinks I was a no-show, too, and leaves without discussing brunch.*

Denise, Portia, and Simone used to have Sunday brunch at least once a month, before they stopped attending church regularly, if at all.

Following the sermon, the senior choir belted out a powerful rendition of "Work It Out" that could have made angels descend from heaven. The congregation was elated. Bodies bopped to the rhythm. Peacock feathers in big tawdry hats lurched, doing the shimmy. Ushers and deacons danced shamelessly praising the Lord. Potted plants perched atop twin mantels on each side of the podium vibrated in tune with the synthesizing keyboard. Touched by the Spirit, the believer in Simone soul-clapped, tapped her feet to the tempo, and hoped, *One day the hoity-toity will stop acting like being saved on Sunday morning is the latest fad and church is the place to be seen sitting in the front pew.*

Singing and praising it up, Pastor Cox and Caroline marched the choir down the aisle out to the vestibule. Church was dismissed. Pastor Cox posted up on one side of the oak doors and Caroline was on the other blessing, and shaking hands of parishioners as they left the sanctuary.

Simone searched high and low, row by row for Portia, but didn't see her anywhere. She then scrambled to keep up with the rush to leave. Children hurried to reconnect with their chaperones in the lobby, while Denise schemed on Deacon Brown as he, too, blessed and shook the hands of parishioners on their way out. From behind, hair stylist TraNeese tapped Simone on her shoulder, praising the Lord. "God is good."

Simone turned and replied with the standard, "All the time."

"He's been so good that I've been able to make time to visit Nathan's school and speak with his teachers. We agreed that a weekly progress report would be in his best interest. I even volunteered to do lunch duty every other Monday."

Happy-go-lucky Nathan whizzed by Simone and raced into his mother's adoring arms.

Simone didn't notice Nathan because she was distracted watching Pastor Cox eye Denise as she vied for Deacon Brown's affection. Pastor Cox discreetly left his post, walked to Denise and ministered unsolicited marriage counseling.

"Sister Hightower, tell your husband Jackson he's welcome here anytime."

When Simone saw Pastor Cox tactfully resume blessing parishioners, she gave Denise a hint of reality.

"Your future is not with Deacon Brown. Look at him. He's not paying you any mind. Think about Dorion and Dillon. Salvage your marriage. Reconcile with Jackson. And don't forget, God don't like ugly."

"He ain't too fond of pretty, either," gushed Sister Pritchard, head of the hospitality committee. She yanked Simone into the bosom of her teal-green dress, which smelled of spicy Fendi perfume. "It's nice seeing you this glorious morning. Where have you been?"

"Well, I've been kind of going through something personal." When Simone's upbeat demeanor cracked, Sister Pritchard slipped her arm through Simone's.

"Walk with me to the nursing station. We can talk privately there."

Walking away with Sister Pritchard, Simone made eye contact with Denise, "Think about what I said. We can talk later, okay?" She whispered as she walked by.

Denise replied with a nonchalant "Sure," while locking her gaze on Deacon Brown.

In the triage unit, Simone went through the emotionally daunting task of explaining her fibroid condition to Sister Pritchard.

"God never gives you more than you can handle. If you're grounded in faith, then you should understand He would not have revealed the horrible circumstance to you at such a critical time in your life if He didn't think you were prepared to weather the storm." Sister Pritchard lifted Simone's chin with a perfectly manicured finger. "Keep your head up. We've all felt it hard when we least expected trouble to come our way. Never forget a problem shared is one less burden on your cross. Stay prayed-up. Are you hearing me?"

After inhaling deeply, Simone exhaled, "Yes. Thank you for encouraging words."

28

COTTON AND STEEL

The spirit of the Word delivered Simone to the cotton and steel of the Miller family. She hadn't seen or heard from her mother Claire since refusing to honor her liquor store request. Simone hoped the Sabbath Day was a safe time to make amends.

She pressed down on the bell, hard and long, knowing her mother's hearing was not what it used to be. Just her luck it started to rain. She pressed the bell longer. Claire didn't answer; Simone thumped the doorknocker several times. Then she called out to her, "Mother, open up. It's me!"

The door opened slightly. A nearly sixty-year-old face studied Simone through the narrow slit. Her mother opened the door wider, shifted weight off her arthritic feet, and rested her side against the casing for support.

"Why are you keeping up all this noise like you ain't got the good sense God blessed you with?"

"Mother, I was worried when you didn't answer the bell. Plus, my clothes are getting wet."

"Never mind about your clothes. Worry about catching pneumonia."

Simone sucked her teeth, Claire held her at the doorway. Impatient, Simone grumbled, "Can I come in? If I stand here any longer I'm going to become a puddle."

"Child, get your vain behind in here. Remove those wet shoes before you go tracking up my floor. I almost pulled a back muscle scrubbing it." Claire stepped aside to eyeball Simone's next move. Simone sure as heck wasn't about to mess up the floor her mother almost pulled a muscle scrubbing. Since childhood she'd been a disciplinarian with immaculate housekeeping skills, which Simone had yet to perfect. Her mother was always meticulous. When Simone was young, she used to tease her mother, saying "When you die I am going to bury you with a gallon of Pine-Sol."

Claire watched Simone remove her shoes and leave them on the small rug placed neatly by the door. She watched Simone until she sat on the flower-patterned settee.

Reaching into her bag, Simone withdrew a wrapped package.

"Here. I brought something for you."

Her mother moved closer, staring at the package. "Something like what?"

"Please, just take it and stop giving me a hard time. And please crack a window and let some fresh air in this stuffy place." The look Claire gave Simone was dirtier than the last.

"Ain't no windows being opened around here. Turn on the fan if you're warm," she said tersely, opening the box and rummaging through pastel tissue paper to remove the glass object. Her face softened at the sight of the gift. She twirled the Austrian crystal pineapple that Simone bought to add to her collection of knickknacks. "Well, ain't you sweeter than a piece of cake."

Simone laughed. "Yeah, right. The other day I was a box of lemons because I wouldn't run you to the liquor store."

"Sweet, sour, and mouthy. Either way this sure is a fine piece of crystal. It looks awfully expensive, but I do appreciate it."

Her mother found a place for the knickknack among the many figurines on her glass curio shelf, then she walked to the kitchen.

"It's a little something I picked up for you at the mall," Simone gushed with pride as she followed her. The first thing Simone noticed in the kitchen was the once white paint was now discolored and the walls chipped. Adhesive paper borders curled at the edges and away from the surface. The kitchen was past due for an upgrade, but overall the dining area was organized. The linoleum flooring was spic and span with a penny shine to it. Helping herself to iced water Simone inhaled the aroma of a Sunday meal in progress.

"What's for dinner?"

"Pot roast, 'tata salad, and greens. Next time wash your hands before you open my refrigerator."

Gulping the last drop of water, Simone rinsed the glass and returned it to the strainer before her mother could lecture about dirtying up dishes. Not completely resigned about the chipped and faded paint, Simone tried to convince her mother to remodel the kitchen, a mini-project she and her sister Susan had discussed taking on when and if Susan got her money right.

"Mother, I thought you were changing the color to canary yellow to match the Annie Lee art I gave you for Christmas?"

"Ain't got time to think about paint. I'm tired and getting on in age. My bones the reason I ain't been to church steady."

Her mother sat at the kitchen table and started peeling potatoes to prepare the potato salad. A bunch of collard greens soaked in a bowl of baking soda. Smoked turkey wings simmered on the stove. The pot roast was already done. For as far back as Simone could remember, her mother always preferred getting her meat out of the way early, so she could focus on side dishes while humming southern hymns that could have shaken up a wretched soul.

"Oh, stop whining," Simone teased. "You're only as old as you feel. Find a hobby besides shopping for odds and ends at Wal-Mart."

Her mother pointed the potato peeler at Simone, "Don't forget, um grown. I'll whine if I want to."

"Mother…" Simone spoke softly, twiddling her thumbs, admiring the matte plum nail polish.

"Somethin' botherin' you?" Claire whispered, she was superstitious about the walls having ears.

Simone bowed her head to tame her troubled emotions.

"What's the matter? The cat got a hold of your tongue and won't let it go? Open your mouth and speak. Don't say it's no big deal either. Now that I got a good look at you—" her mother gave her the once over—"Susan was right. That belly does look a little swollen. Something you forgot to tell momma?"

"For goodness sake, I wish Susan would stop nitpicking about my stomach and start worrying about her own business!" Simone griped, crossing her arms in front of her stomach.

Claire slammed the peeler on the table Simone tensed up as if she knew a left hook was coming. When it came to laying down the law in her house, Simone's mother wore the pants, dress, and the skirt.

"Raise your voice in here again!" She warned Simone. "I hope you don't think you're too old to take a whooping. I still got my strength for that, you know."

"Mother, please," Simone said exasperated, "I need to talk to you about something."

"Then stop lippin' off and tell me what's got you sitting in my kitchen so anxious."

"It's a female thing."

"A female thing like what?" Claire gave Simone a wary look as she lifted a Mason jar of liquid off the Corian countertop. She jiggled the ice cubes, took a swallow, and returned the jar to the surface.

Simone frowned, "What are you drinking?"

"Nothin'," Claire, quipped, downing another swig.

"You should be drinking prune juice," Simone snickered.

"Never mind what um drinkin'." She paused to take another swallow of nothin' before reminding Simone she was a grown woman who didn't need permission to enjoy a taste of bourbon-on-the-rocks every now and then to keep her warm and cozy inside.

Simone backed off the jar of nothin' to refocus on the other reason for her visit.

"Anyway, I wasn't going to say anything. I don't want to upset you, but I had an ultrasound because of the swelling in my stomach. The doctor said I have fi—"

"Five months to live?!," her mother interrupted, throwing her hands up in despair. "Lord Jesus, please don't take my baby!" She shouted, nearly knocked the bowl of potato salad on the floor.

"Mother, calm down. You're overreacting. It's not that serious. Really, it isn't. Please, relax before you work up a heart attack. I'm not dying, but I might as well be if complications from fibroids prevent me from starting a family someday."

"A family?" Her mother retorted, ignoring the fibroids announcement. "Is that why you got my blood pressure up?" Claire frowned then secured the mixing spoon to start blending the potato salad ingredients. "Child, you're delirious. Don't bring children into this war-torn world as hard as it is to make ends meet. You can't do it alone. You don't know what hard is until you have to raise a child with one hand tied behind your back. Mess around and come up pregnant and alone and surely you will find out the struggle ain't easy. Parenting is a 24-hour commitment. You had better think long and hard about your baby momma aspirations because I ain't babysittin', no sir-ree."

"Mother, don't judge me. The Bible—"

"Quiet in my house!" Claire scolded and then playfully stuck the spoon in Simone's face. "I know exactly what's written in the Good Book about judging other folks." Claire's specialty was recalling scripture like it was tattooed on the palm of her hands. "Matthew 7:1 warns: *Do not judge, or you too will be judged.* Simone, I know you're grown, but you're still my child. I want you to understand what I have to say today. If the Lord wanted to bless you with a hollering baby, you'd have one by now 'cause I know you ain't no virgin. I can tell by the way you swish and swing those hips." She stood up and gyrated her hips to mimic Simone's walk, except she needed some practice to slacken up her aging bones.

A spark of light brightened Simone's face as she watched her mother attempt Josephine Baker's moves with her old southern hips.

"Ole girl still got it," her mother proclaimed, rocking side-to-side making her way to the sink to rinse and dry the greens before submerging them deep into the turkey-based boiling water. "By the way, what was that young man's name you were nutty about? How come y'all didn't work out? He wasn't husband material?"

"What young man?" Simone asked, even though she knew exactly who Claire meant.

"Clyde. Clown. Clark Kent... You know my memory ain't what it used to be. But he sure had a dip in his stride like he had been blessed with a third leg—"

Simone quickly cut Claire off. "His name was Clay. That was so long ago. I've had two lovers since him."

"Look here, your mouth is running faster than your brain. I didn't raise no sluts," her mother countered, holding a spoon, pretending to whack Simone upside the head with it. "And say what you want to say about your sister Susan. She found herself a husband. He ain't no Harry Belafonte when Harry was handsome like your jive turkey father was, but I reckon an ugly husband is better than not having a man around to help rear children."

"Mother, I'm curious, when did Susan become a model citizen? There used to be a time when she had you wringing the skin off your hands with shame."

"You ain't picture perfect and don't forget what I told you when you snuck off to the park with Clyde, Clark. What was his name again?"

"Clay, Mother."

"Clay? Yeah, that's right, you did just tell me that didn't you? Anyway, like I was saying before my memory failed me, I already raised my babies. My tubes are tied tight. I ain't being saddled down with no more headaches! Now, come on and pray with me," Claire ordered, already in prayer position on the kitchen floor mat. Simone joined in.

"Heavenly Father, please keep working on my baby. She's doing so well with her life. She don't do no drugs. She don't be in the streets raising all kinds of hell. She don't party and drink up her paycheck. Find a way to fix her 'cause I sure would hate for somethin' bad to happen to my baby. I love her with all my heart. She can be a little bullheaded like her ole crude father was, but she ain't never been weak."

Simone was tearing up, and sniffed her runny nose. Her mother kept on praying. "She's always been a strong fighter, determined to break the dysfunctional cycle of drugs, abuse, and debt tearing so many families apart. She ain't a victim of none of that self-defeating behavior."

Simone held back tears.

Her mother carried on. "Father, if you're using her to teach other people how to be brave, then show her the light of happiness. Bless her with the strength of Goliath to beat the fibroids taking over her body and making her worry."

Simone prepared to stand. Her mother held her wrist to keep her down.

"Don't you budge, I ain't through with you, yet. Bow your head."

Back in prayer position, Simone rested her chin on her chest. Claire continued praying for her youngest child.

"Father, please teach Simone how to forgive those who have trespassed against her. Teach Simone and Susan if they can't love each other as sisters, then they ain't got no business loving anybody else that ain't their blood relative. That's all I ask for."

On one accord, they uttered, "Amen."

Claire walked back to the counter, raised the jar of nothin' to her lips, and finished the remaining liquid in one guzzle.

Simone sat down at the kitchen table looking anxious.

Claire took notice.

"You got something else on your mind?" she asked sitting across from Simone.

"I didn't get a chance to tell you about my fibroids, and why I might not be able to start a family to call my own."

"Simone, worry 'bout starting a family when you meet a man worth marrying. Focus on your health. Now, I know a little something 'bout fibroids. A long time ago there was a big write up in the newspaper 'bout doctors performing hysterectomies because they didn't know how to treat fibroids. Hell, I worried 'bout my womanhood being in jeopardy and I didn't even have fibroids." Claire cackled. "But I sure did educate myself 'bout 'em."

"Well, I wish I didn't have fibroids. My life hasn't been the same since. I always gotta pee, I'm constipated, I've got painful premenstrual cramps and my periods are sometimes depressing. And to think that I might not be able to get pregnant."

"You ain't learned from nothing I taught you 'bout listening, have you?"

"Mother maybe if you actually talked to me instead of scolding me all the time, I would listen more. When I'm going through something you act like I should just get over it."

"Simone, baby if you expect me to sit here and encourage you to tie yourself down with babies then you'll be sadly disappointed. If you want fake, I ain't it!" Claire countered with the signature feisty Miller attitude.

"Mother, I'm not asking for advice. I'm trying to lean on you for support. I know at times I act like I have it all together, but honestly, I don't."

When Simone began to cry, Claire put her hand on top of Simone's on the table. "Look at me, Mother. My waistline makes me feel unattractive. I barely recognize myself."

"You're crying because your waist is spreading? Why are you so vain? There's nothing wrong with you child. Any man who can't see that don't deserve you."

Simone wiped away her tears and smiled her thanks.

"So, what has your doctor said about the fibroids?" Claire asked as she checked on the meal.

"Dr. Theery told me to 'watch and wait'. I go back every six months to see if they change in size, or multiply."

"Seems to me you ought to listen, be patient, and stop worrying yourself, and worrying me." Claire walked back to the table, and placed her hand on Simone's cheek. "I know I don't say it enough but I love you and want the best for you. Please be patient. Find yourself a decent man who will respect everything about you, before you think about bearing his children. I ain't trying to stall your life, I'm trying to teach you what my momma never taught me. Babies can wait. You working a temp job and seem to be happy with the flexible time, and still caught up in shopping and getting your hair done. Once a baby comes along all that will change. Don't slow down your life because fibroids got you thinking you missing out on something. Motherhood is a beautiful experience, but it's also demanding, exhausting, and downright expensive, too. And the way you were hanging on my bell earlier worried 'bout your hair, you ain't ready to make vain sacrifices."

"Mother!"

"Don't mother me because you know it's true. Now let me fix you a plate of momma's comfort food."

"Simone stood to leave. "Actually, I have a dinner date."

"Is that right? What kind of person is he?"

"He seems decent and he's a police officer."

"A police officer you say? Hmm. In other words he's a male-whore."

"Mother, they're not all the same.

"Do y'all have an ounce of chemistry?"

"A little, I think."

"A little ain't enough to pass on my home-cooked meal. Claire bowed her head and wrung her hands, in her typical ploy for sympathy. "I sure get lonely for company sometimes."

But Simone didn't give in.

"Mother, another time. This date could be the beginning of something special."

"Alright. Just remember after he pays the bill, sex ain't the proper way for a lady to say thank-you."

Simone left hoping dinner that evening with Jeff wouldn't prove her mother's male-whore theory true. More than anything she needed a distraction from the drama, stress, aches, and pain of her life.

29

TABLE FOR TWO

Dressing for dinner was mind-boggling for Simone. *"Should I go sexy or semi-conservative? Stepping out sexy will win over Jeff's attention, but looking too sexy the night might end with us body slapping to baby-making music."*

Just the thought of soiled diapers and sleepless nights, made Simone decide to play it safe. She chose a semi-sexy cleavage-enhancing cowl-neck dress, the hemline stopped just above her knees. The Lycra body shaper underneath trimmed her spreading waistline. Silver jewelry and black peep-toe pumps with sterling buckles at the ankles made the dress *pop*. Traces of berry eye shadow and matching lip-gloss added a touch of softness to the dark ensemble. A squirt of Dolce & Gabana Light Blue perfume on her pressure points completed the look.

Driving up Route 9, first date jitters overwhelmed Simone. *Breathe, girl, breathe. Take it easy. It's only dinner. You're not meeting his parents, and he's definitely not meeting your dysfunctional family and circle of needy friends.* The bout of angst was committed to her short-term memory, as she parked.

Rushing to be the first to arrive, Jeff and Simone nearly collided at the restaurant's entrance. If a man made the
clothes, then everything about Jeff's tailored sports jacket,
shiny shoes, slacks, crisp shirt, and silk tie confirmed he was
not stingy with the dinero. He was dressed to impress from
top to toe.

Jeff pulled Simone close in a comforting embrace, before
placing a tender peck on her left cheek. His Issey Miyake cologne sailed up her nostrils. Jeff gave an approving nod at her
modest outfit as his eyes traveled up one side of her and down
the other. "Nice legs."

She blushed and praised him in return. "You clean up
nicely." She said as Jeff took her arm and steered her inside
the restaurant.

"McKinley, party of two," Jeff said to a plump, fresh-out-
the-tanning booth brunette who identified herself as Jenny,
their waitress for the evening then led them to their booth.
Jeff pressed his hand into the small of Simone's back. "Ladies
first," he politely said, allowing her to walk ahead of him.

Jenny escorted them to a booth distant from the restroom
and the active kitchen. Simone considered both bad seating
areas in a restaurant.

Once seated, they draped a napkin on their lap and
browsed the menu of American and Italian cuisine. Health
conscience, they eliminated entrees that were high in fat, sodium, and cholesterol. Heeding Dr. Theery's orders, Simone
avoided greasy foods and chose broiled fish. Jeff selected
an Italian dish. Raspberry lemonade was their beverage of
choice.

Then they passed the time asking and answering ice-
breaking questions.

"Tell me, Officer McKinley, what made you join the police force?"

"I always wanted to serve the community as a way of giving back. After graduating from Northeastern University with a criminal justice degree, I went straight into the police academy. Pop retired from the line of duty the same day I took my oath."

"How noble. Your parents must have been mighty proud."

"Yes. I would say so—until tragedy struck."

Simone leaned into the table and softened her voice. "How so?"

"Nine months after graduation, Mom was diagnosed with advanced metastatic breast cancer, which was Stage IV and hopeless. Depression quickly settled into our household after the doctor informed us the cancer had spread to vital organs. She underwent radiation treatment to keep her comfortable, but the doctor cautioned us not to expect her to live beyond three months. Ninety days and a week later she passed."

"Forgive me for asking, but was she getting regular mammograms?"

"We assumed so. Mom was very private. She rarely had much to say about anything. She carried on about life with no outward worries until she became ill. One month she was full of zest—baking pies, rolling dumplings, and whipping up my favorite banana pudding. The next—hospitalized, barely breathing, and dependent on a morphine drip to ease her pain. After the cancer spread to her brain, her will to live couldn't fight the ravaging cancer anymore. One by one, vital organs shut down, eventually her heart stopped beating. She died holding Pop's hand."

Simone's father's long battle with cancer filtered through her head, but she didn't want to overshadow Jeff's emotional moment discussing his death. So, Simone decided to keep the conversation about their mothers, and let Jeff show a vulnerable side she might not get to see again."

I'm so sorry for your loss. I don't know what I would do if I lost my mother. Death is not something anyone can ever truly be prepared for."

"I totally agree. Pop took mom's passing especially hard. She was his one and only true love. He couldn't picture going on without his soul mate. Gosh, I miss her so much." Jeff choked back tears.

"I'm sure she's smiling down on you." Simone said reaching for her glass of water.

Jeff drank some water too, and then said quietly. "Every day."

"So, what else do you do when you're not on the beat and running laps around The Pond?" Simone asked feeling a need to change the subject to a lighter topic.

"Sometimes I help my Pop manage his rental property. Aside from that, I'm a low-key kind of guy."

"Low-key, huh? How many women are in your low-key harem?" Simone asked, bracing for the inevitable truth that all men were dogs and Jeff was leading the pack.

He grinned bashfully and looked around the restaurant like he was expecting the harem posse to walk in.

"I can't believe you're blushing. Well, how many do you have in your stable? Two? Four? Six? Eight? Tell me!"

"As a matter of fact, none. When I joined District B, Pop warned me about women and their fascination for men in uniform. He said that I'd have to beat them off with my nightstick."

Simone laughed. "And the ones you didn't beat off with your nightstick?"

Jeff shifted in his seat as if the question made him uncomfortable. "Gina, my ex-fiancée, she was a keeper until she grew tired of the take-a-number-and-wait routine."

Simone laughed a little too loudly before covering her mouth after the outburst.

Baffled, Jeff asked, "What's so funny? Did I miss the punch line?"

"Well, when you said take-a-number-and-wait, I envisioned cracked pepper turkey and provolone cheese seeing that I've been meaning to get to the deli to buy some lunchmeat."

"That's cold-blooded."

"Admit it was funny."

"I guess so." Jeff smirked.

"So, do you have any burning questions for me?" Simone asked taking a sip of water.

"Actually, yes. How do you make ends meet on a temporary salary? Is that a stable way of earning a living?"

"I'm content and don't want for much after making a decent living, busting my hump over a decade in Corporate America. Besides, I only have me, myself, and I to support. Being childless has its advantages."

Jeff smiled cynically. "All good things have a limit. You know that, right?"

"Don't worry. I'm not taking life for granted, and I don't live beyond my means."

"That's good to know. Do you have any siblings?"

"There are four of us, but my sister Susan and I are the only two living in Boston. And yourself?"

"Only child."

"Are you selfish?"

"I can be. Are you spoiled?"

"Depends on what or whom I want."

"Interesting. Very interesting." Jeff said as the waitress delivered their meals.

"Miso salmon for you, ma'am. Shrimp scampi for you, sir." Jenny carefully placed their meals on the table. "Can I get you anything else?" she asked.

"No, thank you." Simone responded.

Jeff winked. "What she said."

That was cute, Simone thought.

Amused by his dry wit, Jenny laughed and said, "Okay. Well, enjoy," then she sauntered off to tend to other patrons.

Jeff ate every bit of his generous serving of shrimp scampi, flavored with light cream, garlic, butter, and a touch of lemon. Salmon, snow peas, and rice pilaf satisfied Simone's taste buds. Following the entrees, she bypassed a tasty treat from the dessert menu, especially after Jeff said he didn't have a sweet tooth.

Twenty minutes later, Simone answered to her bladder. Shortly after, they topped off their date with a leisure stroll through the upscale shopping center that catered to professionals, yuppies, and buppies. Simone and Jeff loitered at the window of Tiffany & Co., admiring a dazzling array of diamonds and precious pearls. Simone noticed Jeff observing her as she fantasized about a happily ever after.

He caressed her hand and whispered, "Are you ready to move on?"

Move on, they did, eventually coming to a standstill in front of her car.

"Well, here we are," Simone said turning to face Jeff.

"Muffin Top, thank you for a lovely evening."

"No, Officer McKinley, I should be thanking you for the invitation."

"Simone." Jeff whispered her name as he cradled her hands tenderly in his, before brushing them across his lips. "You can thank me later." He then pulled her into his buffed chest and gently kissed Simone's right cheek. "Now that I've covered both cheeks," He said, "I would love a real kiss if you want it as much as I do."

Simone watched as his lips slowly approached her mouth. The scent of garlic assaulted her nostrils. The smell pushed her back, and ruined the possibility of their first kiss.

"Slow down, Officer Frisky."

Jeff chuckled, "It's just a kiss. I'm not trying to bed you after one meal."

"Oh, believe me, it's going to take more than the price of salmon to get under my dress."

Jeff hemmed Simone against the car as if he was making an arrest. "Is that right?" He asked pressing hard against her. She didn't try to break free, knowing she wanted him to do everything Secret Pleasure couldn't do—lick her, squeeze her, sink his teeth into her breast, work her clit standing, laying and sitting. Simone yearned for Jeff to tug her hair from the back and spank her ass until it turned a beautiful shade of brown. Jeff pressed harder, sliding her dress thigh high. In the throes of passion his well-endowed sex pistol stiffened and triggered Simone's inner freak. Juices percolated between her legs just as Jeff spoke tenderly in her ear.

"Can we hurry up and do dinner again?"

His hot breath against her ear was an instant turn on.

"Sure, and dessert is on me, literally," She responded, then the lonely in her groped him passionately, gripping every incredible inch of him. As she gazed at Jeff with seducing eyes, softly she moaned, "Feel me feeling all of you?"

"Be careful, magic fingers. Cameras are rolling," Jeff warned her.

"Shh." Simone silenced him. "If we're caught, blame it on reality television. Now, unzip your pants and show me what I have to look forward to should you round third base and slide in for a home run."

Never taking his eyes off Simone, Jeff turned their bodies so that his back was facing the surveillance camera. Simone buried her face deep into his chest to inhale his manliness. The Issey Miyake cologne caused her juices to flow faster. Love's sugar dampened her thong. Jeff unzipped his slacks to release his sex pistol. Simone secured him in a delicate grip and massaged it slowly and gently. It wasn't long after the massaging started before they became tangled pretzels in the backseat of her Camry. Weak in the knees, Jeff groaned to the rhythm of her teasing strokes.

"Muffin Top, let's go back to my place and finish what you started."

In an instant, Simone's libido deactivated. She struggled to nudge his six-two, 205-pound physique off her five-foot-five, 135-pound body.

"Officer McKinley, you might be above the law, but you're not above disease. Do you have protection?"

"Muffin Top, my .357 Magnum is always loaded with six rounds of lead."

"Slow down, cowboy. That's not what I meant. Do you have a condom?"

"Don't need one. I'm clean."

"Jeff, I can't trust your word alone. I'm not taking any health risks. No condom, no action. It's late. I think we've had our fill for one night, besides sex ain't the proper way for a lady to say thank-you for a meal."

"Simone, relax. I know you're only being cautious. It's not about sex. I was serious about doing dinner again. That hasn't changed, has it?"

"No. Not at all, and for the record, I was turned off by your cavalier attitude toward unprotected sex."

"It won't happen again. Promise."

With a future date on the horizon, and a promise, Simone coasted Route 9, heading home, skeptical about Jeff. *Can I ever trust again? Can a man in his profession love one woman more than he claimed his dad adored his mother?*

"I have my doubts and Mother I hope you're proud that I listened for a change," Simone heard herself say, as she parked in front of her house.

30

GOODIES

Simone was grateful for the peace and quiet on the home front as she parked. The neighborhood was as still as the galaxy of stars above. Peyton Place, as Simone sometimes affectionately called her neighborhood, had lost some of its flare since her flamboyant neighbor Ritchie Calhoun moved away after "coming out" to his father turned into a living nightmare. Simone thought there was no sight more disturbing than a three-legged dog hobbling the streets, until she witnessed a grown man like Ritchie break down and cry over his father's rejection. Ritchie was banned from the Calhoun home to never be welcomed again unless he came back to show off his wife and kids. Ritchie wept so hard he could have filled a bucket with tears. All cried out, he relocated to New York hoping to be judged less harshly there for being gay.

The porch light was off, which Simone thought was odd. She clearly remembered turning it on before leaving the house. A few feet from the door, Simone thought she heard rustling in the lofty hedges along the perimeter. She called for Snow, to come out of hiding. When the fluffy feline didn't show her face, Simone bolted for the door, jammed and turned the key, hurried inside, and slammed it shut to make certain it was closed tight. She disengaged the alarm and turned the lights on.

Simone freed her feet from her pumps to rush around propping chairs under the front, rear, and basement door-knobs for added security. Afraid someone might hear her moving around in the house, she tiptoed upstairs to peer down on the deserted street. There was no movement other than a passing blue sedan. After washing her hands and face and brushing her teeth, Simone slipped out of her dress, and changed into Capri pajama pants, and a cotton nightshirt. She lay back on the bed with her eyes open, both ears alert, with her trusty box cutter under the pillow for easy access.

The soft-top mattress never felt so good. She unconscious-ly gave herself a breast examination, starting on the left, using circular motions with her fingers. She applied slight pressure in, on, and around the areola to detect tenderness or unusual lumps. She repeated the exam on the right breast. In the pro-cess, her eyelids fluttered, gained weight, and slowly closed until she heard incessant barking under the bedroom window.

Simone sat up, patting around for the box cutter. She located the weapon, securing it in a tight grip. She contem-plated calling Jeff. *What am I going to say? I heard rustling in the bushes? A dog is barking? More importantly, why in the heck didn't you say call when you get home?* Her internal babbling ceased as quickly as it settled into her brain. Securing the box cutter, Simone climbed out of bed and peeked through the drapes to find Miss Bonita and her dog Ginger Snap. She almost did a double take when she saw her niece Monica aiming to pitch a rock at the window. Miss Bonita held Monica's wrist to keep her from throwing it.

Simone tapped the glass and mouthed, "Don't you dare." She then tucked the box cutter back under the pillow and ran downstairs at break-neck pace, intending to drag Monica inside. Livid, Simone pushed the chair aside and swung open the front door.

"What are you doing out here? Does your mother know where you are this time of night?" Simone was hopping mad and tired to boot. Miss Bonita didn't need to explain that she found Monica asleep in the bushes. Simone came to that conclusion after seeing dirt on the kneecaps of her painted-on jeans, which explained the rustling in the hedges earlier.

Monica started to cry.

Miss Bonita appealed to Simone. "Spare the rod. Don't chew the child out. She's been through too much already this evening, po' thang."

Simone thanked Miss Bonita for her input, told Ginger Snap, "I owe you a treat," then shouted, "Monica get in this house and start talking—now!"

Simone's phone rang.

"Speak!" she barked into the phone without checking the Caller ID.

"Good evening, Simone. I was calling to see if you made it home. Is everything okay?"

"Oh, hi, Jeff. Yes, I made it home safely."

"Is something bothering you?"

"No, nothing's bothering me. The phone startled me awake."

Monica opened her mouth as if to say, liar, but she closed it when Simone wagged a stern finger.

"Okay, I didn't mean to disturb your beauty sleep. Get some rest."

"I'll try. Good night."

Simone hung up and turned to Monica. "So how'd you get here?"

"A boy named Tyson I met at the library when I went to use the computer because Mummy took mine away."

"I wonder why. Finish."

"He picked me up from my friend Eryka's house to go see a movie and then get something to eat. When he dropped me off after curfew, Mummy wouldn't let me in. She told me to go back where I came from. When he saw I couldn't get in, I told him no one was home and asked him to drop me off at the bottom of your street so he wouldn't know where you live. When I got closer to your door, I saw headlights turning onto your street. When the lights went off I got scared and ran to the bushes. I got tired of waiting for you to come home and fell asleep. Ms. Bonita said she saw me in your bushes when you were coming up the walkway. She woke me up by shining a flashlight in my face. I told her I didn't wanna trouble you and asked if she could drive me home. She said she didn't have a car and that she knew you would understand after you got beyond your anger."

"Monica you wouldn't have to sleep in the bushes if you learn to obey your mother. Focus on getting your lessons in school and stop thinking everyone you meet is your friend. Hanging out with Tyson left you in the streets because you chose to have fun instead of respecting your mother's rules."

"Auntie, why are you yelling at me? I get what you're saying. I'm tired. I wanna go to bed."

Simone rolled her eyes, "So did I before you woke me up. Now, go wash that makeup off your face. You're going home tonight. You and your mother have some talking to do."

"I don't wanna go home. I'm tired of listening to arguments about money, bills, and food. I hate that house of horror."

"When you turn eighteen, you can get your own place. Until then, you need to apologize to your mother before I let you spend the night here. Besides, you have school tomorrow. I bet school was the furthest thought from your mind when you were riding around with Tyson. And what are your plans after you graduate from high school?" Simone asked when Monica had calmed down. The sudden question went unanswered as Monica gave her a blank stare. "You have no idea what you plan on doing with your life after high school, do you?"

Monica looked down at her sneakers. "No, not really because I have two more years before I graduate."

"Did you steal something?"

Monica looked at Simone somewhat miffed. "Huh?"

"You were looking down at your feet like you're ashamed. When someone is speaking to you, be confident, look them in the eye. Come sit on the sofa for some girl talk." They sat. Simone lead the conversation.

"Do you know what I would've said if someone had asked me what I want to be when I grow up?"

"No."

"Has anyone ever asked you that before tonight? Your mother? Teacher? Guidance counselor? Peers?"

"No. Only you."

"When I was your age, and even as young as six, if someone asked me what I wanted to be when I grow up, I would proudly say a lawyer, a businesswoman, a stewardess, a hairdresser, anything that popped into my head. One last thing, When you're surfing the Internet what sites do you visit most often?"

"Chat rooms. Facebook. Oh, and I check my e-mail accounts."

"What have the chat rooms and Facebook taught you about yourself? About life? About people? About the future?"

Monica shrugged "Nothing, I guess. I don't know. It's fun."

"Stop wasting so much time having fun learning nothing. Average grades won't get you in the college of your choice. When you set your sights high and reach for the stars, there is no limit to what you can do, who you can be. The possibilities are endless. Now what's this I hear about you settling for C's in school? You're a bright girl. Why are you slacking?"

"I don't know. I haven't been studying as hard as I should."

"Name something you're good at—reading, cooking, computers, math, science, anything."

"I like biology and computers."

"Do you know what kind of job you can get with a biology degree?"

"No."

"Do you care?"

"Yeah."

"Then I suggest you stop chatting and find out. Put your mind to good use. There's absolutely no harm having fun in the process of making something of yourself. Don't get side-tracked hanging out with boys, especially if they don't have good intentions. Focus on education and start giving more thought to preparing for your future, so when you meet that special someone you don't have to depend on him to feed, clothe, and treat you like an employee on his payroll." Simone sighed. "Monica, you're young. You need your mother's guidance. Being disrespectful and thinking you know everything could lead to trouble in the streets. There's a lot to be naïve about when you get too big for your britches. Do you understand what that means?"

"Yeah. I'm acting too grown. Same broken record Mummy always plays."

"Then don't you think if you're hearing the same tune from two people who love you dearly that you ought to make some changes before you get yourself in trouble making mistakes that are not always easy to fix? And I hope you're still a member of the Virgin Club."

Monica placed her hands on her maturing hips and proudly said, "Auntie, I'm the V-Club president."

"You'd better be. Now, go wash your face."

Monica shuffled to the bathroom. Simone went upstairs to change into jeans and a sweatshirt. She returned with a white T-shirt.

"Take that mess off," Simone said, pointing to the tiny crop top Monica was wearing. "Put this on." She handed the crewneck to Monica in exchange for her top with the word, "Goodies," emblazoned across her budding breasts.

Monica looked at the shirt., "Auntie, this is gonna ruin my outfit."

"It'll save your life, too."

"But—"

"But nothing, Monica. You can have your T-shirt back when you turn eighteen. Now hurry up so I can get back and get some sleep."

31

FOOLISH

When Simone and Monica arrived at the Miller-Taylor residence, a black-and-white police cruiser had just completed a three-point turn and sped away. Simone sensed trouble and called Susan from her cell phone.

"Simone, what's up?"

"I'm with your daughter outside and a police cruiser just drove away."

"Yeah, I know. Barry and I had words. It's nothing to worry about. Why is Monica with you?"

"Where'd you expect for her to go? She's only sixteen."

"I told her grown ass if she chooses not to follow the curfew rules, then she can't stay here. Since she got so much mouth, I left it to her to figure out and it sounds like she did."

"That's some tough love, Susan. She's still a child."

"A child who needs to respect her mother."

"Susan, we're coming in."

"Go home Simone and take Monica with you because I don't want to deal with her tonight."

"I will do no such thing. Monica needs to be home with her mother, not at my house running away from grown people's problems. We can finish this discussion inside. Simone then hung up without waiting for an answer.

"Monica, get out and open the door while I get something out the trunk." Simone unlocked the trunk to locate what she was looking for. She kept searching until the tire iron came into view. She gripped the handle tight and lifted it from the trunk.

Perplexed, Monica asked, "Auntie, what are you gonna do with that?"

"Don't worry about it. Now, open the door," she ordered, standing on the bottom step, holding the tire iron solid like a bat, prepared to swing like a maniac if she learned that Susan's husband put one ungrateful hand on her.

"I lost my keys." Monica was embarrassed to admit.

Simone chastised her, "How irresponsible! Maybe if you spent less time chatting on the Internet, you'd keep up with things. Am I clear?"

"Crystal," Monica replied, hanging her head.

"Hold your head up and bang on the door. Where's your mother anyway? I just told her we were coming in."

Monica banged on the door until Dallas and Sasha let them in.

Dallas rushed to Simone on the doorstep, wearing his Ninja Turtle pajamas. "Auntie, I want to go home with you," he cried.

She rubbed his back. "Fathead, don't cry. It's okay." Sasha seemed unfazed by his crying and gave Simone a lackluster hello.

"Where's your mother?" Simone wanted to scream, but she was too exhausted from Monica's foolishness.

"In her room, I think." Sasha answered, looking over her shoulder in the direction of Susan's bedroom.

"Dallas, where's your father?" Simone tightened her grip on the tire iron. Her palm grew moist with sweat.

"Mummy told him to get out and don't come back until he finds a job. Mummy called the cops. They made Daddy get his stuff and leave. Can I play with that?" Dallas said all in one breath, before reaching for the tire iron.

"Little boy, get back before you get hurt."

He whimpered. Tears rained down his sad little face. Simone rubbed his head to console him some more. Dallas then sat cross-legged on the floor, cradled his cheeks in his hands, and didn't breathe another word.

Sasha shook her head like, *whatever. Heard it all before,* and then said, "I'm gonna check on my science project to make sure Dallas didn't touch it."

Simone made a mental note to acknowledge the project at some point during the visit.

"See, I told you. This is a house of horror," Monica mumbled.

"Shame on them. They have no right bickering in front of you kids. Monica, take Dallas to your room. Stay there until I find out what's going on around here."

Heated enough to melt glass Simone ventured off to deal with her sister. At the bedroom door, she shouted, "Susan Miller-Taylor, open up. Don't make me break my toes kicking this door down."

Susan replied from inside, "I told you to go home. I've got our family matter under control."

"Not if Monica is riding around with a stranger wearing tight jeans that are screaming yeast infection; and Dallas is practically begging to live at my house, and Sasha is acting like she doesn't give a damn. Either you deal with me, or answer to Child Protective Services. Hurry up and make up your mind. I don't have all night for you to realize you need to do right by your children," Simone warned, still gripping the tire iron.

"Go home, Simone."

"No! The kids are upset. What happened between you and Barry?"

"Same song he's been singing about doing this and doing that once he finds a job."

"Apparently, he's taking advantage of the 'for better or for worse' part of the wedding vow. You, Monica, Sasha, and Dallas can't survive on an empty promise that things are going to get better. Fall behind on your bills the collectors will start calling. Hard times might even push you back in the streets doing something with your body you aren't supposed to be doing for money."

The bedroom door creaked open and Susan emerged. Disappointment coated her face. Her eyes were tomato red again. Simone could see she had been crying about whatever caused the quarrel between her and Barry.

"Simone, what are you trying to say?"

"I'm not *trying* to say anything. You need to get your house in order. Have you seen yourself this evening? Have you taken a good look in the mirror?"

"I don't understand how this concerns you. It's between Barry and me. Now, unless you're here to fix a flat, you can take your tire iron and go home."

"If I leave, CPS will be at your door before I reach my driveway. Now, is it going to be me or a Social Worker asking questions?"

Susan caved. She invited Simone into her bedroom. Emotionally drained, Simone sank down on the carpeted floor with her back pressed against the wall. Susan lounged on the safari-themed comforter on the bed. The matching shams and bed skirt showcased a healthy balance of femininity and a touch of masculinity that gave her husband an undeserving sense of belonging as the quasi-head of household.

Susan tugged at her loose spiral curls, training her attention on the portrait of a man and a woman crafted in perfect artistry. Simone tracked her gaze and imagined being the petite woman in the portrait whose head leaned slightly on a man's shoulder for unconditional support. She imagined that Susan wished for the same type of support.

Midnight struck. Their sibling bonding session was still going strong.

"Simone, Barry and I are emotionally distant and irritable around each other. We're never in the mood to cuddle anymore. Gone are the nights when I would snuggle up against him and we'd spoon until daylight. These days I stay on my side of the bed, and he stays on his."

"What's causing the friction in your marriage?"

"I think it's the stress of keeping up with the bills and raising these kids on only my income because Barry can't seem to keep a job. Besides that, I don't want to have this baby. I need a loan to get an abortion. Can you help me out?"

Susan's abortion comment sucked the oxygen out of the room. The tire iron crashed to the floor.

Simone lost her cool, "I knew it! I knew it! You always manage to squeeze me for money. Stupid me walked right into your money trap. How much this time? And how'd this pregnancy happen?"

"An abortion will cost about $700, but I only need half. "

"We're not discussing money until you answer my question. How'd it happen?"

"We had sex. Silly." Susan answered, slightly annoyed.

"That's not what I mean and you know it. I thought you were on birth control."

"I was but a couple times we were too hot-in-the-moment for me to insert my diaphragm."

"So laziness is the reason you want me to subsidize the death of my niece or nephew? Uh-unh. No way! I got enough of my own guilt to lug around. You're on your own in this life or death decision." Simone picked up the tire iron to leave.

"Sis, hear me out." Susan jumped in front of the door. "I started thinking differently about my pregnancy after you put a bug in my ear about the dangers of Down syndrome, learning disabilities, and whatnot."

"Susan, leave me out of it. Insurance plans cover abortions. Call your primary care provider."

"I don't want them in my business. Please, Simone, I want to do something with my life besides raising another baby. I'm serious about culinary arts school. Look, here's the brochure. It came in the mail yesterday."

"Alright, I'll loan you the money on one condition. Take a home pregnancy test in my presence, and that stick better turn royal blue!"

Susan pulled up her nightshirt to publicize a developing baby bump.

"This is real. I'm eight-and-a-half weeks along and need to have the abortion before Barry finds out. There's no need for a home pregnancy test."

"Are you saying he doesn't know you're expecting? What kind of marriage is this? You live in the same house and don't communicate.

"My body, my choice. Isn't that what you said when you got rid of your headache some years ago?" Susan asked, hitting Simone a little too close to her heart.

"You're out of line talking about what you don't know about. When I tested positive for that unplanned pregnancy, I didn't even have a friendship ring to brag about, so shut your face."

"What difference does it make whether you had a ring or not? Having one shouldn't justify how you feel about your child. Are you going to loan me the money or not?"

"Let me think about it some more and get back to you because you don't like to pay back what you borrow."

Simone walked out and checked on the kids with an ear to the door of Monica's bedroom. She knocked once before entering. Monica pretended to be studying, but Simone knew better. Dallas was sleeping like an angel nuzzled under a blanket. She hurried along to say good night to Sasha.

"Pretty girl, that's a cool rainforest that you constructed out of a shoebox," Simone said about Sasha's science project. "It's very creative. Keep up the good work and first place will be yours."

Behind the saddest sleepy eyes, Sasha asked, "Auntie, if I win the contest can I come live with you?"

"Sasha sweetie, I would love for you to visit any time you wish, but you can't live with me. Your place is with your mother, brother, and sister, but if you ever want to talk to me about anything, I'm always a phone call away."

"Okay."

"That's my girl."

The bell rang. Simone told Susan she would get the door on her way out. Lo and behold, her brother-in-law, Barry strolled in suited up like a Fortune 500 CEO.

"Simone." He nodded to acknowledge her.

Short and bittersweet, she responded, "Husband."

"I beg your pardon. I've got a name."

"That means what to me?"

"It means you need to use it for a change."

"And if I don't, *Husband?*"

Barry and Simone exchanged glares that communicated their disdain for one another. Susan quickly stepped between them. "Simone, stop. Barry, what are you doing here?"

"Tell your sister to back off," he told Susan before kissing her on the forehead. Susan batted her eyes and trembled like a lizard slithered up her spine. The miso salmon in Simone's stomach churned at the unsettling thought of Susan reuniting with Barry after their extremely brief separation. *She's my sister, but she makes me sick with her gullible self.*

"Babe." He kissed her again. "What do you mean what am I doing here? What God has joined together let no man…" He paused mid sentence to leer at Simone, then looked back at Susan, "…put asunder. I'm back to work on my marriage. For better or for worse, I'm in it to save it." Barry then turned and taunted Simone, "What's the problem? Your subscription to *Essence* expired?"

"Slick ass," Simone hissed.

Barry walked away with a pimp roll headed to the bedroom.

Simone shouted at his back "If you really want to know what my problem is, I'm tired of your wife swindling me for money, which means I'm tired of picking up your slack. You see this tire iron?" She raised it up high for him to get a good look at it, "I brought it to remind you that you are not too good to get your hands dirty towing cars. Triple A Road Service is hiring."

Ignoring her rant, Barry walked into the bedroom and then shut the door behind him.

"Simone, be respectful," Susan admonished.

"No. That useless sap doesn't respect me. Why should I respect him?"

Monica thundered out of her room wearing coverall-footed pajamas, to stand next to Simone.

"What's going on?"

"Stay out of grown folks' business and go back to bed," Susan snapped.

"Mummy, blood is thick. Water evaporates. Auntie Simone *is* my business. At least she didn't lock me out like someone I know."

"I'm not going to tell you again. You're already on thin ice around here."

Pleasantly surprised, Simone said, "Monica, I'm impressed. What women's lib book have you been reading?"

"Simone, do not encourage my child to disrespect me. I won't stand for it under any circumstances."

"Susan, I'm not. But you obviously don't see the error in your ways. Monica is acting out her frustrations. Truth be known, you've been doing a good job of setting a poor example for Monica and Sasha. As their aunt, it's my responsibility to empower my nieces to become self-sufficient, confident women. We have to break the cycle of dysfunction in this family, starting with them."

"I know one thing, Monica better take her behind to bed before I beat her into a coma."

"Aaargggh," Monica growled. "When I turn eighteen, I'm out of here. I swear I am." She stomped off madder than Simone was about the prospect of loaning Susan $350. As far as Simone was concerned, Susan didn't have the financial means to birth and support another child, but she also didn't want the guilt of another abortion on her conscious. With that thought, Simone had some reservations about financing the abortion.

32

DECISIONS. DECISIONS.

Not only did Simone agree to subsidize Susan's abortion expense, she chaperoned Susan to Brighton Clinic located in the seclusion of a residential neighborhood on the outskirts of Boston.

Simone drove into the asphalt-paved lot and parked in the drop-off/pick-up section. She killed the engine but left the key in the ignition and faced Susan.

"This is the end of the road for me. I'm not coming in. This place brings back too many sad memories of when I did what I had to do."

"Sis, you don't have to come inside. Wait for me in the car. I'll be out before you know it."

"I have my follow-up appointment this morning to review the ultrasound results and go over my treatment options. I can't stay even if I wanted to. I have to take care of me too, you know."

"I understand. Can Big Sis have a hug before I go and do what *I* gotta do?"

"Of course. Love, support, and loyalty, that's what family is for."

As they hugged Susan's eyes welled with tears. Simone gently dried the teardrops on Susan's face with a tissue.

"It's not too late to change your mind. You can drop me off at the hospital, take my car, and pick me up later. It's as simple as you jumping into the driver's seat. Tell me something. The clock is ticking. I have to get going before traffic picks up."

"Simone, I'm going through with it. Could you at least wait and leave after I complete the paperwork?"

"Sure. Don't you think your husband needs to know what's going on? He has rights where the baby is concerned. I mean, I don't have love for the man, but it is his child that you're carrying."

Susan heaved a sigh as if it were her last breath. "More like his burden. As it stands, I'm the sole provider for essentially everything in the house—food, clothes, bills—you name it I'm paying it. I can't depend on Barry from one day to the next. Birthing another child into the equation will only make matters worse. My number one priority is starting culinary arts school, not starting over with another baby."

"I realize you have aspirations to do more with your life, but your husband still deserves to have his feelings heard about the abortion, that's all I'm saying."

"Sis, as you always say, everything ain't for everybody. Husband or no husband, he's not going to convince me to have a child I don't want. And, no matter what differences we may have in the future, this stays between us."

"You have my word. Just remember, a secret is not a secret if it involves two people. Speaking of, I don't appreciate you hinting to Mother what I told you in confidence about my kangaroo pouch. She was upset and carried on like somebody had died."

"That's Mother for you, especially when she's got liquor in her system. Come on, let's get this over with," Susan said, and then clutched Simone's hand and led her up a short flight of stairs. They waited on the landing for a few seconds before they were buzzed in. Simone tried to get comfortable in the lobby while Susan disappeared inside a private room to complete and sign consent forms authorizing the clinic to suck life out of her womb.

As Simone waited, she blocked out the business-as-usual atmosphere and thought back to her own abortion, remembering the nurse's words.

"It's going to pinch a little. The needles will dilate your uterus. Inhale. Exhale. Take deep breaths. Try to relax. We'll take good care of you." It was over fast. In what seemed like only a few minutes later Simone was waking up in the recovery room, with a hot water bottle resting on top of her stomach. Numbed by what she had done, Simone snacked on crackers and sipped ginger ale. Her only regret after the fact was not walking away from Andy when he called seven days later to see if she was still alive. His absence hurt more than the death of her child.

"Hello. Hello. Earth to Simone."

Startled, Simone shook off the past when Susan called her name.

"You look like you just saw a ghost. Are you okay?"

"This place makes me sad. Simone reached inside of her wristlet and removed several dollar bills. "Here's cab fare. This should also cover idle time while you get your penicillin prescription afterward. Be brave. I'm out of here."

Susan slipped the money into her purse while Simone rushed to Women's Hospital to tackle the state of her health.

A half hour later, Dr. Theery confirmed the presence of benign uterine fibroids, precisely what she had suspected from the initial pelvic exam. Several myomas, as Simone had come to know them from the sporadic reading of various sources of literature, were growing in and on her precious uterus. They ranged in size from three centimeters up to a whopping ten.

Simone weaved her clammy fingers together, and placed them in her lap, as she listened to Dr. Theery, occasionally furrowing her brows to express bewilderment.

"Ms. Miller, because of their location and growth pattern, subserosal fibroids, such as yours, are apt to grow rather large and cause the abdomen to expand creating a false impression of pregnancy and invariably compression in the pelvic area. That explains the pressure you've been experiencing in your lower abdomen. One microscopic subserosal fibroid is in close proximity of your bladder. Another submucosal fibroid is attached to the outer wall of your cervix, the neck of your womb."

"Dr. Theery, can you tell me more about subserosal fibroids, like what makes them subserosal?"

"Good question. Fibroids are classified according their location. Subserosal fibroids grow from the uterine wall to the outside of the uterus and tend to affect other organs, which could explain your constipation, and frequent urination," Dr. Theery explained.

"I see. And what about submucosal fibroids?"

Submucosal is a name to specify its position relative to other fibroids. It grows from the uterine wall into the uterine cavity. It can cause a great deal of pain and heavy bleeding during menstruation. Although that particular type is the least common, research studies have determined they can block fallopian tubes and prevent eggs from entering the uterus altogether. Essentially they can cause infertility."

"I'm concerned about the myoma near my cervix. What are my chances of conceiving should I want to start a family?"

"So you do want children someday?"

Simone unlaced her fingers and made use of her hands to talk. "Children are not a high priority, and I'm not in a serious relationship. But one day I might be and I want to have the option of having children," she explained. Dr. Theery listened attentively, jotting notes on Simone's chart. Dr. Theery then sat the pen atop the manila folder, stood, and walked from behind the desk to stand in the path of Simone's vacant stare.

"There is a strong possibility the fibroid near your cervix might lead to infertility, but research indicates—"

"Dr. Theery," Simone quietly interrupted the doctor's research spiel. "With all due respect, let's face it. I am an at-risk Black female approaching thirty-five with no male prospects remotely in my life whose sperm can backstroke up my cervix and make a love connection with, I presume, my fertile eggs. Therefore, if that pain-in-the-ass fibroid renders me childless, no one would be the wiser."

Tears streamed from the corners of Simone's weary eyes and slid down to her jaw. Dr. Theery retrieved a box of tissue from her desk and held it out to Simone, who nodded and took two sheets to wipe her face.

Dr. Theery returned to her desk seemingly in search of encouraging words. "Ms. Miller, this is a lot of information to take in. Do you need a minute? Would you like some water?"

"No thank you. What are the treatment options for fibroids?"

"Well, depending on their location and the severity of your pain, treatment can range from hormone replacement therapy, which induces shrinkage; uterine artery emboliza-tion, which blocks blood flow to tumors resulting in degeneration; an abdominal myomectomy, which is surgical extraction; and to the extent of excising your uterus by way of a hyst—"

"That won't be necessary. I'd rather crawl in pain before contributing to that disparaging statistic." Simone interrupted before the off-putting word hysterectomy could roll off the doctor's tongue. "And, according to published data, minority women undergo hysterectomies at a much higher rate than our counterparts."

"I see you've been reading about fibroids." Dr. Theery smiled approvingly.

"Yes, I have. To credit books, the Internet, and ongoing research, I've learned a little about my health choices and the associated risks that come with the territory, including quality-of-life changes: mood swings, fluctuating sex drive, and intestinal issues. Because of my research I know that I don't have to consider an irreversible option like a hysterectomy as treatment since the ultrasound reports my ovaries are hale and hearty, and my uterus as remarkable, in spite of the myomas. For the time being, I have to find a way to live with fibroids and suffer through the consequences of that choice until I decide which treatment option is in my best interest."

"I think that is a healthy and wise decision. Let me back-track a moment. The birth control pill is another option avail-able to you."

"Dr. Theery, I refuse to take any more chemicals; I was pill-dependent in my early to late twenties, and I've got the adverse affects of peach fuzz under my chin to prove it."

"Very well, then I suggest we watch and wait, and monitor the fibroids every six months for any change in size, quantity, as well as any new growths that may occur. In the interim, take Ibuprofen as needed, exercise regularly, drink plenty of water, and increase your fiber intake to help regulate your bowel. If the pain worsens, then we can discuss our next step."

Dr. Theery's suggestions segued into the inevitable bad news. Duty-bound, she cautioned Simone, "If you elect the abdominal myomectomy procedure to extract the fibroids, more could potentially develop in new locations. In addition, the fibroid near your cervix is in high-risk territory. If extrac-tion is attempted, internal bleeding is a probable complica-tion during surgery."

The grave notion of hemorrhaging gave Simone consider-able reason to worry. *I could die on the operating table like Traci's mother.*

The irony of suffering the same fate as Doreen put a hys-terectomy back into consideration.

33

BAMBOOZLED

D riving to Quest Financial, Simone mentally prepped to endure eight hours of rubbing elbows with her workplace family. Instead of wasting gas circling the massive lot for a parking space, she parked a few blocks away and speed-walked to the shuttle bus.

Now, if I could just exercise on a more consistent basis to maintain blood circulation, strengthen my bones, and keep my heart healthy, I could probably trim a layer off my muffin top. In her head, speed walking burned fifty calories.

Shortly after, she entered the premises and rode the elevator to Quest Financial Services, recently voted the number one family-friendly employer in the country. On the ride up, her father's battle with cancer filtered through her mind like a movie trailer on constant replay. Nearly fourteen years to the date of his death, a dignified yes or a firm no would determine the quality of health care she would receive: limited coverage provided by Crown Employment Agency or full coverage, including preexisting conditions, compliments of Quest Financial.

Smiling and upbeat, Simone glided through the doors of Quest. Her colleagues would have never guessed the burden on her shoulders. The majority of Simone's workday was spent completing new hire paperwork. Pierre from maintenance, worked feverishly to replace a blown bulb above her cubicle, which was furnished with a flex back chair, flat-screen monitor, and a loaner laptop for outside appointments. Congratulatory good luck wishes and a box of Godiva gold-ribbon chocolate welcomed Simone as a permanent employee.

Ms. Hedley wasted no time extending an invitation to her office so she could announce Simone's initiation task as team leader. Simone didn't rush to sit in the hot seat again. Minutes after the friendly welcome wore off it was glaringly clear why she was apprehensive: her first assignment was revamping the entire mutual fund pricing system—more than eighty funds, including international indices. Simone almost fell out of her chair while reading the scope of the project.

"How many times has the fund overhaul been attempted?" After the words escaped her mouth, Simone realized the question probably didn't paint her as capable, and up-for-the-challenge. Her subliminal thinking didn't get by Ms. Hedley.

"You seem troubled about the project. As I said when I explained the position to you, high-net-worth clients can be very demanding. They expect timely and accurate reporting, and I personally think as team leader, your many years of experience in the field are why you were the most qualified candidate for the job. To answer your question, there were a few attempts. But, what matters most is that Mr. Graham wants the over-haul done before year-end." Ms. Hedley added, twisting her fountain pen.

"Please pardon my reaction. I guess I'm just anxious to get started. The history you provided can help me get off to a good start. Considering the looming deadline, I have to assemble a steering committee, assign roles, and set deadlines as soon as possible," Simone responded with more confidence than she actually felt.

"See, you're already thinking like a seasoned manager. I knew you wouldn't let me down."

What the pessimist in Simone really heard from self-serving Ms. Hedley was, *if I want to shine in my role as team leader— now that I'm permanent with healthcare benefits and a hefty bonus—I have to exceed her expectations and appease Mr. Graham.*

Simone silenced her internal voice, and stood up. She brushed her hands across her skirt to smoothen it. Surprisingly calm and incredibly cool, she chose to end the conversation on her own accord.

"I need some air. Please excuse me," she nodded at Ms. Hedley.

"Sure. Take as much time as you need."

Glaring back and forth between the fountain pen, now lying on a yellow legal pad, and the elephant figurine on the desk, Simone made up her mind to take an extended lunch break because at that moment she wasn't feeling so lucky. Once again, the hurricane she called life had brought her to another challenge. Her inner voice switched on again. *What else could possibly top fibroids?*

Back in the corridor, Pierre watched Simone exit Ms. Hedley's office. He stopped wiping fingerprints off glass doors to search through his cluttered utility cart, assumingly for a tool of some sort. Friendly as always, he ceased searching when she was close enough for him to exercise discretion in what he had to say.

"Congratulations."

"On?" Simone asked, confused.

"The team leader position."

"How do you know about that? I just heard the news minutes ago myself. Who told you?"

"I have my sources."

Simone's suspicions roused. "Who told you?"

"Don't fret about who said what right now. It's a setup. Take my word for it."

"A setup!" Simone was shocked. "By whom?"

Pierre grinned. "Ms. Hedley." His grin exposed a capped front tooth. A gleam of radiance ricocheted off his gold-tooth.

"Are you implying that Ms. Hedley is trying to bamboozle me—in other words, play me for a fool?"

Poker-faced and brazen he corroborated her suspicion. "I most certainly am."

"For what purpose? What you're saying doesn't make sense. If you've got the inside scoop, please share it with me, so I can rethink the offer."

"Come with me. I'll tell you more in my office."

Simone hesitated.

When she didn't budge right away, he said, "I'm harmless."

Simone reluctantly trailed a short distance behind Pierre as he wheeled the utility cart until they reached a steel door. He unlocked the door and pushed it open with a calloused, ashy hand. He flipped on the light switch and illuminated the enormous storage room composed of heavy-duty steel shelves, exposed support pillars, and dust.

"This way." Pierre gestured and guided her behind a stack of archived boxes, piled to the ceiling. Dust whirled in the air. Simone fanned it away from her face. Pierre parked the cart and turned on a digital radio. All smiles, he gazed at Simone. "Oldies but goodies, jazz, soft rock, rhythm and blues? The choice is yours."

Annoyed she threw up her hand, "Please, no music. This is too important. I don't need any distractions."

"What the pretty woman wants, the pretty woman gets."

She was suddenly troubled by his physical reference. It dawned on her that she had wittingly entered a secluded location without questioning his intent for their impromptu meeting. Simone's impatient look was intended to squash any intimate notions Pierre might have had about them ever being more than just colleagues.

"Spill the beans, and make it quick. I feel like these walls are closing in on me."

"Okay, as you wish. Every time Ms. Hedley attempts to implement phases of the conversion project, stress causes her staff to drop like flies."

"Which means Mr. Graham would expect Ms. Hedley to pick up the shortfall if she wants to stay on his short list for regional director of funds processing."

"Yep. You got it. And talk around here says stress is the reason the project has been nicknamed WCS."

"Pierre, enlighten me. What's WCS?"

"Workman's Comp Season. If you have any doubts, hang around the water cooler to learn something."

"So water cooler-talk is your source for information, and WCS explains why Ms. Hedley didn't consider hiring internal employees."

"You're learning already," he beamed a gold toothed smile.

"Pierre, why haven't you offered your expertise? You seem to be in-the-know. Surely, you have useful skills and talents that exceed pushing a broom and snaking a mop across the floor."

"Politics, my dear. Politics. There's a certain-type I see pass through these doors all the time. Young, college graduates, twenty-five years my junior. I hit my prime when they were earning their degrees. But I don't fret. My job might not be fancy and glamorous, but you won't ever hear me complaining about a backbiting boss and money-hungry clients. I'm taking it all in stride until retirement."

"That's something to look forward to *and* envy. I've got a ways to go before I start collecting checks."

"I have twenty-two years with Quest, and I'm fully vested in the company's pension fund. After thirty years of service, I'm taking advantage of the early retirement plan so I can re-search my family roots in Tennessee," Pierre proudly shared.

"Okay, so what else can you tell me about this so-called conversion project?"

"Guess how many times the implementation process failed?"

"I don't know where to begin counting. Do you have any insights on how I should rally the team members so we can be successful? I mean, I am the newbie on the block. I have to build trust, get them to buy into the project, and most impor-tantly, get it done according to Mr. Graham's expectations."

"Let me share something my father used to tell me when-ever I failed at mowing the lawn 'the right way'". He would put his hand on my shoulder and say, 'Son, if you want rightness, do it yourself.' Now hear me good. I have spent the last ten years watching everything and everybody in this office. Would you be surprised if I told you that I have a master plan for the project's success under lock and key?" Pierre tapped his temple to indicate his brain was the lock and key.

"Let's hear it," Simone said.

"Email all the fund data values to me when you get them, so I can work on them from home. I'll send them back to you the next morning.

"Great!" Simone was excited for success. "I'll assign an anal-retentive team member to proof the data for discrepancies, and delegate the task of revising to someone meticulous. Then I'll export the files to Excel to create graphic illustrations."

"Simone, how are you going to get that all done before the meeting?"

"It's simple. All I have to do is press and hold the F11 key to graph the data. Select the bar graph and pie chart options. The last step would be to modify the charts to make them aesthetically appealing and easy to read. Which reminds me to enlist a keen-eyed member to proof the charts prior to delivering the final version to Ms. Hedley for constructive criticism." Cautious not to leave any mishaps to chance, Simone sarcastically mimicked the words constructive criticism using quotation marks.

"Run them by me first. My sources claim Mr. Graham is a stickler for details. Word is, he's been known to clear the conference room at the smallest flaw in a report," Pierre shared.

"Gotcha! We should use external e-mail accounts to cover our tracks."

"Smart thinking, Dear." Pierre said and wrote his email address on a scrap piece of paper and handed it to Simone.

"By the way, why are you so eager to help me?" She asked receiving the paper.

"You've always been kind to me. You say 'good morning', 'please', and 'thank you', and 'have a good evening' on your way out. Most of the people who work here, treat me like I'm invisible. So I don't mind watching your back."

"Well, I'm thankful to have you in my corner, Pierre."

"Don't mention it."

"Now, how do I get out of here without tripping the busy-body alarm?"

"The service elevator is waiting. It'll take you to the ground level. When you get to the bottom, head toward shipping and receiving. You should know your way around from there."

On the ride down for some fresh air, Simone thought, *no matter what, I must consider my agenda and stay the course for the sake of eradicating these fibroids from my womb should they continue to grow, multiply, and persist to being aches and pains in my ass.* At that moment, her cell phone calendar beeped a reminder: SECOND DATE WITH JEFF. DON'T BE LATE.

34

MIXED MESSAGES

Simone retrieved her favorite jogging suit from the bottom drawer, shook the cobwebs off her running shoes, and geared up for a rendezvous at The Pond. While getting herself together for her second date with Jeff, Portia called.

"Hey Simone."

"Oh hey. Listen, I've got one foot out the door. I'm on my way to meet Jeff for our second date."

"Really! Does this mean he's got potential?"

"A little. But there are some things to clear up."

"Like what? You just met."

"I need to know where Jeff's head is at and where our situation might be going. I need to know if he's still stuck on his ex-fiancée Gina or screwing his rebound Daphne or any other woman he may have picked up on his beat."

"Basically, you want Jeff to tell you he's a player." Portia laughed.

"No. But I do want to be cautious."

"Hmm. Someone's catching the love bug." Portia teased.

"Hardly. I just want to know what I'm dealing with. I've had enough disappointment with men, and don't want to get in too deep with Jeff if he's only looking for something casual. I'll call you later. Smooches."

Simone hung up then wrapped her hair and covered it under a pink baseball cap.

Ten minutes later, she pulled up to Jamaica Pond. Jeff arrived in his spanking-clean onyx Maxima 3.5 ES and rushed to greet Simone.

Jeff held her close. Simone let her body melt into his like butter on a hot potato. She felt safe in his soothing arms. "Muffin Top, is everything okay?" Jeff whispered against her cheek.

"Can we walk and talk?"

"Sure."

Arm in arm, they strolled on the shoreline. Simone told Jeff about the job offer, Ms. Hedley, and the conversion project.

"Is the pay decent?" he asked, as if money was the cure-all for her problems.

"Money isn't the issue."

"Then why the sad face?"

"Ms. Hedley had her agenda and I had reservations from the outset, but these fi... Never mind. Just forget it."

"No. Please. Go on. What were you about to say?"

Pride prevented Simone from discussing her fibroid diagnosis and the possibility of future surgery with Jeff.

"It was nothing, just me babbling."

"Come here." Jeff slowly turned her to face him. He playfully swiped his thumb down the bridge of her nose. "Muffin Top, you're a smart woman. I enjoy your company, but if you don't believe in yourself, why should I waste time entertaining your insecurities?"

"That's an interesting perspective. I never thought of it from that angle." Simone's thoughts trailed away from the present moment. *I finally know what attracts me to Jeff. It's his ability to communicate. I've never felt that with anyone. Communicating is an innate gift. I never thought I would say this so soon after meeting someone, but I think I'm falling for him, and it scares me.*

"Hey." He pinched her arm to get some attention. "What are you thinking about?" "

When she attempted to conjure up something brilliant to say, Jeff's lips covered her mouth. He kissed Simone and then nibbled her bottom lip. His sex pistol hardened with anticipation. Simone caressed, and fondled his nature. Taking control made her feel so powerful, wholesome, and wanted. She could feel her libido shifting into high gear, turned on by their public foreplay.

Jeff panted warm breath in her ear, "Flash-flood warning. If your magic fingers keep performing like that, I might have to haul you in for an eleven-ninety-nine."

"And what might that be, Officer McKinley?"

"Scanner code for Officer In Distress."

They laughed, talked, and walked until returning to their starting point. Simone and Jeff snuggled against a tree to watch the great ball of fire navigate its way west.

"Are you thinking what I'm thinking?" he asked, towering over her.

Simone gazed up to see his Crest White smile and dimpled-cheeks. Turned on, she leaned in and tongued her way up his strong neck. His skin tasted sweeter than saltwater taffy. She stopped tonguing him and purred, "What are you thinking?"

Jeff squirmed and whispered a proposition, "We should go back to my place and finish what we started."

Simone squeezed his soft lips together using three of her fingers. "Shh! I have a better idea. Don't move." She eased her hand down the front of his sweatpants.

Jeff stuttered, "You are s–s–s–so amazing. I love surprises." His eyes rolled to the back of his head.

She began stroking him steadily and unhurriedly. The more her slender and graceful fingers stroked, the louder Jeff ooohed and aaahed a lustful symphony. At the rate their chemistry was brewing to a powerful climax, the second date was destined to let whatever was going to happen between them happen.

Back at his apartment, Jeff carried Simone to his platform bed. She locked her hands behind his neck and relaxed her head on his broad shoulder. She held on tight and didn't want to ever let go, fearing their fling was bound to end by her undoing, or Jeff living up to the rumor that all men in uniforms were dogs.

Jeff sat on the edge of his bed with Simone in his lap. She pulled his athletic shirt over his head to help him undress. Simone then got down on her knees and reached into his sweatpants to gently stroke the shaft of his protruding sex pistol.

"Take it," he insisted, placing his hand over hers.

"Got it. Now what would you like for me to do with it?"

"Blow my mind like you'll never see me again," he said, moaning with pleasure. Simone pulled his pants and boxers to his ankles. Jeff finished undressing himself and then grabbed Simone's hands. With their fingers entwined, Jeff stood and pulled Simone to her feet and they fell back on the bed. When Jeff covered her mouth with his, their tongues battled each other like crazy.

When they came up for air Simone cooed, "Oh, I want to lick you like a fudge Popsicle oozing chocolate down my throat."

Jeff unzipped her sweat jacket, eased his hand under her tank top, then released the bra clasp to expose and fondle her perky tits. The sounds of their passion filled the room as they found each other's pleasure points. Ms. Hedley may have had a hidden agenda and Simone clearly had her own, but one thing was certain, Jeff had no qualms about making his intention known. In the back of her mind, Simone wondered if his pep talk at the pond was just B.S. to cop some ass.

While she was lost in her thoughts, Jeff's sex pistol was arrow straight. He parted her legs, and slipped his hand between her thighs. Simone heated up. Her Lady pulsated for a deep penetrating thrust. Sound judgment surfaced before foreplay could lead to reckless sex.

"Slow down, Officer Frisky. Do you have a condom?"

Staying in control of the situation, not only was Jeff required to produce a condom, Simone expected him to test for every STD under the sun and share the results.

"Muffin Top, I don't need protection. I'm clean."

"Jeff, I told you before, you've got to wrap it up. What brand of condom do you use because certain ones give me a yeast infection."

Jeff's voice now had a slight edge, "I'm clean. Look at me. Do I look sick? Do you see any lesions on my body?"

"Inspecting your body wouldn't prove anything to me. I'm not taking any risks." Simone eased out from under Jeff and jumped off the bed, straightened her clothes, and then stuffed her hair back under the baseball cap.

"Are you insinuating that I'm taking risks?" Jeff asked.

"Well, you're acting like the word condom isn't a part of your vocabulary, so yes."

"Muffin Top, it's about you and me. There's no need to worry."

"Even if we consent to a monogamous relationship today, I wouldn't engage in reckless sex," Simone said walking towards the door.

Jeff became aggressive. "Stop being so difficult. I want you so damn bad. Can't you tell?" He grabbed her hands to keep her from walking out. He asked Simone to stay but she didn't want to hear it.

"Let me say something Jeff before I go. Perhaps I sent mixed messages coming back to your place, and I'm sorry. I'm not sure what I feel, but I feel something for you. Our chemistry freaks me out. I don't want to mess this up with sex because you've already shown me that you will take it if I'm willing to give it so freely. And you also don't seem to mind having unprotected sex."

Jeff's mouth tightened and he abruptly released her hands. "Hold on. Don't go getting all self-righteous now. It seems like you've made up your mind that sex is what you want from me. I said this before and I'll say it again. I have to respect your wishes to slow things down. I'm capable of treating you like a queen, but if you show me the only thing you have to offer is sex, then don't complain when I treat you how you show me you want to be treated."

"Are you implying that I was being a *slut*?"

"Not at all," Jeff answered, calming down, as he palmed the small of her back. To Simone's surprise, he didn't pressure her about staying or leaving. He escorted her to the door when sudden hammering on its surface and yelling from the other side shocked them both to a standstill.

"Jeff, open this door and bring your crime-fighting, low-down, two-timing ass out here now!"

Simone frowned in confusion. She stared hard at Jeff and asked him, "Expecting an angry fiancée are you?"

He tried to laugh it off. "Not to my knowledge. Stay here. Let me see who it is." Simone noticed that Jeff was nervous. He cautiously opened the door and attempted to close it before Simone could get a glimpse of the irate woman fuming outside.

"Jeffrey McKinley, don't you dare shut this door in my face!" The woman yelled furiously.

He quickly positioned his back against the door.

"*Jeffrey?*" Simone sneered. "Sounds like she knows you. Has your fiancée Gina returned to claim her man?"

"No. She's not Gina. I'll explain everything later."

"Jeffrey," Simone mocked with a trace of Miller attitude, "why can't you explain now? Never mind. You must have something to hide. Excuse me. I'm leaving." When Simone tried to brush past Jeff, he pressed his back firmly against the door to stop her.

"Where are you going?"

"You were showing me out, remember?"

Simone pushed him out of her path, turned the knob, and stepped into a snake pit. The long-in-the-face woman with blonde streaks throughout her Hawaiian Silky mane was visibly vexed to see Simone.

"Who the hell is she, and, why is she here?" the woman spat at Jeff.

"Don't worry about her. She's invited company. What are *you* doing here?" Jeff asked her matter-of-factly.

"You knew I was coming," she said.

Jeff said, "That was yesterday. Today is a new day. You should have called or made new arrangements."

"Asshole, I left messages all over the place. You act like I don't exist. What's going on? We *ova* or what?"

"Over? Jackie, when did we begin?"

"I don't believe this," Jackie shrieked. "Why do you insist on playing childish games? First, your fiancée Gina, then Daphne, now this uppity looking chick." She cut her eyes over Jeff to examine Simone head to feet as though she was trying to decipher what Jeff saw in the competition that he didn't see in her. She locked eyes with Simone and asked, "Who is Jeff to you anyway?"

"Jackie, right?" Simone retorted with the feistiness that flowed unapologetically in her bloodline.

Jackie sucked her teeth and tilted her head. "You heard him right the first time!"

"See, Jackie, I wasn't going to interrupt your lovers' quarrel until you put me in it. But I gladly accept the invitation since you don't seem content acting high school alone. Now, let me be clear, I don't owe you an explanation. Ask Jeff who I am to him because this could be a moment of clarity for us both."

"Don't get snippy because I will slap your uppity ass right off your high horse. I already ran Gina out of town and stole her man. Ain't that right, Jeffrey?" Jackie snarled at Jeff who was cold busted up to the sweat glands raining puddles in his armpits.

"That's enough! Everybody calm down and listen. There will be no fighting. Jackie, not another word out of you." Jeff turned to Simone. "Let me explain," he said, trying to hold her hand. Simone flinched. Eyes squinting, nostrils flared, if she could blow flames she would have roasted his whorish ass to a charred crisp.

"What else haven't you told me?" Simone asked.

"Alright," he said after a few moments of silence. "Yesterday, I invited Jackie to my place so I could break it off with her. I really want to get to know you better. You don't have to believe me, but it's true. She did come between Gina and me, but a combination of cold feet and working around the clock cost me someone I thought was irreplaceable, until our conversation at The Pond."

"So your selective amnesia prevented you from telling me that you were involved with someone at that time? Even after I asked you about Daphne following the Spade's incident, you still didn't think this was something I needed to know? You got me wondering if it was quality time that Gina wanted, or your inability to keep your penis zipped in your pants." Simone then sounded off in her head. *I knew something in the milk wasn't clean! His lies are curdling to the surface.* As she seethed in silence, Jeff was still pleading his innocence.

"Yes and no. I–I–I have been seeing Jackie on and off, but it isn't serious. Simone, cut me some slack. When I first met you, I was on duty responding to a domestic violence call. When I ran into you unexpectedly at The Pond, I was enamored with your quick wit. I liked the flow of our conversation. I thought I could get to know you better over dinner or a drink. I didn't intend to try to run game on you. I thought my intentions were clear."

Simone rolled her eyes at his pathetic effort to save face in front of the mad woman he probably cheated on his fiancée with.

"Jeff, please find yourself another fool and toy with her mind because I'm not here for head games." Simone said frowning her doubt.

"Jeff, you are such a bad, bad, liar. Your nose is growing!" Jackie announced to the world, and then gave Simone an earful of deal breakers that sealed Jeff's fate. "Ms. Uppity, I don't know what lies he's been feeding you, but Gina broke off the engagement and moved to California when she discovered he was sleeping with Daphne *and* me. We still have threesomes. Isn't that right, Jeffrey?"

"What?!" Simone gasped. "Jeff I can't believe you expected to have unprotected sex with me! I want no part of your community dick!"

Jeff scowled at Jackie, entertaining unlawful thoughts. Simone acted as if she knew just what he was thinking. If she were in his shoes she would have been thinking the same. *I ought to shoot her in the mouth, rip open her throat, yank out her tongue, and choke her with it.* Simone snapped out of her criminal mind just in time to hear Jeff lambast Jackie with a few choice words.

"Jackie, you're being dramatic! I told you about showing up whenever you feel like it. You don't live here and you don't have papers on me, so technically you're trespassing."

"I wasn't a trespasser when you cuffed me to your bed, slurping all up in my beaver, now was I?" Jackie said, shooting a sly look at Simone and then said, "Ms. Uppity, I bet you thought you were special."

Simone struck back with her infamous Miller Attitude. "Honey, don't start smelling yourself too strong because I can serve up a supreme dish of vagina soufflé. An hour ago Jeff would've been choking on my cream pie, and screaming mercy as my name. So, please don't underestimate the power of my puss—"

"Enough of this nonsense!" Jeff shouted. He then turned to Jackie, "I meant what I said about trespassing."

Unmoved, Jackie gave Jeff a serious stare-down. "Here you go again, throwing around your keystone cop authority."

Fed up, Simone walked away.

Jeff ran ahead to block her path. "Wait. Don't leave because of what she said. Come inside. I'll explain everything. I promise."

"Promises, promises, promises," Jackie hissed eyeing Simone, daring her to set foot back inside his apartment. Simone glared back tearing her to shreds with her eyes then decided to call Jackie's bluff. Simone marched back inside Jeff's apartment like a one-woman army and stormed out to see if Jackie really had an ounce of fight in her bitter body.

Jeff wedged himself between Simone and Jackie to keep tempers from escalating to a vicious catfight. The whole scene was nauseating for Simone. Everything she once liked about Jeff's Crest White smile, dimpled cheeks, Ford-built physique, and communication skills, transformed into an ugly, boldface lie. Disgusted, she lit into Jeff, "Fighting over a man is beneath me. Have a nice life liar!"

"Wait." He gently secured her wrist.

She pried his hand away and shouted, "Don't touch me!"

Smirking, Jackie watched them bicker from the sideline.

"Simone, we should talk. You can't leave angry. I won't let you," Jeff pleaded.

"What are you going to do, arrest me?" Simone asked sarcastically.

Jeff was silent. All of his denying and apologizing couldn't keep Simone by his side. She adjusted her baseball cap, and then approached Jackie to bring a proper end to their squabble. Jackie assumed a boxing stance, poised to land a knockout punch. Simone stopped in front of her. The two women faced off like fierce felines.

Addressing Jackie, Simone attempted to be civil. "Woman-to-woman, no hard feelings. It's not in my character to argue over a man. You can have Jeff even if you don't want him."

Jackie relaxed her stance to plaster a winning smile on her face.

Jeff scowled at Jackie. "You make me sick."

Jackie sneered. "And you can't get enough of my beaver. Deny it. I dare you."

At that point, Simone had heard enough, and seen enough for one day. Teed off, she got in her car, and blew blistering air all the way home. "From now on, it's gonna be Secret Pleasure, fibroids, and me!"

Two hours later.

"Portia, hold on. Let me see who's nagging me." Simone clicked over to answer an incoming call. "Say your piece." She spat into the receiver.

"It's Jeff. Please don't hang up. Jackie means nothing to me. I'm done with her. Yesterday, I intended to end it for good, but she never showed up. I swear on my mother's grave. God rest her soul. You have to believe me."

"Jeff, I think your games with me have only just begun. Good bye."

"Wait, Muffin Top, before you hang up, I called out sick to be with you. I'm serious about trying to get to know you better."

"I'm flattered, but there are ninety-nine unsolved murders in the city of Boston that deserve attention. If you call and harass me again, I will see to it that permanent desk duty, pending a suspension hearing, is the beginning of the end of your career." Simone said and clicked over to Portia. "I'm back. Guess who that was?"

"Girl, I don't have to. You know men can be a trip around the world sometimes."

Simone sighed. "I guess the rumor about men in uniform is true after all. It just goes to show that we never know a person's true character because they only show what they want people to see until their mask of deception is stripped away."

"At least the experience taught you something."

"It sure did, *the only thing to gain from a lie is the truth*."

"That's right." Portia agreed adding her perspective about the truth. "You can twist it, churn it, bend it, *and* ring it dry, but it's still gonna come out clean in the wash."

"It sure will."

"Truth hurts, doesn't it, Simone?"

"And pisses you off."

"Weakens you."

"And strengthens you because there will be no second chances."

"Are you sure about that?"

"Absolutely. Jeff's harem ran the gamut from kissy-pooh Daphne, to crude Jackie, and probably many more. The trust factor would be a constant thorn in our relationship. I don't want to add more stress and aggravation to my life."

"Can you forgive him if he asks for forgiveness and wants to start over?"

"Portia, I still couldn't trust him with my mind, body, and spirit. Forgiveness will come in due season."

"So, how have you been feeling health-wise?"

"Good, actually. Oh, I forgot to tell you that I accepted a full-time position with Quest Financial. My first assignment is a major overhaul of the mutual fund reporting system."

"Congratulations. You can handle the challenge. I'll have to pamper you with a complimentary spa treatment after you slay those corporate goons with your brilliance. Blush Cosmetics recently launched an amazing moisturizer. You can be my guinea pig. And while we're on the subject of skin," Portia said giggling, "when are you going to start wearing makeup to enhance that pretty little face? I can do wonders with those mysterious eyes."

"How many times do I have to tell you that I only flow naturally and don't need to represent Picasso to feel beautiful?"

"Okay, Beautiful. Have a better night."

"You as well. Smooches."

"Smooches."

35

DEEPEST FEAR

One month after accepting the team leader position, the pressure weighed heavily on Simone the morning of the presentation. As soon as she approached the elevator bank on the premises of Quest Financial, fear of failure snatched her confidence and numbed her inside out. The feeling was reminiscent of the preliminary fibroid diagnosis when she thought her life would be over after hearing the word tumor.

Nevertheless, the day's darkest hour had arrived. Anxiety filled her esophagus. Simone felt her windpipe narrow and complicate her breathing. Numb, she felt like she was floating on air. Her parched tongue clung to the roof of her mouth. She craved a rejuvenating drink of water before delivering the highly anticipated presentation in the Vault conference room.

The closer she got to the door, the more she wanted to give up before getting started. *Face your demons or they will conquer you.* She reminded herself. Beads of perspiration bubbled on the bridge of her nose. Hives peppered her arms. A familiar feeling fizzed in her stomach. "Here comes the vomit again," Simone said. She paused to see if the fizzing would pass. When it didn't, she ran to the bathroom and didn't stop running until her face met the poop throne where she barfed up Satan, the beast in her belly. At the sink, she swallowed quenching tap water down her throat, sprinkled droplets over her face, and patted dry with a paper towel. Staring in the mirror, Simone called to mind an excerpt from *Deepest Fear*—the inspiring words of Marianne Williamson in her book *A Return To Love*—to muster up courage to complete the project according to Mr. Graham's expectations.

> "…*who am I to be brilliant, gorgeous, talented, and fabulous? Actually, who are you not to be? You are a child of God. Your playing small doesn't serve the world. There's nothing enlightened about shrinking so that other people won't feel insecure around you. We are all meant to shine*…"

"And shine I will" Simone whispered with a boost of confidence. Heading for the conference room where the managing director Mr. Graham waited, she vowed, "I will not fail. I cannot fail." Warily nervous again, she wobbled, walking along the wall for support to keep her knees from buckling.

"Morning Dear. You look mighty spiffy." Pierre said, then offered moral support and words of encouragement, "As my mum would say whenever she had worries, 'If a princess can face her fears, then so shall a queen.' Now, go get 'em!"

Simone somehow managed to eke out, "Thanks." Her confidence returned.

"Here you are. I've been looking everywhere for you."

"Yes, Ms. Hedley, here I am; ready, willing and able to deliver a performance to be remembered."

"Well, don't stand there. We don't want to keep Mr. Graham waiting. Let's get the presentation underway." Ms. Hedley ushered Simone to the executive boardroom.

One month later and at the precise hour of accepting the team leader position, Simone stood front and center with the powers-that-be, facing a challenge that could either affirm or ruin her professional career.

Relaxed in a black skirt suit, a white rayon top and conservative medium-heel pumps, Simone walked to the front of the boardroom. The scenic Charles River, spanning from Boston, Cambridge, Watertown, and through Newton, created a serene and scenic backdrop.

Composed, she took her place behind the podium with her head held high.

"Good morning, everyone," she articulated clearly.

The audience responded, "Good morning".

She arranged a sheet of paper containing talking points within arm's reach, just in case she lost her train of thought or forgot the order of the slides. Ms. Hedley grunted. Simone's paranoia overwhelmed her. *Is that the surreptitious code for saying all bets are against me?* Her suspicion nearly eclipsed her focus, but she maintained her composure and stayed the course. After all, it was her moment, her time to shine brighter than a diamond.

After a slight nod from Ms. Hedley, Simone gave tech support a subtle cue to dim the lights. She then launched into the presentation. Slide number one entitled *Quest Quick Response Reporting System* in bold green letters appeared centered on the drop down screen. She hesitated briefly before stating the objective, the cost benefits analysis, fund validation process, action steps, and contingency plans. Eyes were fixated on Simone as she executed the presentation with the finesse and ease of a seasoned employee. The delivery was seamless and thought out to the dollar. She then came to the conclusion.

"Quest Quick Response Reporting System will guarantee real time fund updates. It will not cut into the company's profits. It will help us retain clients and attract new ones from our competitors. Real time reporting will not only justify a monetary increase in our transaction fees, it will give our clients a clear market advantage. Colleagues, before I close, I would like to stress that my team and I are committed to conducting ongoing research to identify and secure opportunities to reduce operating expenditures and increase client satisfaction. Thank you for your time."

Mr. Graham gave an appreciative two-thumbs-up. The meeting adjourned with applause that vibrated the conference room under Simone's feet. She exhaled a breathy sigh of relief.

What seemed like eternity, panned out to be ninety minutes tops, including a rather lengthy question-and-answer period followed by praise, praise, and more praise from Mr. Graham. Standing very proud, he emphasized his approval with an extended applause and more praise.

"Simone, that was outstanding. Perhaps the best execution I've seen around these parts since I came onboard as managing director. You certainly did your homework. Aptitude not attitude is my mantra," he said with a touch of sarcasm. It humored Simone to see those who have allegedly "paid their dues" squirm in their seats.

"Please, be my guest of honor." Mr. Graham motioned Simone to get comfortable at the head of the table, in his chair. "I've heard great things about you and I must say you are a positive addition to Quest. The report, might I add, was well organized, thorough, and convincing. Listen," he said resting a palm on her shoulder "if you stick with Quest, I have no doubts you will make a fine regional manager."

In earshot, smug-faced Ms. Hedley cleared her throat again. Mr. Graham's attention averted to the bevy of refreshments on a cloth-draped table where staff members mingled over bagels, coffee, tea, and bottles of Poland Spring water.

"Ms. Hedley, help yourself to some water to relieve that itch because I'm going to need your help persuading our rising star—" he stopped talking in mid-sentence and looked at Simone with a glint in his eyes—"that she has a bright future here at Quest."

Once again, if looks could kill, Ms. Hedley would have dug Simone's grave and pushed her into it.

Simone walked to her cubicle. En route, Pierre was hauling a huge plastic trash bag down the corridor. When he noticed her approaching, he sat the bag at his feet to remove his industrial gloves.

"So, how did it go?" he asked impatiently.

"Excellent. I owe you big time."

"Simone, may I have a word with you?" Ms. Hedley asked catching them off guard. Pierre quickly changed the subject.

"Ms. Miller, I'll find a spare chair for your cubicle immediately." He said then snuck in a quick wink.

"Thanks. As always, I appreciate your help. Yes, Ms. Hedley." Simone said all in one breath.

"Great job."

"That's it?"

"That's it."

"Ms. Hedley, while I have your attention, do you have a few minutes?"

"Sure."

"Can we talk in private?"

"Let's go to my office", Ms. Hedley said leading the way. A few moments later she sat at her desk and offered Simone a seat. "What is it that you'd like to talk about?" she asked, twirling her fountain pen.

"Just to give you ample notice, I have a medical issue to mull over and decide if surgery is the best option to alleviate some occasional discomfort. Female stuff." Simone gave a hesitant smile before sharing more details. "My doctor said if I choose the most invasive surgical procedure, the recovery period could take six to eight weeks. I hate to spring this on you now, but I'm sure Mr. Graham would approve."

Ms. Hedley placed the pen on her desk and leaned forward. "This doesn't leave the room..." As she spoke guardedly, she arranged the elephant figurine so that it was aligned along the edge of her desk. "Your health is more important than any job. Wait until you experience menopause."

"Menopause!" Simone echoed.

"Yes. 'The change'."

"I see," Simone said, containing the other half of her thoughts. *I should have known. The mood swings were apparent all along.*

Ms. Hedley smirked. "Don't worry. Your job will be here when you return, and your office per Mr. Graham."

"My office!" Simone responded completely surprised.

"Yes. He seems to think you've earned it."

"I–I don't know what to say."

Ms. Hedley clasped her hands across her plump belly, and rocked back and forth then chuckled. "I'm sure you'll think of something. Have a good day."

"You, too."

Simone returned to her cubicle to call her mother and share the good news. As usual, Claire was fussy and curt, but proud of her daughter, nonetheless. Simone thought to call Jeff to let him know that all her insecurities about the job were nothing more than her being insecure. Using better judgment, she decided it was in her best interest to move forward and keep that chapter closed, even if Jackie really meant nothing to him. She then frowned at the phone, "Humph, that's what they all say when they get caught."

"Is this the end of the road for us?" Pierre's question blind-sided Simone. She didn't feel his presence lurking over her shoulder.

"Not a chance. We are Bonnie and Clyde, thicker than thieves. And you are truly the keeper of wisdom and you deserve all the credit."

"Don't mention it. Will you be staying on?"

"For a short while, then I will entertain teaching in the public school system as my way of giving back to the community."

"Teaching might be your calling. The students will be blessed."

"Pierre. You're the best. Thanks a million for everything."

"Bonnie."

"Yes, Clyde?"

"You will always be a friend in my heart."

36

PAYBACK

Approximately two hundred miles south of Boston, in Westchester County, New York, Keisha was staked out in her rental car, two doors from the luxurious home of Mr. and Mrs. Gordon Upshaw. The lavish bleached-brick house was nestled on a sprawling, leafy landscape. The Upshaws were clearly living the good life on at least an acre while Keisha was cooped up in a cramped one-bedroom rental.

After exchanging an affectionate good-bye kiss with her beloved husband, Mrs. Iris Upshaw stood in the doorway. Her hair was tapered in a glossy chin length bob. She wore very little makeup, if any at all. Her nails were freshly painted in neutral clear base with French manicure tips.

Keisha's eyes were green with envy, "Aww, isn't that sweet? Look at the twinkle in her faithful eyes. This is going to be a piece of cake, almost too easy." As she watched the missus wave her cheating husband out of sight, Keisha prepared to make her move up the driveway, pretending to be lost.

Iris was about to close the door when she heard a car door slam. Keisha swayed her hips, striding in classic corporate boardroom attire and patent leather Jimmy Choo pointed toe pumps, compensation from Mr. Upshaw.

"Good morning, Miss, can you tell me how to..."

Iris cut her short and looked down her nose at Keisha.

"It's *Mrs.* Upshaw. Mrs. *Gordon* Upshaw. You must be lost," she said sarcastically.

"Yes, and I was wondering if you could tell me how to get to the business district."

Keisha was in full character, according to Simone's script, claiming to be in town on a business trip and panicked after taking the wrong exit off the expressway.

"I'm sorry that you're lost." Keisha could tell she was actually sympathetic, which made it hard for Keisha to dislike everything about her, including the ritzy home and the fifty percent stake in the bank accounts that Keisha knew the missus had at her disposal. But she dug into her purse preparing to deflate Mrs. Gordon Upshaw's snooty bubble.

"Mom, I'm ready. When is Mr. Ferguson coming?"

"Son, where are your manners?"

The little boy standing at his mother's side greeted Keisha with a cheesy smile. "Good morning Miss."

"Hey there, tiger." Keisha smiled and gritted her teeth. *Damn, he's not supposed to be home. What in the hell would Simone do?*

"Franklin, wait for me in the kitchen. I'll be in to pack your lunch in a minute."

"Okay mom." He smiled at Keisha. "Bye Miss. Have a great day."

"Thanks." Keisha zipped her purse closed. She didn't have the gall to spring incriminating pictures on Mrs. Upshaw and witness the hurt in Franklin's face, too.

It was back to the drawing board for Keisha.

Seated in her rented car at her wit's end, she pulled out her iPhone and dialed up Simone and left a message.

"THERE'S A LITTLE OBSTACLE I DIDN'T PLAN FOR. CALL ME ON MY CELL ASAP!"

Two afternoons later, Keisha watched from her car as Iris answered the door.

"Good afternoon. I have a special delivery for Mrs. Gordon Upshaw."

"I am she. May I help you?" Iris answered like a proud soccer mom.

"I have a package for you. Sign here." The disheveled mail carrier directed her to the signature line before handing her the padded envelope. She followed instructions and signed her name. In exchange for her signature, she received the portrait-sized envelope.

"Have a good day, ma'am."

"Why thank you, sir," she replied cordially before closing the door while studying the package absent of a return address. Its two day-old postmark was stamped New York, New York.

As planned, everything was going according to the revised script. Hell hath no fury like a woman twice scorned. Keisha was hell-bent on adding to her home wrecking shenanigans. She drove discreetly away to park two houses down on the residential road. Wearing Jimmy Choo leopard print flats, she exited the car scrutinizing her immediate surroundings for possible witnesses to the trespassing misdemeanor she was plotting to commit on private property. Keisha snuck around the rear of the house trampling day lilies and tulips in search of a window with a view. She crouched low in the delicate flowerbed, and watched through a panoramic picture window that exposed sections of the foyer, the exquisite formal living room, and chef-style kitchen.

Iris went from the kitchen to the living room after attending to pasta boiling on the stove. She pulled the strip marked with an arrow and followed the instructions, TEAR SLOWLY IN THIS DIRECTION until an opening was created large enough to insert her hand and withdraw a smaller unsealed envelope. Three photographs fell out and landed face down. She bent over to pick them up. Flipping them over her mouth fell open, at the same time the remaining contents in the envelope fell to the floor. She knelt slowly to collect one more photo. There were four pictures in all. Just as she was about to examine them, Franklin appeared in the living room with his Batman cape tied around his neck.

He asked curiously, "Mom, what are you looking at?"

"Daddy sent me a surprise birthday gift. Run along to your room. I'll call you when the spaghetti is ready."

Franklin did as he was told, chanting the *Batman* theme song all the way to his bedroom. Iris assembled the photos neatly on the marble coffee table and then shuffled through them like a view master in action. Speaking softly to herself, she carried on a rhetorical conversation while sitting on the plush powder blue sofa. "Gordon and another woman? Gordon got another woman pregnant? How could that be?" she asked analyzing each picture of Gordon and his pregnant mistress knotted in unflattering sexual positions. She wept. Tears floated down her cheeks and dropped gently in her lap. She then stood up abruptly and hurried back to the stove to turn off the pot of pasta. At the stove, she wailed, "I knew he was up to no good! I knew it!"

Franklin raced to the kitchen with the cape trailing behind, "Mom, are you okay? Did you burn yourself?"

"No, son. I'm okay. Please, go back to your room."

"But Mom, you're crying."

"Go to your room, I said!" She slammed the pot down on the stovetop. Spaghetti splashed in the air. Droplets of cloudy water splattered on her hand. "Ouch!" she groaned, then wiped up the water with a dishcloth. She ran her hands down the front of the apron to dry them.

Franklin whined but his mother was in no state of mind to cater to his emotions. Her head was too foggy from the pictures that told a story of infidelity.

"Gordon will pay for this, and I do mean *pay*," she said, settling into the plush sofa again, and forgetting all about feeding Franklin.

Waiting for Gordon to return home seemed interminable. The day wore on. The pasta turned soggy. Iris finally crawled out of her miserable funk to microwave a bowl of Chef Boyardee spaghetti and meatballs, smeared I Can't Believe It's Not Butter onto a slice of wheat bread, and sat the plate, a fork, napkin, and a cup of apple juice in front of Franklin. Sitting at the breakfast nook, she talked to Franklin while he happily ate his food.

"Son, you know I love you more than anything in the whole wide world, don't you?"

"Yes," he answered after swooping up a fork of spaghetti. He slurped the pasta and licked tangy tomato sauce off his lips.

"Good, and don't ever forget it."

"Okay."

"Promise?"

"Promise."

An hour later, Iris heard the garage door chirp, and Gordon accelerating his Lexus LS460 sedan to park on his side of the garage. She read the kitchen clock, and realized, "He's home early."

"Son, I think you've had enough already. Go brush your teeth and clean up your room. I'll check on you in a little while."

"But Mom, I'm not done," Franklin whined.

She rubbed his head, "I know baby, but mommy needs some alone-time with daddy. You can eat the rest as a late night snack. How does that sound?"

"Okay," Franklin planted a wet, sloppy kiss on her cheek.

She kissed him back. "Don't forget who loves you," she reminded him before he dashed off again.

"Don't forget who loves you back," he gushed, running fast to brush his teeth.

She left the dishes on the table, hurried to the master bedroom disappearing from Keisha's view.

"Shit!" Keisha cursed. "All that I can't see will have to come from eavesdropping. That's what Simone would tell me to do."

In the bedroom, Iris plopped down onto the La-Z-Boy chair to shuffle through the pictures like it was the first time she was seeing them. She was steaming mad, desperately trying to establish the place, the time, and the opportunity for Gordon's torrid affair. She started to cry and agonize some more about where, when, why, and who had fulfilled her husband's intimate desires. She just couldn't believe that an entertainment attorney found time to cheat because Gordon always appeared to be bogged down with caseloads, writing depositions, and rotating weekly carpool duty with their neighbor Mr. Ferguson, transporting their boys to school and karate lessons.

She lounged in the chair; reminiscing about the day she met the boy sporting the legendary number 23 on the back of his high school basketball jersey. The same boy she later married and now depends on for her livelihood. She entered into matrimony thinking it would be love everlasting, or until death parted them, not because of her short temper, or Gordon's inability to resist worldly temptations of voluptuous women in miniskirts. Feeling betrayed Iris waited.

"*How could Gordon do this to his only son?* Was the last question she thought before her husband showed his face in the bedroom doorway.

Iris didn't let him breathe a word before she charged and pounded him on the chest with the pictures. "You cheating, no-good bastard! When were you going to tell me? I trusted you. I've loved you from the day we met. I did everything for you. I gave you a son. Is Franklin not enough for you to be faithful for once in this marriage?!"

Gordon blocked her blows with his hands. "Honey, calm down. What's gotten into you?" He tried to snatch the pictures from her. She yanked them away, almost frothing at the mouth.

"When were you going to tell me you'd gotten another woman pregnant? Tell me. When? These pictures don't lie." She fanned them in front of her face. "I want answers. How long were you going to keep this secret from me? Until the baby was born? I should've known that brain between your legs would make you lose your mind. But, remember this. I'm still your wife. And as long as we stay married on paper you will respect Franklin, this house, and the oath we made to each other at the altar."

Gordon looked confused. "Iris, all this about another woman being pregnant is ludicrous. What woman? Honey, come on. Let me see the pictures so I can defend myself because I honestly don't know what you're bitching about. I swear I don't."

"Kiss my ass, and defend that!" she yelled, racing to the living room to retrieve their wedding album. She ran back to the bedroom, and pitched it at Gordon's head. He ducked. The book crashed into the wall, photographs of happier times spilled out.

"Iris, what is wrong with you?"

"You have to ask? I gave you ten years. Count them! Ten solid years of my life and almost died trying to have your babies, every one of them. I suffered three miscarriages before Franklin was born. How could you forget all that we've been through?"

"Honey, I could never forget. Have you been taking your medication?"

"Medication?" Iris echoed. "Not only are you dumb in the brain, you are an insensitive, no good motherfu…" In the midst of her rampage, Iris asked God to forgive her before she spewed more profanity.

Gordon tried to reason with her, "Give me the pictures so I can see for myself what you're accusing me of."

"And give you a chance to lie your way out of it? Say it wasn't you? Well, this time around, save your lies for the judge."

"Lower your voice. We don't want to upset Franklin."

"No! As of today, I'm not living by your rules. To hell with Prozac, Zoloft, and Xanax. If not for your unfaithful ways, I wouldn't need medication to maintain my sanity. I was cursed the day I married you." Iris scrambled barefoot around the room frantically searching for something else to throw at him. Gordon tried to grab her, but she jerked away.

"Touch me and an assault charge will get you six months in jail," she sneered frostily.

"Okay, you win." He retreated, putting space between them. "But if you go forward with these accusations, my lawyer will call those pictures bogus."

Again, Iris sneered. "And mine will call them checkmate, fifty percent, your ass is homeless, and more. Now try me!"

Gordon lunged for the pictures. She escaped his reach, ran, and locked herself in the master bathroom. He attempted to make peace with her through the door. On the other side, she opened the air vent cover and hid the pictures inside.

"Iris, come out and talk to me like an adult. This is getting ridiculous and giving me a headache."

"Your head? Ha! You would have to go up your mistress's, ass to find it. Now take your things and leave."

"Woman, I don't know what's gotten into you talking that silly nonsense in my house. My money pays the bills around here. I pay for Franklin's private school and karate lessons. I have the law degree, property, and prestigious club memberships. Don't forget, you married *up* when you married me." Gordon promptly reminded Iris she was nothing but a commoner from Alabama when he married her and will be even more anti-depressant dependent if she filed for divorce.

She peered through the door and scowled angrily, "Well, now, rich boy, you can rest on your laurels for rescuing the poor girl from the backwoods of Mobile, Alabama, but do your resting with your tramp and bastard child because Franklin and I deserve better. Starting today, attorney Gordon Upshaw, you are no longer welcome in *my* house."

She left the bathroom and hustled Gordon to the side entrance off the kitchen that led to the garage.

"Mom! Dad!" Franklin cried from the top of the stairs.

"Franklin, go back to your room," Gordon yelled.

Franklin whimpered off.

One foot out the door on the brink of losing everything he had worked for, Gordon broke down and confessed "Honey, I have something to tell you. All this nonsense about another woman carrying my baby is absurd. Now, what I'm about to tell you will fan the flames."

"Go ahead. Burn the house down. You already struck the match making a baby outside this marriage."

"There is no baby! But, you need to get tested."

"Tested for what?"

"HPV."

"HPV, as in genital warts?"

"Yes. I'm sorry."

One would have thought lightning struck Iris on her feet. That's how fast she hauled tail to the kitchen sink and back in Gordon's face wielding a frying pan, aiming to bash it into his skull.

"Gordon, how could you be so stupid?"

"Iris put the pan away. And, what do you know about HPV?"

"Evidently, more than you know about me. After I see my doctor you better pray all I have is HPV, otherwise you will have hell on your hands dealing with me in divorce court. Now get out! Get your germy ass out of my house before I beat the sin out of you."

Gordon knew Iris was country when they met, but he never thought he'd see the day she'd brandish a pan threatening to end his life. In hopes of one day making partner at Bingham, Fields & Poole, he vacated the premises.

At that moment, Keisha crept to the side of the house and watched Gordon leave before she ran fast to her car and sped off into the sunset.

37

ISSUES

Held up at a red light a few days later, Simone attached the earpiece to her mobile phone to get Portia on the line to announce that the presentation was spectacular.

Groggy and incoherent, Portia answered, "Blessed and highly favored." Her voice was so low Simone could barely hear her.

"You don't sound too blessed. Who died and didn't make it to heaven?"

Portia's spirit filled with laughter. "Girl, you need to be a comedienne. Anyway, cramps are doing me in."

"Oh, boy, I can relate. Mine don't kick they drop atomic bombs. Can I bring you anything to make you comfortable?"

"Orange juice would be nice."

"You've got it."

Half an hour later, Simone traveled north toward Washington Street, up Fort Hill, parked, and rang Portia's bell.

"Who is it?"

"Is it safe to come up?" Simone joked.

"Very funny." Portia said and buzzed her in.

Inside the condo they greeted each other with air kisses.

Portia took the orange juice from Simone and a bottle of Midol off the table and went to the kitchenette. She popped two pills, chased them with the juice, and then returned to the living room.

Simone didn't hold back her thoughts. "Mind if I ask if your decision to sever ties with Lonnie came with or without controversy?"

Completely ignoring Simone's inquiry, Portia said, "Would you like a glass of O.J. so we can toast to your presentation success?"

"You're deflecting as usual, which means you're still his punching bag."

Portia rolled her eyes, finished the juice and placed the glass atop a coaster on the mahogany table. "You know what Simone, at times you can be one persistent little witch. Come to my office. I want you to read something."

In the workspace Post-it reminders of sales goals covered the walls. Plastic bags of Blush product samples were piled in a corner. Portia reached into the desk's top drawer and then passed a folded sheet of paper to Simone. She unfolded the certified letter from Portia's condo association. It read along the lines of tenants complaining to the Board about disruptive noise coming from Portia's unit and the numerous times police have responded to disturbance calls. It also informed Portia she was in direct violation of the noise ordinance code of conduct clause outlined in the fine print of the association's bylaws. The tenant organization demanded Portia take immediate action to correct the chaos in her condo, otherwise the association would pursue the matter in court.

Simone folded the letter and gave it to Portia. "I bet you were too caught up making excuses for Lonnie's behavior to see that complaint coming. How did he react to the not-so-good news?"

"He asked me to marry him." Portia held up her left hand to show off a lovely diamond mounted on a gold band. She smiled proudly at the engagement ring. "What do you think?"

Amazed by the grape-sized stone, Simone was rendered momentarily speechless. "I think it's absolutely beautiful and would look gorgeous on my finger. And from the size of that stone Lonnie is not a broke man. Did he hit you when he gave it to you? Oopsie." Simone slapped her hand over her mouth. "Did I just say that? Forgive me. I meant to ask if he *hit* the lottery."

Head in the clouds, high on sunshine, Portia ignored her cynicism and gleamed with pride at the sparkling diamond. "You can crack jokes all day, but money is money. No matter where it comes from, it all spends the same. I don't care how he got the ring. It's perfect, and what I've always wanted since I was a knee-high little girl."

Simone couldn't believe her ears. "*Hello*, let's play common sense for a minute—"

Portia interrupted her. "We can play common sense as long as we can agree that my common sense is not your common sense."

"Fair enough. But you told Lonnie no, right?"

"Not exactly in those words. I told him I would take some time and think about his proposal. He told me to wear the ring until I made up my mind."

"Portia, if or when you say I do, remember you are going into marriage knowing what you know about his abusive ways.

Don't expect him to change overnight, if at all. Scrap the proposal, and buy a poodle or a cat to keep you company."

"Simone, owning a pet is not the same as having someone to talk to, someone to hold me tight when I'm feeling all alone, especially on those cold winter nights. I don't know about you, but I'm tired of hugging my pillow when I go to sleep. Shoot, I want to hold some muscle for a change, and so should you."

"Geesh, you've got issues if you think marrying Lonnie is the cure for loneliness. Thank goodness your common sense is not the universal standard. But, hey, it's your life, I can't control your feelings and needs, but I think accepting Lonnie's marriage proposal could be the beginning of a tragic ending to your life in many ways, starting with your health and happiness."

"Miss Perfect, you don't have issues?"

"Of course I do. But Portia, you can't mask your issues with lipstick, concealer, and blush because Lonnie beats it off you quicker than you can smear it on. Furthermore, I don't care how tired you are of being alone. Lonnie is not the man for you. He's abusive, controlling, disrespectful, shiftless, and did I mention, abusive?"

"Simone we have disagreements. We fight. So what! He has other redeeming qualities that will shine after he gets help for his anger problems and childhood trauma."

"What's redeeming about Lonnie? Is he a great listener? Does he support your business endeavors? What common ground do you share outside the bedroom? After sexing it up, what else do you have in common besides body fluids?"

Portia shrieked while laughing, "Simone, that's disgusting."

"But it's true!"

"Simone, it's also true that people in glass houses should never throw stones without a shield because the stones you pitch might ricochet a reality check. Your relationship with Andy wasn't sweet peaches and cream either. You stayed with Andy when he was making you an emotional wreck, but that was none of my business. I could say more, but I won't."

"First of all smart ass, I'm no longer with Andy. Second, if you got more to say, *say* it."

"Simone, if you weren't lonely you wouldn't have used closure as an excuse to sleep with Andy again. But sleeping with him was your prerogative. Now, will you be my maid of honor if I say yes to Lonnie?"

"Nope, and as a friend, I can't give you my blessing either." Simone pouted to protest Portia's future decision to marry her abuser.

"Why not?"

"Because marriage won't change Lonnie. I don't care how much *help*," Simone gestured with air quotes to emphasize her point, "he gets. And I hope you don't deplete your bank account for the joyous occasion since Lonnie isn't working a steady gig and can't collect unemployment anymore. It's not like he can afford to whisk you off to Bora-Bora, unless you're paying for the honeymoon, too."

"Simone, how do you know about Lonnie not working and his unemployment situation?"

"Your loose lips have tongues wagging about your personal business at Tresses."

"Yeah, apparently they're wagging too damn much."

"Portia, gossiping happens to be sport for some people. Keep your business to yourself and you won't have to worry about people telling it all behind your back."

"They still need to worry about their problems and stop gossiping about mine."

"Portia you have to take responsibility, too. By your own account, Lonnie is shiftless *and* abusive."

"Simone, you're being messy. I can't believe you'd throw gossip in my face. Some friend you are."

"Don't blame me for your loose lips. I love you like a sister and would never betray you by perpetuating gossip." Simone started toward the door. "Consider the orange juice my wedding gift. It's time for me to head home and put my groceries away before they go bad in the car."

"Wait. Don't leave yet. I understand your concern, but Lonnie and I talked about him attending anger management sessions to address his rage before we actually start planning the wedding. Deep down inside, we're in love and have committed to walk in lockstep throughout life, equally yoked. We even found the perfect scripture to prepare us for the walk in matrimony. Philippians 2 states *complete my joy by being of the same mind, having the same love, being in full accord and of one mind.* So, if one of us wears a hole in the sole of our shoes before the other, then we will brainstorm survival strategies. If it is beyond our repair, we will invoke the name of Christ through prayer, counseling, and therapy, if need be. Simone, I don't want to be single and alone for the rest of my life and die an old maid. I just don't. If I tell Lonnie yes, are we still going to be girls-for-life?"

"Of course. But, I can't bring myself to think about what might happen if you do say yes. And I wasn't trying to be malicious and hurt your feelings with gossip. As a true friend, I only want you to make a healthy choice."

"I know you do, but I prayed about it. My heart revealed the truth. I'm in love with Lonnie and I intend to follow my heart. Hugs?"

They hugged a hug that apologized for their rare spat. But, Simone had one more thing to add.

"Portia, this is coming from a good place because it seems like you already said yes. Anyway, I know you haven't seen your dad in years so you might appreciate knowing that growing up I watched my father abuse my mother. Had I stayed with Andy, I would have perpetuated that cycle of emotional, and mental abuse. Believe this or not, Andy's mom divorced his father for the same abusive reasons my mother left my father. So, as trailblazers you and I can stop the vicious cycle of domestic violence in the community and lead as resilient women with our heads screwed on right when it comes to whom we trust with our heart. When and where it ends is up to us."

Suddenly, their waterworks began to freefall. They embraced and cried for their own personal reasons. Simone stepped out of Portia's hug and wiped away a tear with her finger. Portia reciprocated and dried Simone's tears.

"Simone, I hear you, but Lonnie is slowly changing. He served his time in jail for petty crimes he didn't think would ever catch up to him. He did many stupid things that have slowed him down. Don't forget we met in church. I believe we can work our way back to the house of worship together. We're not getting married tomorrow, or next week for that matter. It's going to take some time, but we'll get there. Somehow we will get there."

"Portia, I adore you as a friend, but I've grown tired of dealing with your relationship woes because you refuse to sleep alone. But I guarantee you it's safer than marrying an abusive zebra like Lonnie who can't change his stripes. He is who he is."

Portia wanted to grab Simone by the shoulders and shake her. "Simone, please stop! Stop! Stop! Please stop! It's not about you and how you see life. Some things are not open for discussion, and the man I choose to marry is one of them. It's about me, my special day that's prayerfully in the near future. The day I marry my soul mate. I started dreaming about getting married when I was a little girl playing dress-up in the mirror. My dream is going to come true. I can feel it."

Simone shook her head sadly. "Well, at least you have the something *blue* covered. And I wouldn't be surprised if you already got the wedding dress picked out, altered, sling back sandals, teardrop earrings, and matching bracelet tucked away nice, and neat in your closet."

"Don't get me started on the hidden pleasure in your closet," Portia teased.

"Honey, you know nothing about the pleasure I got in my closet."

"Girl, go home and enjoy your dildo."

Simone giggled, "At least he never disappoints. The only thing that's going to let me down are the batteries."

Portia and Simone laughed like they never laughed before. Honesty, transparency, and trust cemented their bond. They knew each other too well and valued their friendship. Simone and Portia hugged again, and began reciting the Prayer for a Friend to protect their friendship.

Cruising up Seaver Street, Simone merged with the oncoming traffic traveling up Blue Hill Ave. Her Nextel chirped.

Denise's name flashed in the screen. She quickly connected the earpiece for safe driving.

"Hi there. What's up?"

Denise moaned, "Not a whole lot. I'm stuck on Blue Hill Ave. as we speak."

"Same here. Are you heading home?"

"Actually, I'm going to Bible study and thought I'd give you a call to make the drive more interesting."

"Denise, you've been going to Bible study after hours a lot lately. Are things getting better or worse between you and Jackson?"

"Things are slowly improving."

"And Deacon Brown, are things improving with him, too?"

"Not as of today. Jackson wants to come home and work on rebuilding our marriage. We had a talk about his gambling, and him spending more time with the boys, and less time throwing dice at the casino. He wants me to work harder at ignoring his mother's snide remarks and accepting her for who she's always been: a control freak who needs a little mattress action to chill her out—his words not mine, by the way."

"Jackson said that about his mom?"

"Yes, he did. Anyway, I told him I would try to mend fences, but she has to meet me halfway. Can you believe she wants me to cater to her, call her all the time and run behind her like some lost puppy? She'll grow old waiting because I don't even sniff under my *own* mother like that. Jackson is gonna see to it that she respects me as an adult and stops acting like she gave life to my boys. But I warned him if she continues her overbearing antics, we won't let them spend the weekends with her bossy behind."

"That's not playing fair. Don't use the boys as pawns. It will break her spiteful heart if she can't see her *grandbabies*."

"I don't care what it breaks. All I know is her phony behind needs to volunteer somewhere and keep her two cents to herself."

"Has your mother-in-law been a thorn in your marriage all these years?"

"Absolutely. How do you think I felt not being able to sit comfortably during the holidays with her scowling? Every time she saw me she always had something negative to say about my hair, my jewelry, my clothes, anything. That's why I started hosting family gatherings at my house. If she declines my Thanksgiving dinner invitation, that's gonna be her problem, not mine."

"Denise, speaking of refusing to participate, remember when we met downtown and you mentioned something about Portia showing me something?"

"Yeah."

"Was that something an engagement ring?"

"So she finally lowered the boom on you, too? Did you give her your blessing?"

"No and I explained why. Did you give her yours?"

Denise sighed. "If Portia wants to marry Lonnie, let her. I'm sure she has her reasons for believing she wants to spend her life with him. As women and friends, we can't be a substitute for the love she yearns for in her heart."

"You're right."

"Simone, I just pulled into the parking lot. Let me go handle my business with Deacon Brown. Toodles."

A few moments later, Denise rapped lightly on Deacon Brown's chamber door. The door opened slightly. Sister Pritchard, head of the hospitality committee eased it open to a crack while quickly adjusting her bra. "May I help you?"

"I'm here to see Deacon Brown. Is he here?" Denise asked, mildly irritated.

"Yes, but he can't meet with you now."

"And why not?"

"The deacon is in a meeting. You need an appointment to see him. If you would like, I can schedule some time on his calendar."

Denise smirked, "Miss God Don't Like Ugly, is that what he tells you when you sink to your knees under his desk? I know the sneaky things you do here after hours, and it's not typing announcements, prepping sermons for sunrise service, or polishing his shoes either. I've had a keen eye on you ever since I joined New Baptist. I see the way you shake your panty-less tail around Deacon Brown and cross and uncross your legs perched in the front pew in direct view of Pastor Cox. Only the devil knows what you would do with *him* if given half the chance to be his holy piece on the side."

"I beg your pardon but I don't know what you're talking about."

"Sister Pritchard, I'm talking about your lips coiling around the deacon's private behind closed doors. If you want your sin to remain a secret, then politely move out of my way before I forget that I'm saved and move you myself."

Sister Pritchard scooted aside. "The deacon is all yours."

Denise entered his quarters. Hands on her hips she made the purpose of her visit known. "Troy, I'd like to have a minute of your time. Is that possible because the gatekeeper doesn't seem to think so?"

"Call me Deacon Brown in the Lord's house. And why are you here? Didn't I promise to call when I could make time to see you again?"

"Never make a promise you don't intend to keep."

His voice deepened. "So what brings you here today?" Poking around on his cluttered desk, Deacon Brown picked up his leather-bound agenda and started leafing through his monthly calendar. "Hurry up and say what you have to say. I've got a schedule to keep." His abrasive tone pulled a frown out of Denise.

"I'm here to end our affair so I can work on reconciling my marriage."

"A phone call would have sufficed." Almost sounding indignant, Deacon Brown walked to the door, opened it and stepped aside. "You don't want to keep your husband waiting."

Glaring at him, and feeling humiliated, Denise grumbled, "You don't have to be nasty."

"I'm a single man, and you're a married woman, which means in the eyes of God you have forfeited your right to protest anything I do. However, my bedroom door will remain open should you have a change of heart. Until then, go home to your husband."

As ruthless as it was for Deacon Brown to be truthful, it pained Denise even more to hear that she was just a booty call to him.

Simone lifted two plastic bags packed with groceries onto the granite kitchen countertop. She then dashed to the bathroom and submitted to the call of her pushy bladder. Shortly thereafter, she put away the groceries, rushing the task with unusual urgency. Fruits loaded with fiber, vegetables high in vitamins, whole grain fat-free rice cakes, shelled walnuts, wild salmon, skinless poultry, Lactaid milk, calcium-enriched orange juice, and hydrating spring water were placed in their respective compartments of the brushed nickel refrigerator.

Cleaning supplies were stored in the utility closet. Last of all, she doubled back to the kitchen and removed a variety pack of Ramen noodles from the maple cupboard above the stove and threw it in the trash.

"Healthy eating starts today!" she exhaled. "InternetRomeo, here I come." Simone rushed to her computer.

Seated in front of the monitor, she fired up the computer and didn't miss a keystroke composing an email to her cyber confidant.

INTERNETROMEO,

ONCE AGAIN, I NEED A MAN'S PERSPECTIVE ON A RELATIONSHIP MATTER. A FRIEND IS MARRYING HER ABUSIVE LOVER. PERSONALLY, I DON'T THINK SHE IS MAKING A WISE DECISION. HER HUSBAND-TO-BE HASN'T EXACTLY PROVEN TO BE RELIABLE, MUCH LESS RESPECTFUL OF HER BODY AND FEELINGS. SHE CLAIMS TO BE TIRED OF WAKING UP ALONE. CARE TO SERENADE ME WITH YOUR POINT OF VIEW?

Simone hit send.

Logging off, she thought, *what if Andy and I got married? What if?*

38

SOME THINGS NEVER CHANGE

Early birds hadn't yet eaten the worms before Simone welcomed the break of day. At the light of dawn, she rolled out of bed to do some therapeutic cleaning around the house and even try to put a dent in her laundry. A few hours later, exhausted, she took a break from her chores to reflect on what faith had carried her through over the past two months. Through reflection she realized life's lessons could only make her stronger, wiser, fearless, and even more resilient in times of adversity.

"God doesn't put more on me than I can handle," She recited, drawing back the curtains to officially welcome the June sun. The weather forecast for the day was hazy, hot, and humid, with a possibility of a thunderstorm. Basking in the radiant glory, Simone smiled widely and thought, *today is the perfect day to implement my thirty-minute walking plan to stay fit in body and sane in mind.*

Standing at the window she did a double take as Andy pulled up and staggered out of his Lincoln Navigator, clearly drunk out of his skull, and walking like he had two left feet. Simone angrily and quickly took off her pajamas and tugged a pair of jeans over her spreading hips, slipped on a shirt, ran to the bathroom to gargle peppermint mouthwash, and then ran downstairs. She unlocked the door, ready to scold Andy for showing up again without calling. He was leaning heavily on the doorframe; he could barely stand up straight. His low Caesar haircut hadn't seen a brush. His clothes were a tousled mess. His shirt was shoved haphazardly into his pants. He looked like he hadn't slept in twenty-four hours, much less showered. He reeked of alcohol and the stench was making Simone queasy.

At a loss for words, Simone just stared at the staggering drunk.

"Are you gonna make me pee in my pants?" Andy slurred.

"Why not? Like I told you before, dogs pee outside."

"Woman, stop acting like you're not happy to see me, and let me use the bathroom."

Simone rolled her eyes in disgust, "Andy, the more you try to change the more you stay the same. What is your problem? You are in no condition to be driving, putting everybody's life at risk, including your own."

"Sweetheart, aren't you going to invite me in for old time's sake?"

The longer Simone stared at Andy, the more the blinds shifted at Miss Bonita's house. Without a trace of sympathy for Andy, Simone frowned, "Get in here before you give Miss Bonita a reason to fetch her camcorder to broadcast my business to the Neighborhood Watch Committee."

Andy swung around to face Miss Bonita's house, then boldly grabbed his crotch. "This'll give that nosy old prune something to talk about. "

Moments later Miss Bonita appeared under her porch awning and preached scripture to Simone, "Young lady, *wisdom will save you from the ways of wicked men.* You'd better be mindful of the company you keep because that man right there is the devil." Ginger Snap barked. Miss Bonita yanked the dog inside by its collar then slammed her door.

If Simone could have rolled her eyes any harder at Andy, she would have burst a blood vessel.

"That was disrespectful and uncalled for. Get in here so I can sober you up."

Simone stepped back to let Andy stumble his way into the living room. He looped, wobbled, rocked, and swayed before plummeting like a cinder block onto the sofa.

"Hey! Take it easy!" Simone yelled. "Your money didn't buy anything in this house, so don't come over hear tearing up my furniture."

"I'll buy you another couch," Andy slurred. "I never liked the color anyway. It's boring and looks like puke."

"I'm gonna let your B.S. slide today. You've had too much to drink and can't be thinking rationally, especially if you offend your elders. The only reason your disrespectful ass is sitting in my living room is because you're in no condition to drive."

"See, that's what I like about you, Simone. You're a compassionate bitch. Sweetheart, have I ever told you that I like when my bitches care about me?"

"*Bitch*?!" Simone echoed loudly, "Andy, at one time this bitch was your doctor and your dealer. "In fact," she laughed, "you were clinically addicted to my Lady drug. Now shut up before I knock your disrespectful teeth down your throat, and watch you choke on them. In fact, I'll do you one better. How do you like your coffee, so I can sober you up and get your ass the hell out of my life?"

"I don't want coffee. I'll take a slice of you if you're on the menu. Please, just a sample will sober me up. Help me out. It's for a good cause."

"Sorry, we will not have a repeat performance today or any other day. Let's concentrate on getting you sober and home safe."

Andy nodded and slurred, "I don't want sober. I want you. Come sit on Poppa's lap and let me tickle your baby fat."

Normally Simone would have laughed but she was trying to move on in life and not in the mood for jokes. She didn't want to sit on his lap, she wanted to make mincemeat out of the alcoholic, bag him up, and set him out with Thursday's trash. As frustrated as Simone was, she still felt a tinge of pity for Andy before realizing she couldn't stand the sight of him.

"Andy, I'll make some coffee and you're gonna drink it to sober up because I want your disrespectful ass out of my house!"

He flapped a hand to gesture no to the coffee and sank deeper into the cushion, nodding off, drooling from the corner of his mouth.

Simone thought, *what if we got married and started a family? Would his drunkenness be the misery I'd have to battle every day?*

Consumed with the ridiculous possibility of marriage joining them together, she tugged on Andy's arm to lurch him off the couch. "Get your drunken ass up and hit the road."

His dead weight was too heavy for Simone to heave. Her hold on him weakened. She tumbled backward. Her pride touched down before her body hit the floor. Andy slumped back deeper into the sofa. She wanted him up and out. Back at tugging him again, she inhaled deeply, counted to ten, then hoisted him up. They both tumbled to the floor. Pride aside, she attempted with all her strength to drag him by one leg to the door. Winded and physically exhausted, Simone barely made it a few feet away from the couch. Defeated, she ransacked his pockets and pulled out a few coins, his wallet, and finally his keys before calling for a cab.

"Let's go. The meter is running." Once more, she hauled Andy to his feet and mustered the strength to push him out the door. The driver helped her situate Andy in the backseat of the taxi. He slumped over and conked out snoring a drunken melody. Simone followed closely behind, driving the Navigator, knowing their unresolved issues were testaments that love was breakable, which left her no choice except to bid adieu to another fruitless romance in spite of her desire to love Andy.

Guilt-free, Simone left Andy sitting on his stoop cursing obscenities at her back.

In place of cranking down the glass and poking her head out to defend her womanhood, Simone peered out the rear window of the taxi and blew a good-bye kiss to the end of an emotionally draining era. Then emotions looped in her head. *Andy's negative energy isn't going to crowd my space anymore. In order to make things right between us, I have to keep on moving on. I don't know where I'm going, but I'll know when I meet a morally disciplined companion with compatible interests, values, and goals. Someone spiritually, emotionally, and socially balanced. But more importantly than a library card, and a stellar FICO Score, the ideal companion must be health conscious, respectful, and mature.*

"Where to Miss?"

The cabbie's question interrupted her thoughts. Simone blinked out of her trance, and gave the cab driver her address. She then closed her eyes and relaxed until she arrived at home sweet home.

39

GOOD NIGHT, AMERICA

Back at home, cyberspace was the conduit that continued to be Simone's escape to a world that allowed her to forget where she was and who she was, if only for a minute. Curious to know if InternetRomeo had responded to her message, she booted up the PC and typed in her user name, and password. As expected, her inbox was inundated with bulk mail, and political rhetoric. Simone deleted everything except for Keisha's e-mail bearing no subject header. She opened and read it.

SIMONE,
I BROUGHT HOME THE GOLDEN STATUE!

Laughing hysterically, Simone typed back,
I'M GONNA PRAY FOR YOU!

After clicking send, an instant message alert popped up. InternetRomeo never let her down. Anxious to get a man's point of view, Simone clicked, Read Now.

SIMMY,

AS I RECALL, A FEW YEARS AGO, I WAS JUST AS CONCERNED ABOUT YOU WHEN YOU WERE DATING A GUILTY PLEASURE WHO WAS TAKING YOU FOR GRANTED. REMEMBER WHEN YOU REACHED OUT TO ME FOR ADVICE? NOW, YOU ARE TRYING TO TOSS THIS PERSON A LIFE PRESERVER, BUT IT SEEMS HER BOAT HAS DRIFTED TOO FAR OFFSHORE TO RECEIVE IT.

YOUR CONCERNS ARE VALID, AND I HAPPEN TO AGREE WITH YOU. I WOULD PROBABLY BE JUST AS CONCERNED IF MY FRIEND WAS MAKING POOR CHOICES, TOO, ESPECIALLY WITH WHOM THEY MARRY. IT'S TOO BAD THAT SHE DOESN'T ACT LIKE SHE DESERVES TO BE TREATED BETTER. SOMETIMES WE MAKE DECISIONS THAT ARE NOT IN OUR BEST INTEREST. UNFORTUNATELY, SOME PEOPLE PREFER TO SETTLE FOR LESS IN SEARCH OF PEACE, LOVE, AND HAPPINESS IN ALL THE WRONG PLACES BEFORE FINDING FULFILLMENT WITHIN.

HOWEVER, THIS PERSON'S LIFE IS NOT YOURS TO STRESS OVER. DON'T MAKE HER ISSUE YOUR ISSUE. LET GO. GET OUT THE WAY SO GOD CAN DO HIS WORK.

IF SHE DOES NOT VALUE YOUR INPUT, THEN YOU WILL HAVE TO RESPECT HER DECISION TO ENTER MATRIMONY AND PRAY SHE IS NOT

MAKING A DEADLY MISTAKE. COME WHAT MAY, I PRAY SHE WILL HAVE A TRUSTWORTHY SUPPORT SYSTEM IN PLACE IF THE MARRIAGE CRUMBLES ON THE HONEYMOON. AND TO SAVE YOUR FRIENDSHIP, PLEASE DON'T SAY I TOLD YOU SO, INSTEAD, TELL HER TO DIAL 1-800-799-SAFE OR VISIT www.ndvh.org OR www. dvinstitute.org FOR HELP.

After reading InternetRomeo's response Simone signed off and powered on the television in search of something intellectually stimulating to watch. She increased the volume to listen to a live news report.

"Earlier today, residents hailed from Roxbury, Dorchester, and Mattapan in historic numbers to rally on the steps of the state capitol demanding the governor take back the city. When asked what they were most concerned with, some who live in those communities, many all their lives, voiced frustrations about the overwhelming number of shootings, unsolved murders, and lack of police presence. Here's what some of the protesters had to say."

"I'm afraid to let my children play in the backyard. Stray bullets don't have names."

"I had to adjust my hours at work so I could drive my wife to the train station and pick her up after work. She's afraid to walk alone."

"I have three sons ages thirteen, fourteen, and nineteen. I don't sleep well at night because I fear one day the police are gonna knock at my door to tell me that my boys are dead."

The camera panned away from the crowd and back to the reporter preparing to wrap up his coverage.

"Clearly, emotions are running high today. The community wants action. The governor's office simply released a 'No comment,' but assures hope is not lost. I can guarantee you that these concerns will be at the forefront of the governor's state of the union speech in the coming weeks. Paul Lupey, reporting for WHUB News. Good night, America."

"Good night is right," Simone repeated as she picked up the remote and zapped off the television. She then walked to the kitchen, where she filled a saucepan with tap water, sat it on top of searing blue flames, and waited for the liquid to boil. When the water was piping hot, she steeped a cup of Vanilla Nut tea and retreated upstairs with the mug. She was destined to retrieve her journal. In a corner, underneath a reading lamp, she kicked back on an easy chair to collect her thoughts and write down her opinion about the community rally. After penning a final thought, Simone took pleasure in the last drop of tea. She then showered and prepared to take a nap.

Lying back in her sleigh bed on the pillow-top mattress, she tucked her palm under her head. Stretched out, she performed another breast exam, starting on the left using circular motions with her fingers. She pressed in, on, and around the areola looking for tenderness and abnormal lumps. She applied the same circular motions on the right side. Suddenly, her body heat tingled up her spine, causing her Lady to pulsate for Secret Pleasure. Simone stood, walked to the closet, rolled the sliding doors down metal tracks, plowed through the train of shoeboxes, and retrieved the velvet container set deep in the back on the top shelf. She removed the lid, reached inside, and tenderly caressed Secret Pleasure. Back on the bed, she propped a pillow under her head, ready for mechanical intimacy.

Following her session, Simone laid in the dark palming her stomach dreading the next day—the first official day of summer, and the hazy, hot, and humid crime ridden days that often follow.

EPILOGUE
FIBROIDS, MYOMAS, AND TUMORS

On a mild summer day in June, all was calm in Simone's working-class neighborhood as she rounded the corner of Gunther Road and parked at the foot of her driveway. She purposely let the engine idle while her mind was stuck in neutral.

Spent and drained of her last drop of energy, Simone lowered the visor and massaged her stomach as she looked at the bags under her eyes. She stopped massaging her stomach to turn off the engine, and lower the window to catch a breeze. A wave of thick air enveloped the cabin and moistened her thirty-four-year-old skin until it glistened in the sun. She reclined her seat to relish in the moment.

As expected, Miss Bonita, the Neighborhood Watch Committee member, reported to duty. Simone was her object of scrutiny.

"You seem mighty tired there, young lady. Are you okay?" she asked, standing at the driver's side door with Ginger Snap loping at her feet, tail wagging.

Please, don't let her start meddling, Simone thought then quieted her inner voice, faked a happy face to answer Miss Bonita's concern.

"A little tired. I didn't hear you and Ginger Snap coming. How are you this evening? " Simone asked, hoping Miss Bonita heeded the tired cue.

"Aside from the humidity sucking the moisture out of my press and curl, it does me no good to complain about the jungle heat blanketing the city, because frosty winter temperatures make my arthritis act up, and the spring rains flood my basement. Either way, God got me out of bed this morning with more strength than I had yesterday. There's no other man like Him. You know that, right?"

Listening to Miss Bonita sing God's praises centered Simone in a positive space. She was in full agreement as she began an anxious search to locate her cell and wristlet. After a brief hunt, both items were located exactly where she had stored them, in her workbag.

She rolled up the window and exited the car feeling as free as a butterfly shedding its cocoon. "In God I do trust because tomorrow is never a promise." Simone said closing the door.

"Amen." Miss Bonita agreed "And young lady, I've been meaning to say you've gotten a little rounded in the hips and filling out some there." Miss Bonita patted her potbelly spilling over the rubber waistband of her cranberry polyester pants to specify what "there" she was referring to.

Simone stared dumbfounded, unsure if she should laugh at how ridiculous Miss Bonita looked patting her belly, or dart inside to avoid further scrutiny. Instead, she drifted across the weathered green lawn as free as a butterfly flapping its delicate wings in the thick, humid air. Pausing at the door to retrieve a stack of mail, she turned to give Miss Bonita a nod before going inside.

"Have a good evening."

"You do the same and young lady get some rest because I don't want to get used to seeing you look a mess."

Simone forced the best smile her lips could shape as she entered her house with not a care in the world. Inside, she disarmed the security system and rushed upstairs to pose sideways in the floor length mirror to study her jut round belly.

Again she asked, "Why me?" Simultaneously her stomach grumbled, "Feed me."

⚬

Simone freshened up and settled in for a quick bite to eat. Albacore tuna on rye, unsalted potato chips, and lime-ade enabled her to muster the energy she needed to spruce up her garden of hardy perennials that were overrun with weeds.

On the step leading into the house, Snow nibbled on the leftover tuna in the tin and then licked her matted fur clean after enjoying her meal.

At some point on her green-thumb mission, Simone heard a screen door creak open. She lifted her head discreetly, and looked across the street as Miss Bonita appeared on her porch wearing a change of clothes. She meandered toward Simone. The fringes on the lavender shawl swathing over her back shimmied wildly and frightened Snow away.

"Young lady, I see you got a second wind to pluck those weeds. It's a good thing you got out here before dark catches up to you."

Simone acknowledged her presence and removed the garden gloves, dropping them into the spiky needles of Kentucky blue grass.

"Please, join me for a cup of tea." Simone's offer was a feeble attempt to distract Miss Bonita from addressing her physical appearance again.

Miss Bonita obliged the offer. Simone led her inside. Miss Bonita wiped her feet clean on the mat then settled all of her plumpness on the soft chair. The cracking of her old bones as she squatted, brought a smile to Simone's face as she gained a soft spot for her elder.

"On second thought, no tea for me this evening." Miss Bonita politely declined, waving her hand. "If I drink this hour of the day I'll be going to the bathroom all night. That's what happens when you get up in age. Your body undergoes so many changes. You can't keep up with them then the doctor wants to prescribe all sorts of medication. I tell mine all the time, no thank you, I ain't buying what you're selling. Pills can't do the Lord's work."

"Well, I'm not your age and I've been having some medical issues of my own to manage. My ultrasound revealed I've got multiple uterine fibroids."

"Fibroids?" Miss Bonita repeated. "Is that so? I had those myself when I was around your age. Pain in the butt, ain't they?" She laughed lightly, shifting and wiggling to get comfortable in the chair.

Simone tried to smile, but couldn't quite form her mouth into one.

"I try not to think about my fibroids until around the time my cycle is due to wash down. I agree they can be grueling. Between us, what I've been experiencing is enough to make a man thankful he was born with a pool stick and two cue balls—" Simone winked— "if you know what I mean."

Miss Bonita's upper back and shoulders shivered with glee from her internal laughter. "I know exactly what you mean, with your fresh self." Her bashful grin revealed her dentures. "Got me blushing. You ought to be 'shame." The color flushed from her raisin-in-the sun skin. Miss Bonita used her hand to cool down. "Woo! It's warming up in here."

Simone smiled, then asked. "Would you mind sharing your fibroid experience?"

"Well," Miss Bonita sighed, "there ain't much to tell. I had a hysterectomy to get rid of my tumors soon after my late husband Henry was crushed to death on a construction site where he worked as a foreman. The impact of a steal beam literally knocked the wind out of him. Soon after his lungs collapsed, his heart stopped pumping blood. He died at General Hospital before I could get there and say my last good-byes. When God called Henry Home my dream to birth children died right along with him. Another thing, I did not have one iota of pain after them doctors took my uterus away. What are you doing about yours?"

"I'm in watch-and-wait mode. My doctor wants to monitor them every six months for any change in size, as well as any new growths that may occur. And if I have to choose between one of the many treatment options now available, including herbs and home remedies, I would seriously lean toward the uterine artery embolization."

"Isn't that the same procedure Condoleezza Rice had?"

"As a matter of fact, she sure did. It's a non-surgical intervention and supposedly the least invasive treatment with the shortest recovery period. I'm also somewhat on the fence about the abdominal myomectomy, though I'm not crazy about going under the scalpel knowing the odds of new fibroids emerging are stacked against me. Not to mention the recovery period can be anywhere from six to eight weeks."

"Young lady research and treatment have come a long way since I had fibroids years ago. Back then doctors didn't know much of anything about them, except they were benign tumors. Because of their ignorance, doctors were recommending and performing hysterectomies like they were picking cotton out of folks. Just pray on it. Put some serious thought into your decision. Consider the long-term effects, not a band-aid solution to the problem. Don't be hasty. Make darn sure you get a second opinion. Ask questions. Entertain theory. Get the facts before you let those doctors open you up."

"Thanks for the advice. I've been reading books and mulling over options that my gynecologist outlined for me. I plan on living with the fibroids as long as they allow me to function and have a normal lifestyle. I won't rush a medical decision I might regret in the end. But a hysterectomy is completely out of the question!"

Miss Bonita shared more knowledge through wisdom. For once Simone appreciated the meddling nature of her neighbor.

"Whatever you decide, don't let them doctors cut you unless it's absolutely necessary. Put your health in God's care. Scripture says: *In his hands is the life of all creatures and the breath of all mankind.* As my late Henry always used to say: 'Once the air enters your body them organs might go haywire and start fighting with each other. Next thing you know, something else will be wrong with you.' Young lady, don't let those doctors coax you into taking risks with your body because it's the only one you got, and besides you got babies to start thinking about. You're still young and I presume fertile, ain't you?"

Simone tuned out the drone of her biological clock and proudly said, "Call me Fertile Myrtle. I menstruate every twenty-eight days just like clockwork."

Miss Bonita chuckled and rose from the chair readjusting the shawl over her fragile shoulders. "Well, I won't take up any more of your time. I best get going 'cause I know Ginger Snap is hungry for a treat."

After seeing Miss Bonita out, Simone turned the telephone ringers off to guarantee a moment of uninterrupted "me time". She retrieved *Dreamgirls* soundtrack from the CD tower, inserted the disc into the play chamber, skipping every song until she reached "I Am Changing" by Oscar winner Jennifer Hudson.

While the music was strumming softly in the living room, Simone hurried upstairs to strike a sideways pose in the mirror. She stood there looking at her reflection and absorbing Jennifer Hudson's heartfelt and inspirational lyrics of escaping the mistakes of her past. Simone felt lifted and hopeful as she looked in the mirror envisioning she was gazing at an image of herself and her future companion entwined in each other's arms waltzing in a grand ballroom without a care in the world. The soaring lyrics claiming that *nothing was going to stop me now,* snapped Simone out of her fantasy and once again she was faced with the reality of her jutting belly in the mirror.

Eyeballing her kangaroo pouch with contempt, she repeated the question that had been plaguing her since her initial pelvic exam, "Why me?" Troubled about the state of her health, Simone's voice trickled down to a weary whisper. "Uterine fibroids. Myomas. Benign tumors. What if they ruin my chance of conceiving some day?"

As fate would have it, Simone's body was indeed changing. The adage of birds flying and flocking together was painfully true. Simone's fibroid diagnosis may not have been synonymous with Keisha's HPV, Portia's abusive relationship, Denise's broken marriage, Susan's unwanted pregnancy, or Monica's ignorance of consequences, but every disease, circumstance, decision, and outcome they faced would undoubtedly leave an indelible mark of dissent, emptiness, resentment, and ambivalence in their hearts.

Again Simone repeated "Why me?"

MY PERSONAL STORY...

Although the story you've just read was purely a work of fiction, it was inspired by my own experience with fibroid tumors. Much like Simone Miller, I too started getting, shall I say, somewhat thick in the middle around the same time a strange discomfort plagued me during the onset of premenstrual syndrome. Pants, dresses, and skirts increased in size to accommodate my expanding waistline. Buttons on blouses were several deep breaths from popping at the midsection! My physical condition evolved seemingly overnight. One day I was curvy all over, and the next, I had the "booty-do" thing going on. You're probably like, booty-*what*? The way it was explained to me, booty-do is another way of saying my stomach protruded outward more than my butt did in the back. As ridiculously funny as it may sound, it was pathetically true and a sore sight in my youthful eyes. My once tight little body that had men checking me out on the sly had become disproportionate, and with disproportion came a heap load of confusion and fear of the unknown.

I thought age was definitely a contributing factor in the metamorphosis of my outer appearance, especially since physiological changes in my cycle often occurred around my birthday. Over the years, my periods became increasingly unpredictable. The blood flow increased, decreased, and quarter-sized clots, sometimes bigger, would drop in the toilet. Moreover, my least favorite attribute of womanhood—cramps—would mysteriously subside only to sneak up and knock me off my feet with the force of a mighty blow.

My plumbing system didn't take too kindly to Extra Strength Tylenol, as much as it responded to aspirin. I was cognizant of potentially harmful side effects of ingesting the tiny white pills, particularly stomach irritation and thinning blood. So, I limited my aspirin intake to "as needed."

Fast forward to my diagnosis. At the time of my discomfort and obvious biological and physical changes, I frequented a local neighborhood clinic that became a devastating ordeal. My then primary care physician (PCP) commuted from north of Boston, but I didn't learn about her daunting commute until she resigned in favor of a lateral position closer to her hometown somewhere in the state of Maine.

After my PCP resigned, my ultrasound results remained unaccounted for in the clinic's database. It was convenient for the director to blame the missing report on a computer glitch. So, I started asking legal questions that warranted truthful answers.

What I learned: When it comes to serious matters of the mind, body, and spirit, I would not make the mistake again of entrusting my well being to a one-stop-shop clinic, especially if I experience prolonged and chronic symptoms.

Following the "glitch" and recovery of my results, I immediately contacted patient records and signed a release form authorizing the clinic to forward my entire medical history to a reputable hospital in Boston that specializes in fibroid treatment.

REFERENCE GUIDE

You only have one life to live, put your health first.

Got health concerns? Questions? Need answers? Get in touch with your mind, body, and spirit. Research, seek professional advice, and get the facts!

Alcoholics Anonymous
www.aa.org

Breast Cancer
1-800-ACS-2345
www.cancer.org/breastcancer

Centers for Disease Control and Prevention
www.cdc.gov

Domestic Violence—The National Domestic Violence Hotline
1-800-799-SAFE
www.dvinstitute.org
www.ndvh.org

Fibroids Readings
It's A Sistah Thing by Monique Brown
Sex, Lies, & the Truth About Uterine Fibroids by Carla Dionne

Fibroids
Signs and symptoms
www.fibroidnetworkonline.com

HPV
http://www.cdc.gov/hpv/Domestic Violence

Sexual Assault — RAINN (Rape, Abuse & Incest National Network)
https://www.rainn.org

Violence Against Women and Children (Facebook Page)
https://www.facebook.com/ViolenceAgainstWomenChildren

READING GROUP DISCUSSION GUIDE

1) After reading the title, did you immediately think sex, health, a combination of both, or neither?

2) Was there any one character that you could relate to personally? Why?

3) Why do you think Simone is so cynical about relationships?

4) Do you think Andy and Jeff were sincere in their pursuit of Simone? Why? Why not? Did either of them deserve a second chance? Why? Why not?

5) Do you believe in second chances? Why? Why not?

6) Why do you think Keisha finds fulfillment in pursuing married men?

7) How do you think Keisha would function in a relationship with a single man?

8) Do you think Portia's reasons for staying in her abusive relationship has anything to do with her not having a relationship with her father?

9) Women, parenthood, and marriage: Why do you think Susan and Denise feel they sacrificed their livelihood to start a family?

10) How familiar were you with the health issues raised in the book, in particular fibroids?

11) What theme(s) in the book resonated with you most: education, health, community related, or relationships?

12) Do you think women rely on relationships to make them complete? Why? Why not?

13) Who should provide the condom in a relationship?

14) Did the novel inspire you to be more attentive to your health?

15) Do you ask questions during your medical appointments? If not, after reading this novel will you start asking clarifying questions about your health?

16) The book was written to raise health awareness. Do you think the author accomplished that objective?

If you have/had fibroids, feel free to share your story/experience at: sh@sonyaharris.com

Like Facebook Author page: https://www.facebook.com/ author_sonyaharris

Follow me on Twitter: @author_sonya

Like Facebook page: https://www.facebook.com/Violence-AgainstWomenChildren

My next novel, *I Love Him But...* will aim to raise domestic violence awareness.

Until then, be light.